FOREVER WITH HIM

STACY TRAVIS

FOREVER WITH HIM

STACY TRAVIS

Cover Design: Alyssa Garcia, Uplifting Author Services

Editing: Red Adept Editing

Publicity: Social Butterfly PR

PROLOGUE

AIR FRANCE BUSINESS CLASS – July
Nikki

CHRIS LOOKED like he was moving through water, making his way toward me at a pace that seemed impossibly gluey and slow. He held his cellphone out in front of him as though it was contaminated from the conversation he'd just had.

The words he'd just uttered, "We have a problem," continued to ring in my ears, but because it was Chris and because he really didn't seem to have unsurmountable problems, I chose not to be overly alarmed. Maybe he'd left the script for his next project behind at his house. Maybe his neighbor had forgotten to water his plants and they'd all died. And while I didn't relish the murder of ferns, I couldn't help but hope for their demise over other more dire options.

The signs were not great. His eyes were glassy, and he ran a hand through his hair, which meant he was stuck in a mental gymnasium. It was clear he was concerned about something more significant than whether the in-flight meal contained dairy.

"Like, 'Houston, we have a problem'?" I asked, not liking the look on his face and hoping to counter it with levity. "Are you searching for a parachute, or is your assistant just worried because you're on a commercial airline? Because you might distract the pilot with your pretty face and we'll crash? Because frankly, I'd be concerned about that too."

"You're funny," he said dryly, settling into the window seat next to mine and getting out of the way of the flight attendant who was passing a tray of champagne flutes to the passengers in business class. He wasn't smiling and he didn't fasten his seatbelt, so I wasn't sure if he planned on staying.

"I'm glad I can amuse you in the face of a problem. But what's wrong?" I asked.

I wasn't used to this. He was unflappable. I was the one who freaked out over trivial things, such as whether I'd put too much salt in my salad dressing or whether the black town car that ferried us around was eco-friendly. And then freaked out at the very existence of a black town car that ferried us around.

His expression was giving me a new thing to freak out about. Gone was the relaxed vacation visage I'd stared at for two weeks, as well as the I-might-be-in-love-with-you face I'd seen a few minutes earlier. Chris looked like he had more than just a problem. He looked concerned and confused, which made me concerned and confused.

"Chris, what's going on?" I asked again. In his silence, my brain had time to conjure a few possibilities: he couldn't fly to LA with me just yet, which wouldn't be the end of the world; he'd made a mistake and decided he didn't want a future together; or his wife just called and reminded him to be home in time for dinner. Considering anything but the first scenario was enough to make cold pinpricks break out across my skin. My carefully guarded heart had already edged open in the few minutes since he'd professed his desire to be with me beyond our time in France.

Close down! Abort mission! Just beat quietly like the organ you were meant to be.

I waited with my heart somewhere in the vicinity of my throat for him to tell me the rest of the story, which I was pretty sure I didn't want to hear. No, that wasn't true. I wanted to hear it. I wanted to help.

"Sir, all passengers need to fasten their seatbelts," a flight attendant to his left said. Chris turned, glassy-eyed, to see who was talking to him, as though she could impart critical information needed to solve his current problem. I wondered if he was considering bolting.

When he fastened his seatbelt but still didn't look at me, I fabricated new concerns. Maybe his managers or agents or whatever handlers controlled his movements got wind of the fact that he wanted to move to LA with me and freaked the hell out. Maybe they told him he would be disowned—or whatever managers, agents, and handlers did when an actor didn't behave according to the marketing plan. Perhaps he was suddenly less marketable if he had a girlfriend, and therefore, he would be parachuting out of the plane once he came to his senses mid-flight.

At his continued silence, the pit in my stomach started growing into an immovable choking object. A sheen of sweat broke across my forehead, and my concerns grew to somewhere on the temperature scale between melting ice cream on a warm sidewalk and a bottomless pit of hellfire.

I inhaled a deep breath and tried to settle my brain into regular angst instead of full-on crippling neurosis. We had eleven hours together, I reasoned, so there was no rush for him to start talking.

I would just sit and wait. I would take a leisurely glance at my surroundings.

Having never flown business class, I noticed how much more space the rows had between them. The cup holders were larger than in coach. I wondered if larger drinks would be served. There were nice-looking headphones.

Who cares about the headphones. Why isn't he talking? Stop freaking out.

I put a hand on his leg, needing to make some sort of contact. He put his hand on top of mine but still faced out the window.

The flight crew went through the motions of checking the plane, and his silence continued as the pilot taxied us and got the jet into the air. It was a side of him I hadn't seen, and I was struck by the realization that with the abrupt end of our vacation time together came a different side of Chris. Whatever was happening, whatever his problem ended up being, it needed a real-world solution. It felt like an unwelcome intrusion into the way Chris and I had related to each other so far. He seemed like a different person.

Finally, I couldn't take his silence any longer. I turned my hand so my palm faced up and curled my fingers around his. He responded, interlacing his fingers with mine. "Chris," I said.

He turned to look at me, and the expression on his face unnerved me. He looked defeated.

I instinctively wanted to reach out to him, because he didn't seem to know how to ask for help. "Talk to me. Let me help you. What's going on?"

He inhaled a jagged breath and let it drain out of him. "I don't even know where to begin..." He shook his head. I was concentrating on not freaking out, really concentrating, which meant a muscle in my cheek had started uncontrollably twitching. "A while back, I dated a woman for a month or so. It wasn't ever going anywhere, but we had a good time..."

I didn't like the continual pauses in his story, because they gave my brain a chance to spin into all kinds of unwelcome territory. So I was thinking about the "good time" he and I had just enjoyed over the past two weeks and wondering if their "good time" was similar. Or better.

"Chris, just tell me. What's going on? Is she sick? Are you getting back together? Is she your baby mama? What?"

He looked surprised at the question. "What? No, I mean, yes, but no. Definitely no."

"Um, which part? Explain?"

"No, we're not together. Yes, apparently now, she's pregnant. And she's told one of the tabloids that I'm the father." He turned to me, his eyes plaintive. I didn't know if he was unnerved because he'd just learned he was going to be a father or if he just didn't like having to tell me.

"Oh."

"Oh?"

"Yeah. I mean, I don't know."

"It's not true. There's no way it's true."

"Okay. Has the tabloid printed the story?"

"No. Not yet. Hopefully not ever."

"That's probably wishful thinking, don't you think?"

He closed his eyes, and I knew the answer. My first instinct was to wrap him in my arms and try to shield us both from the outside world, the way we'd been for the past two weeks.

I swallowed around the lump that was forming in my throat. Whether it was true or not, one thing was certain: we'd left our euphoric vacation bubble behind. Chris's "problem" was a sharp reminder that we were back in his world, and his world included pregnant ex-girlfriends who went to the tabloids before they talked to anyone else. It included paparazzi and his face on magazine covers. If I wanted to be with him, I needed to figure out how to deal with all that.

I also needed to reassure him that everything would be okay, even though I had no idea that was true. I put my other hand on his. "I'm sorry she went to the tabloids before talking to you. That sucks." That part *was* awful. I could be objective about it. But then there was the big steaming dinosaur pie on the runway.

"Is there a chance it's true?" I asked.

He pinched his temples as though to keep a headache from forming and shook his head. "I don't know. I've been wracking my brains for the past half hour, trying to remember the timing of when we were… together. I don't want to sound like an asshole, but it wasn't that memorable."

"Well, I don't want to sound like a jealous asshole, but… okay, that's just fine by me."

For the first time since he'd taken the phone call, his lips twitched as if they might consider working their way into a smile. "I still don't have all the details. I don't know how far along she thinks she is, so I can't look at a calendar to see if the dates even match, but she's already given the interview, and they're threatening to publish the story later this week. Apparently, they were reaching out to me for comment."

"And you said nothing, I hope." I'd been trained to think that way. Without even trying, I'd slipped into the role of public relations fixer. I'd seen a lot worse—real cases of bad behavior and wrongdoing that needed to be cleaned up before the tabloids printed anything, which turned into PR nightmares if they did.

"I haven't talked to them yet. My assistant ran interference, and my publicist and my lawyer are getting into it with the tabloid."

"Okay. Let them handle it."

He nodded. "That's what they told me."

"Good. Listen to them." He didn't look at all convinced that it would be that simple. I moved my hand to his leg and rubbed circles that I hoped were soothing. "Chris, what are you thinking?"

"I just… I feel awful about this. Partly for her, I guess, if she's knocked up and scared. But I'm pretty sure she's full of shit, so I'm withholding my sympathy for now. And I'm here because I want to have a relationship with you, and this is not the way I planned on starting it."

I nodded. "I know."

"Thank you for being so… okay about it."

My nod quickly turned to me shaking my head because he had the wrong idea. "I'm definitely not okay. I'm still processing it. but I'm… I don't know. I'm just confused. Maybe… what should I know about her?"

"What do you want to know?"

"Not her personality or favorite flavor of ice cream. But did she seem like the type who'd fabricate a baby and go to a tabloid?"

"I don't know. Is that a personality type?"

"You know what I mean. Did she seem genuine?"

"Nik, I barely remember her."

"Do you remember if you were careful? Did you have a lapse in judgment?"

He looked offended. "Of course not. There's no question about that."

"How did it end? Could you have given her the wrong idea and maybe she wants to trap you to get you back?"

"It ended because it was casual and I left to film a movie. It was barely a relationship. I think we dated for a month."

A knot tightened in my stomach, and a dullness spread through my chest. I looked away from him. He didn't need me to say that a month was twice as long as he and I had been together.

"Hey," he said, tipping my face to look at him. "We went on a few dates. Yes, I slept with her. But I didn't feel even a glimmer of what I feel with you. You're… it's not even in the same universe. Please know that. I want more with you. I've never been able to say that to anyone before."

His words calmed me, and I worked to shove my concerns about his old relationship aside and focus on what Chris planned to do next. And how I could help him. I knew I wanted to help, and I hated that some people tried to use celebrities like him for their own gain. I was irritated on his behalf, because I could see how kind he normally was and how much it hurt him to have someone say he wasn't a standup guy.

"Okay, well, I'm here for you."

"Even if I turn out to be the father?"

"Let's cross that bridge if we need to. Honestly, the fact that she went to a tabloid before she came to you kinda screams extortion. That's not the kind of thing you do when you want your baby to have a good relationship with his or her dad. It's the kind of thing you do when you want money. Either money to make the story go away or money to help raise her celebrity baby."

"I know," he said, as though he didn't want to say all of those things out loud. "That's generally how these things go."

"You mean, because this has happened before?"

"Not to me. But I know people who've dealt with it. The worst I've had is a couple of stalkers."

"Oh, is that all?" I asked. He smiled at my sarcasm. "Anyone armed and dangerous?"

"Armed, but she's a bad shot, so not particularly dangerous."

He rubbed his hand over the back of his neck. For the first time since he'd taken the phone call, his expression bordered on calm.

"Okay. So get on the plane's Wi-Fi and have your publicist and lawyer reassure you that what she's doing is a money grab. I'm surprised the tabloid hasn't offered to bury the story for a tidy sum."

He looked surprised by my assessment. Maybe he thought I was evil incarnate for being so comfortable with such a scheme. "You said you're good at your job, but clearly, nonvacation Nikki is tough, savvy, and *very good* at her job."

I had no doubt that my cheeks turned hot pink at the compliment. "You're just lucky I've been toiling in the publicity salt mines for the past few years, so these things don't shock me. But plenty of other stuff still does, so don't think you're off the hook from my hysterical reactions."

"I don't want to be off the hook. From any of it." He reached his hand to my cheek and kissed my lips. His gaze charged at me, and I was done for, as usual. I could have stared at those hypnotic, deep-brown eyes for the rest of the flight. His fake baby mama could have given birth and followed it with a lap dance, and I wouldn't have noticed.

Chris ran the back of his hand over my cheek and brought it around until it rested against the back of my neck.

I'd stopped trying to fight the heat that lit every place he touched on fire the second I felt his hands on my skin. "It's gonna be okay," I told him. I had no way of knowing that, but we both needed to believe it.

"I don't even remember what we were talking about," he said. He bent toward me and leaned his forehead against mine.

"That's a very good sign."

His lips swept across mine in the same gentle way as they had many times over the past two weeks. Chris turned more squarely to face me and pulled me toward him, deepening the kiss and our connection. I felt his vulnerability and his need, and I tried to answer it with my own. It was the way we'd been with each other since we'd met, and really, it was the only way we knew how to be. As we fell back into a familiar closeness, the optimist in me hoped a smidgen of our vacation love would follow us back into the real world.

CHAPTER ONE

Nikki

OVER THE COURSE of the flight, Chris had spent a good two hours firing texts and emails back and forth with his lawyer, his publicist, and his manager, all of whom agreed that his ex had contacted the tabloid because she wanted money or fame by association. She didn't seem to want Chris himself, which made the situation more manageable. Once she learned that she couldn't manipulate Chris, she would probably back off, his reps assured him. The first order of business was to take a paternity test to find out if he was in fact the father.

"I swear, we were together a couple times at most," he'd told me again plaintively.

"It only takes one time," I said. I felt like a middle school sex ed teacher.

"True. I'm always careful."

I believed him. He was a good guy. He didn't do reckless things, and he wasn't abusive to anyone's feelings. I didn't know his ex-girlfriend, but I already didn't like her. I didn't want to be suspicious and disdainful of another woman without knowing all the facts, but from what I knew so far, she sounded manipulative.

At the same time, I wasn't so evolved that I really wanted to hear all the details about their time together, something Chris felt the need to recount as he hashed out the scenario, going through the three—he'd decided there were only three—times they'd had sex. All three times, they'd used a condom, and all three times were in the month of March. That meant she was four months pregnant.

A paternity test would quickly put her accusations to rest, one way or the other. "I guess there's nothing to be done until that happens. A lot more digging will have taken place by the time we land. My lawyer will look at her social media posts to see if she has pictures with other men during the time she likely conceived. And they'll subpoena a DNA sample for the paternity test. Then they'll slam the tabloid with a cease-and-desist order, threatening suit for defamation without proof. Nothing will be printed without confirmation." He grabbed my hand and brought it to his chest. "Thank you."

"You're welcome, but I haven't really done anything except talk you down."

"That's what I needed. You're right. I can't let it get to me. Again, if my assistant hadn't called me all crazed, I probably wouldn't have worried so much. I think I internalized her fear."

I decided I didn't like his assistant. I knew I couldn't go forward disliking all the women Chris interacted with, and that wasn't my intention at all, but I couldn't help feeling a bit protective of the man I'd given my heart to. I wanted our tentative beginning to unfold without drama. I wanted us to have a chance. I also knew none of it was up to me.

He was a celebrity. His life was dramatic by default.

~

THE AIR FRANCE jet landed gently on the runway in a feat that always seemed impressive for an impossibly heavy metal flying machine that defied my general understanding of physics. I'd barely felt the wheels touch down, and before long, the brakes slowed the giant bird to a quiet, uneventful roll toward the gate. It wasn't until the plane slowed that I realized I'd been holding Chris's hand in a death grip. I unclenched my sweaty fingers and unwrapped them from his.

"You okay there?" He smiled at me in that way that went straight to my heart.

"Just a reflex. I wasn't scared, but your hand was there, so…"

"Happy to have you use my hand for moral support."

"It was a reflex."

"It's okay if you don't love flying."

"I'm good with flying. Not so good with thinking about flying. Planes are metal and heavy and I don't understand the aerodynamics that keep them afloat."

"You should learn about draft and lift. It would probably make you more comfortable when you fly."

I pulled his hand to my lips and kissed his knuckles. "Later, please teach me about draft and lift. For now, thank you for letting me crush your fingers."

Chris kissed my cheek like a parent reassuring a child that everything would be okay. I tilted my head and looked at the contour of his handsome face, outlined by the sun streaming through the airplane window, and the plush line of his lips, whose touch always left me wanting more. We were still taxiing, and I could see from the cloudless sky that LA had delivered another flawless summer day.

I unwrapped the piece of chocolate I'd saved from the dinner service hours before and popped it into my mouth, savoring the last taste of French anything. At least I assumed it was French. For all I knew, Air France could source their chocolate from anywhere, and I would have been none the wiser.

We agreed to set the paternity allegation aside until we knew more, so I did my best to let it go, and Chris did his best to make sure I was plenty distracted, mostly with his lips. I'd flown next to Chris for more than eleven hours, feeling blissed out and high on my overwhelming feelings for a guy who'd just made a huge life change and decided to move from New York to LA to be with me. I still couldn't really believe he was thinking beyond the two weeks of vacation that I'd convinced myself were all we could ever have.

While he'd napped intermittently, watched a couple movies, and read a couple scripts, I'd spent most of the flight lost in my thoughts, staring at him, taking in my surroundings in business class and marveling at a feeling I'd never experienced. My heart was so full it was in danger of spillage.

Several times, Chris had looked at me, seeming a little curious that I wasn't occupied, and asked something like, "You want to read something on my iPad? Watch a movie? Anything?"

Each time, I'd shaken my head, zombie-like, needing to hole up with my thoughts and spend the flight just sitting there, taking it all in, and marveling at the impossibly gorgeous, too-good-to-be-real guy sitting next to me.

But he was real. It had been a whirlwind couple of weeks with him, and I needed to process his sudden decision to move to LA. I still didn't know what it really meant, and my mind had gone to all sorts of questionable places.

Am I ready to have a guy move across the country for me? Do I know him well enough to think it could work? Can I handle media scrutiny? Will I need to?

By the time we landed, I'd pulled myself together. I wasn't one to shy away from challenging situations, and if dating a global celebrity was my only life hardship, I'd consider myself supremely lucky. Long before I met Chris, I'd learned an important thing about myself through my job and years of living on my own: I was comfortable in my own shoes, and I didn't need approval from strangers for my own validation.

That was, until we stepped off the plane.

As we weaved our way through customs, I noticed how many people were acutely aware of Chris and, by association, aware of me. I looked down at my faded travel pants, which were really unflattering yoga pants I'd bought in the wrong size because they were on sale. As such, they were unfit for anything but sitting—heaven forbid getting fancy and bending anywhere. My hair was loose from its ponytail and made even more messy by Chris running his fingers through it while we made out on the plane… I knew I didn't look like a celebrity's girlfriend ought to look. Maybe I did want a tiny bit of validation.

"You'll get used to it," Chris said, entwining his fingers with mine. Even after knowing me for only two weeks, he could see my comfort zone receding in the distance and kept a tight grasp on my hand.

"How? How do you get used to people looking at you all the time?" My reaction wasn't only about me. I found myself feeling protective of Chris. I wanted people to get out of his personal space and stop gawking. It felt unfair that he couldn't do something as simple as pick up luggage at baggage claim without people snapping surreptitious selfies with him in the background.

"Concentrate on what you're doing and what's in front of you, like a nearsighted person who isn't wearing glasses."

"I am a little nearsighted," I admitted.

"Perfect. Focus on what's in your immediate bubble… That would be me." He pressed a kiss to my temple, completely at ease.

"Looks like your bubble just expanded," I said as moments later, he was agreeing to take a selfie with a female fan and her friend, who were grinning like they'd just gotten braces off their teeth after five years.

"Would you mind?" one of them was asking me, handing me her phone.

I backed up so I could get a better shot of the three of them, knowing to put the phone in portrait mode to get the most flattering shot. I didn't fail to notice that when I was taking the picture, Chris was smiling at me, not looking at the phone screen. I loved him for that.

I handed the phone back, and Chris grabbed my bag from the carousel then tossed it onto a luggage cart. His bag came sailing along the belt right afterward, so in a couple minutes' time, we'd left the fray and made it out to the sidewalk, where a town car was waiting.

Just as a couple people began to notice Chris and point him out, we disappeared into the backseat while the driver loaded our bags into the trunk. Behind the darkened window glass, we were once again protected from the world outside. I knew it wasn't realistic to stay there forever, but I loved the way we were together when it was just us.

The idea of spending more days or weeks with Chris felt like the first layer of ice on a pond that could grow more solid as winter bore on. But until then, our fragility seemed beautiful and precarious, and it wasn't something I was willing to risk just as my heart was starting to believe.

"So in answer to your earlier question about how to get used to fans," he said, putting an arm around me in the car, "I focus on what I'm doing and on the people I care about. I will always oblige and take a selfie if I can, but I try to stay intentionally oblivious to people who just want to stare. What good would it do me to tune in to that and feel like a zoo animal?"

"That makes sense. But what about me? Do I need to up my game, so people won't wonder why you're dating an outlet mall shopper with bedhead?"

He turned toward me, and I saw his expression shift from curiosity to sympathy. "You really don't see yourself, do you?" His eyes roamed my face from top to bottom. "First of all, I'm digging your eleven-hours-on-a-plane look. And I'm not sorry I messed up your hair," he said, raising an eyebrow at the memory. "But the idea that you could possibly reflect badly on me is an impossibility."

"I wasn't fishing for compliments. You do have an image to

uphold." His words were lovely, but he needed to be realistic, or none of this was going to work.

"Okay, sure. If I crash cars and get arrested and beat up photographers, I'll catch hell for it. But who I date is no one's business."

"I think you're being naïve if you don't think people care who you date."

"I don't give a shit about those people. What I care about is you feeling comfortable when we're together. That's all that matters to me."

"I am comfortable when we're together."

"Then to hell with everyone else. Seriously. I will work on this with you until you realize that when I'm with you, all I see is you. No one else matters."

The way his eyes slowly roamed over my face and down my body made me blush. I held tightly to decades-old insecurities about my curvy hips and bee-stung lips that only became fashionable years after I'd been roundly mocked for them in middle school.

Then, as if he could read my thoughts, he wrapped his arm more tightly around me and bent to whisper into my ear. "My goal… is to get you to see yourself the way I see you. Because I can be objective. And what I see when I look at you is a beautiful, bright shining light with a gorgeous brain and a fuck-all sexy body."

He was gazing at me with a look of smitten surrender, and I made a decision: I would not ruin this by second-guessing his compliments and worrying constantly. Instead, I would hear him —really hear him—and believe him. Which was… wow.

"I… don't even know how to respond to that." My heart knew, and it picked up its pace.

"You say thank you… and you admit I'm brilliant."

I grinned at him. "Thank you. You're brilliant."

He slid a hand along my thigh and bent to kiss me. It was a

good kiss, hot and heartfelt with just the right amount of tongue to make me melt.

And even though we'd spent about half the flight huddled into each other, kissing for so long that the flight attendants eventually stopped coming over to ask if we needed anything, I had no problem with the idea of his lips for another ten hours straight.

Kissing him was always a good idea.

THE TOWN CAR snaked through the airport traffic, which was deplorable regardless of the time of day. It felt strange to be back home after two weeks, which felt like two months. What I'd seen on the walls of museums and what I'd eaten in fabulous restaurants made coming back to the same old, same old feel like a letdown. Every street I'd walked had been new to me. The language had challenged me. The blue waters of the Cote d'Azur and the green Seine had mesmerized me. Looking out the window now at billboards, parking structures, and fast food restaurants depressed me. I felt like the city had stagnated while I'd had a worldly adventure. Everything was exactly the same as when I'd left two weeks before.

Then I felt Chris's arm around my shoulder. *Well, not everything.*

I tried not to react to seeing Chris's face on a city bus and two billboards between the airport and the freeway. Eh, whatever. Doesn't everyone look up and see their boyfriend's face on a fifty-by-twenty-foot billboard? Yeah, no. There was no way around it—it was weird.

And… I was getting worked up again. It wasn't just the staggering contrast between his fame and my beloved anonymity. We'd only known each other for two weeks. I was a sure and steady soul. I made logical decisions. Bringing Chris home with me was not logical.

The feel of Chris's fingers massaging my shoulder did a little to calm me down, but not nearly enough. Until he spoke, I hadn't realized I was shaking.

"It's gonna be okay," he said, but when I turned, I saw his look of concern. I wasn't sure that even he, the eternal optimist, so comfortable with his fame that he generally ignored it, really believed we could transfer our vacation romance to the real world without the wheels falling off the cart.

"This is crazy, right? I mean, what makes you think we can seamlessly meld our lives together. I mean—"

Chris put up a hand to stop me. It turned out his look of concern was for me, because he was already anticipating my concerns. Then he closed the privacy screen that separated us from the driver. "What? What are you worried about?"

"I'm worried that you're not allowed to do this. To date me. It seems like you should be getting permission from the celebrity gods or your handlers or whoever's gonna ding your career for moving here to be with me. It's gonna cause stress, and people are going to talk, and you're going to have to answer for your choices. And I'm not sure I'm worth all that. So I'm just sitting here, waiting for you to figure all that out."

I hadn't even articulated it in my mind before that moment, but once I said the words, I knew I'd finally hit on the heart of the issue. I didn't feel worthy of being the reason he was changing his life. I didn't want to meet his gaze for fear that it would confirm I was right, but after a few moments of staring at the floor in silence, I had to look up.

What I saw in Chris's pale eyes was a combination of amusement and maybe a little bit of hurt. "Are you done?"

"Yes."

"Okay, great." He turned to kneel in front of me, which was no challenge in the spacious backseat of the town car. "Phew. I was worried you were gonna wait until we got back from the airport to freak out on me. But now I see you don't waste time with anything."

"Please take this seriously," I said.

Chris was great at lightening the mood, but I didn't want light. I wanted to jump out of the car and run away before *People* wrote an unflattering story about my stretched-out fire-sale yoga pants.

"Oh, I am," he said, but the tone in his voice still told me he found my whole diatribe amusing. He picked up both of my hands and brought them to his lips, where he kissed each one before pulling me forward to rest my hands on his shoulders. "Listen. All that stuff you're worried about… just… try not to, okay? Let me deal with my job and whatever the tabloids feel like writing. I told you, I don't read them, anyway."

"Maybe you should. Then you could be a crazy person like me." I tried to match his lighter tone, but my words felt heavy.

"This is me." He held my hands solidly against him. "The same guy you've spent the last two weeks with. Nothing is different between us except the location."

I wanted to believe him. I wanted to think we could continue falling for each other the way we had every day of our time together. I didn't want that to end. I never wanted it to end.

I looked out the window, where I could see the early-afternoon traffic already backing up on the freeway. In some ways, all the recognizable clutter of cellphone-repair shops, pizza takeout places, and cars was comforting. Always cars in LA. "It's hard to believe you're really here," I said, wanting to fathom some scenario in which our disparate lives could mesh. Maybe I was even starting to believe it—a crack opened just enough to let some light in.

"Believe it. I'm only here for you."

Yes, but he was Chris Conley, a global mega-film star with a gorgeous face and sculpted abs. I didn't make sense in his private-jet, champagne world. I almost felt it was my duty to make him see the madness of his ways.

"I know that, but—"

"No. I don't think you do," he said. He looked into my eyes, hypnotizing me with his stare and his words. "Listen to me. I'm here because this is what I want. You didn't force my hand or give me an ultimatum that I'm going to resent. I chased you down on the plane because I can't stand the thought of being anywhere other than with you." He shrugged like it was that simple.

I nodded as his words sank in. If it was going to work, I had to believe him. I wanted to believe him. "I want to be with you too."

"So stop worrying."

"It's in my DNA."

"Then worry about other things. You don't have to worry about me. I'm crazy about you, and that's all you need to know."

His lips were on mine, sweet and warm and strong, as he slid back into the seat and pulled me closer. He ran one finger along my cheek and traced the contour of my jaw. His other hand tangled in my hair while he deepened the kiss, taking me with him again on the ecstatic freight train I'd been riding for the past two weeks. For a moment, I thought about the driver and wondered if he could see us. And I thought about how Chris hadn't put his seatbelt back on. But to hell with the seatbelt, because it felt too good to have him pressed against me.

By the time we got on the freeway heading northbound toward Santa Monica, I was a dizzy mess of tangled hair, bruised lips, and an insatiable need to get out of my clothes. And I felt unfathomably happy.

So I gave in, tilting my head back as Chris placed a new row of soft, wet kisses along the column of my throat. Then I felt his breath on the part of my neck that gave me chills, and I gave in. I let go of the fears about our future. I let go completely.

CHAPTER TWO

SANTA MONICA
Chris

I COULDN'T BLAME Nikki for being weirded out by strangers asking for selfies, all of it right as I was trying to assuage her fears about the paternity-allegation bombshell. Some women might find it exciting and cool to have a ringside seat to scandal and celebrity, but Nikki would rather run, not walk, in the opposite direction.

Understandable. It was part of what I found lovely and compelling about her—she saw me as a person, not a celebrity. But I hoped her dislike for limelight wouldn't consume her, because I couldn't possibly shield her from all of it.

If we were out together in a public place, people were going to gawk. Maybe that had to mean we didn't go out much. I could handle that. For a while.

Nikki lived six miles from the airport, and it took forty-five minutes to get back to her condo. The traffic was hellish. It was also forty-five glorious, hot minutes in the back of the town car with the privacy screen all the way up. There was no reason to begrudge the benefits of a roomy back seat.

God, I was crazy about this woman. I actually found myself sneaking sideways glances because I still couldn't believe I'd jumped on a plane and chased her to California. But I had no doubt it was the right decision. My life moved too fast for me to spend time second-guessing my choices.

There would be some juggling, to be sure, but once I got my manager and my assistant onboard with the move to LA, things would fall into place. They always did.

As we got closer to her neighborhood, I wanted to look around and get my bearings. I hadn't spent much time in LA, and when I had, it had been for press events and talk shows.

In and out. No time for sightseeing, and frankly, I wasn't all that interested. I could admit to being a slightly arrogant New Yorker who thought that most other cities paled by comparison.

So I hugged her tightly but vowed to keep my hands off the rest of her until we were out of the car. I cracked the window and inhaled the dry, coastal California air. Leaving a city where all of humanity lived on top of each other—in other words, the most dynamic, interesting city on the planet—wouldn't be the worst thing if it meant living by the beach.

"How close do you live to the beach?"

"Six blocks."

"Seriously? I see a walk in our future this afternoon."

"We can do that. It'll help with the jetlag to be outside."

"Oh, I'll want some inside time too, don't you worry."

"I will strive to find a healthy balance."

Once we'd exited the freeway at Fourth Street, I opened the window more and let in a little bit of the breezy ocean smell. Since I didn't know LA well, I was pretty fired up about sightseeing. "What's that?" I pointed at a mammoth, block-wide structure with some sort of metal art piece decorating the side.

"It's a mall. I mean, it's a nice mall, with lots of pretty stores, but still… mall."

"And if a person wanted to buy another person a sexy dress that couldn't possibly be worn with a bra, might that mall be a good place to find such an item?" I knew she wasn't entirely comfortable with me picking out clothes for her, but I felt certain I could find her something she would never buy for herself that would look incredible on her, and I wasn't above pushing her out of her comfort zone.

Her cheeks turned the color of raspberry jam. "I wouldn't know."

I saw an opening in her denial. "No? Something tells me you're downplaying your interest in said mall. You're a secret shopaholic, aren't you?"

"Okay, fine. Not for the sexy dresses. But you might as well know… I do like my shoes."

"Ah, now we're getting somewhere. Is it possible that some of your shoes might benefit from the company of a sexy dress?"

"I'll let you be the judge. I have a Technicolor rainbow of wedge heels and stilettos in my closet, and I'm not apologizing for them. I have a weakness for pretty shoes."

"Then I think we'll get along perfectly. Because I have a weakness for you."

She reached for my hand and turned her face toward the window, but I could see she was smiling. I vowed to eventually make her more comfortable with compliments.

"Okay, we're here. I live on the third floor," she said as the car pulled up in front of her building.

I looked up at the building, which rose about six stories from the sidewalk. It was an older-looking, Spanish-influenced structure. Knowing how captivated she was with the art and architecture in France, it didn't surprise me that she lived in a place with character. She caught me looking, and I guess she felt the need to explain. "I looked forever until I found a unit in this building."

"Why this particular one?"

"It's classic. Old California architecture. There are really two original styles, Craftsman and Spanish. I couldn't live in some modern monolith or cheesy fifties box."

"I like it. Everything's nice and spread out here."

"Different from New York, huh? Do you think you'll miss it?" she asked.

The driver opened the door, and I felt the warm Pacific air and realized how much I already missed being on vacation. There was something steady and calm about the breezy beach climate, and the smell immediately took me back to our time in the South of France.

I shrugged and put an arm around her while the driver lugged our bags from the trunk to the elevator in the building. "Change is good."

"It's okay to say you'll miss it."

"New York has its plusses, but I've been there long enough… and yeah, I'll probably miss it a little."

There wasn't room in the elevator for us, the driver, and our luggage, so we left the luggage behind, raced up the three flights of stairs, and beat the driver to her front door. He rolled our bags down the hallway a minute later. Nikki thanked him profusely for the help, and I shook his hand. I knew a generous tip would be added to the bill by my business manager.

When Nikki opened the door, I was immediately struck by the light scent of plumeria and honey that I'd come to associate with her. Walking in the door was like being enveloped in her, and I gratefully inhaled. She lived in a small but homey condo, and I could see how much effort she'd put into making it uniquely hers. Art was everywhere—paintings, sculptures, even a couple of hanging mobiles that made me think of a Calder exhibit I'd once seen at MOMA.

She kicked the door closed and grabbed for my hand, pulling me toward her. As much as my attention was focused on Nikki and relieving some of the pent-up angst I'd been feeling on the plane, I had to take in our surroundings for just a moment.

On the wall facing the front door, there was a set of six framed mixed-media collages that reminded me of a group of California artists that made lithographs in that style. They were large, each one two by three feet. And they were arresting in their color and composition. She had incredible taste in art. On her reclaimed-wood coffee table in front of the couch, I saw three small sculptures, each worked from different cuts of stone, each one equally striking.

There was more—abstract watercolor paintings on a wall leading to the kitchen, the paint mixed with sand to give it a blotchy, inky look, and black-and-white drawings on a different wall. And that was just what I could see from the room where we stood. She'd surrounded herself with creativity and beauty and I could do nothing but stare in admiration. "You have an incredible art collection," I said, deciding whether I was more impressed with her artistic eye or her bold decision to collect art when most people our age spent money on cars or expensive dinners.

"Thank you," she said, her voice barely audible.

When I turned toward her, curious why her voice was so quiet, she tried again to pull me toward her, away from where I stood, distracted by the art. That only made me more curious. "How long have you been at this?" I asked, wondering how long it took to amass this collection. I wanted to follow where she was leading, especially if it took us to the bedroom, but I was captivated. And interested.

She sighed, seeming surprised that I wanted to talk about the art before I wanted to peel her clothes off and lick her skin. I was surprised, too, but what I was looking at was that beautiful. I couldn't not comment on it. I couldn't not know about it. I would explain later, after I'd peeled her clothes off. For the time being, I looked to her to answer my question.

"I took a painting class in college. A couple painting classes. Then I just kind of got hooked."

My brain was churning, trying to make sense of what she was saying. "Wait, you made all of this? This is *your* art?"

She nodded, and I'm pretty sure she even shrugged. She

wasn't shy about it, not modest, not anything. It was as if we were discussing a cookie recipe she'd made from the back of a box.

"You made… all of this?"

She nodded again, looking at me like I was being dense. "I had a lot of bare walls. It was a fun side project."

I shook my head, not understanding how she didn't see what I did. "This is… isn't some paint-by-numbers side project. I'm blown away. You're really talented. Extremely talented."

She stared at me, her eyes curious and calm, as though she was looking at someone who was possibly mentally unstable. "Okay. Thank you. I'm glad you like it."

"I… we're going to have to discuss this later in more detail."

"Later sounds good. I have a ton of art supplies. We can paint if you think it would be fun," she said, still calmer than I'd seen her most of the time we'd been together. It was as though the art on her walls and the environment she'd created gave her a sense of security and well-being that she didn't have while she was away. She was home, where she felt comfortable being herself.

I understood suddenly why she kept talking about my world as being someplace different, someplace where she might not fit in. Her apartment was her world, and it was magical. "I think… sure. We can paint. Although my idea of fine art is finger painting you with chocolate syrup and licking it off."

She smiled. "We can do that too. Later. Right now, I want—no, I need—to have you take your shirt off. I've been sitting next to you for half a day and thinking almost exclusively about that."

I didn't need an engraved invitation. I pulled my T-shirt over my head and immediately felt her nails drag across my chest and down my abs. I felt my muscles jump at her touch. Jesus, it never got old. "I've been craving you since our last night together in France," I said, wrapping a hand around the back of her neck and kissing her along her jawline. When I got to the neckline of her shirt, I grabbed it in my teeth and tugged, helping it over her head with my other hand from the bottom. "I've been picturing you like this."

She was gorgeous. Her breasts spilled over the tops of her bra cups, and I bent my head to taste her delicious skin. I used the back of my hand to graze the tops of her breasts before reaching around, unclasping it, and letting it fall to the floor.

"Now, your pants," she said.

"People admiring your art makes you kinda bossy," I said.

"You make me kinda everything." She sounded a little breathless. "Sitting next to you on the plane was torture."

"I'd have done this with you on the plane." I wasn't going to lie. If she'd have just said the word, I'd have inducted her into the mile-high club. But I was trying to make our time together more meaningful than what I'd given to past relationships. I didn't think a quick fuck in an airplane bathroom after telling her about my ex's possible pregnancy would accomplish that.

"Ha. You have no shame."

"Nope."

She ran her nails along the waistband of my pants, just teasing the skin. I felt my dick immediately jump to attention as she popped the button and slid the zipper down. I wasn't thinking about art at all anymore.

She licked a trail down my abs, sending a thrill of sensation through every part of me.

I wanted to take my time. Hell, I also wanted to pin her against a wall. I chose to start slow, but she shook her head. "Not after teasing me in the car for three hours. I need you now."

"It wasn't three hours, but I see your point." I kissed her neck, tasting the skin of her shoulder before giving it a little nip.

"Stop. Talking," she said, pulling me closer and backing up until both of us landed on the couch with me on top of her.

She didn't have to tell me twice.

CHAPTER THREE

Nikki

CHRIS DIDN'T HAVE much time to think about missing New York before it beckoned with an urgent plea. He got a call an hour after I showed him the rest of my one-bedroom condo—the walk-in closet, the tiny bonus room I used as a home office, and the kitchen—and learned that production on a film that he'd tried to push back to November couldn't be changed. In fact, it was starting ahead of schedule, and he had to go back to New York immediately for three weeks of prep, after which he would fly to Ireland for a two-month shoot.

His agent wanted to know if he was available.

The way he'd planned it out, he'd be in LA with me for two weeks, and he'd start looking for a place to rent while he was here. Then he'd go back to New York to pack up and fulfill a few commitments there. But with the movie filming locally, he'd be in LA for the majority of the next six months. He told me multiple times that he really wanted to make the move and that I should not feel guilty about whatever legwork that required.

"Are you available?" I asked wryly, expecting him to say no.

He'd already spent part of the plane ride communicating with his manager to finesse the start dates of that very project, and he'd committed to a different movie because it would be shooting on location in LA in four months.

He didn't answer right away, and I could tell that everything had suddenly shifted. Gone were the sweet whispers of an hour before, when Chris told me he wanted to stay inside me forever. Reality had quashed any plans except those relating to his job. I felt a pit settle into my stomach. *Here it goes.*

"Yes. I mean no. I can always say no." He smiled as if he could treat his career with the cavalier tone he was using, but we both knew the truth.

"You don't have to say no. If it's something you want to do, you should do it." I felt strongly about that. I never wanted him to turn down something he wanted to do, especially out of consideration for me.

He looked torn. "I kind of want to do it."

I nodded. It would be fine, I told myself.

"But if you tell me not to do it, I won't."

"Oh no, that's not how this is going to work. If we have a chance at all of being together, you need to work and be happy. I have a job. It's not like I'll be sitting here all day, waiting for you in an apron and bunny slippers. I've got a career to manage too." I was in a bit of denial that I'd be going back to work, but there was no escaping it.

I didn't like the way he was looking at me, like he felt guilty.

"Please. Let's get this right at the outset," I told him. "Go to work. Be your best self. And when you're not at work, come be with me."

Chris sat on my blue denim couch and put his head in his hands. "Ugh, I hate this. You know I want to be here, right?"

"Yes. Chris, I know."

"I could say I'm not available until the November date. They work around my schedule."

"If they could do that, wouldn't they have kept the original date?" I still didn't know enough about how the movie business worked to understand why they moved things around, but I knew there had to be a reason.

"Right. It's a costar issue. She can't do November, and if we don't shoot now, we wait a year, and by then, everything could change."

"Sounds like you have your answer if you want to do this movie."

"But all the things I said… I still mean them. I really do want to be here. I just… can't."

"I appreciate that. I want you to be here too. But we have to start things off right, or we're doomed. Let's make it simple. You were planning on taking this role when it was shooting in November. And you don't have anything—other than me—to keep you from doing it now."

"What if I'd rather hang here with you?"

I sat down next to him. He really seemed distraught over his choices. "Then you're making the wrong decision. Chris, that's a lovely thing to say, and I know you mean it. But I'm not gonna let you start turning down jobs for me."

"So I should go to New York." He didn't sound at all convinced.

"You should."

"Will you come out?"

"Sure. At some point."

"How about next week?"

"I mean… how? I have to work. I just took two weeks off."

"So come for a weekend. I can get you on whatever flights you need, so you can time it with your hours at work."

I nodded, because I understood that he needed to feel like there was a possibility of us seeing each other in order to commit to the film, which I knew was what he wanted. Of course I would try to make that happen. I wanted to be with him. It was worth some redeye flights and a little schedule juggling. "Of course. Sure, I'll come out," I said, having no idea how I was going to do it. I knew I'd be returning to a full in-box and a lot of small fires no one had put out in my absence. The last thing I could do was take more time off. But I had to give Chris the affirmation he wanted. He seemed unable to move forward without it. "I just need to look at my calendar when I get back to work," I said.

FYI, the calendar is going to say "no way in hell."

Chris seemed relieved. Finally, the sad, guilty look was swept from his face. All I had to do was convince him his life didn't have to change in order to be with me.

The reality was that his life hadn't changed. After one night back in LA, during which we'd fallen asleep on the couch despite trying to enjoy our last few hours together, he'd flown back to New York on a private jet.

The next morning, a medical assistant was ferried to the production offices where Chris was meeting with the director to take a cheek swab from him in order to test for paternity. His ex-girlfriend would need a blood test, which so far, she'd refused to get. Once she did, results could be finalized within two to five days. Chris would feel better once he had all the information. So would I.

So instead of spending the majority of the next six months in LA, he'd be spending the next three months in New York and Ireland, with the time after that up in the air.

"You're so great," he told me. I could see his appreciation for bending to allow for his schedule.

But I wasn't really bending. In fact, a part of me had known his offer to move to LA was too good to be true. It was a whim, borne out of his sadness about our vacation fling coming to an end. It wasn't real.

I'd have to see how I felt about starting a relationship from a distance. I had no idea if it would work, but I knew I had to try, because watching him leave this time made me sadder than when I'd said goodbye in France. That time, I'd thought it was goodbye forever.

Why was I sadder when it was only goodbye for a while?

Maybe because it hurt more to want him and know he couldn't be with me for months.

Chris called when he landed to tell me he missed me and to reiterate how grateful he was that I was so understanding of his career. He'd made plans to meet the director the next day over lunch.

He called me again later, after getting coffee from a place on Thompson Street and had chatted with the baristas there because he was that guy, always friendly and open even though he was famous. A few people pretended to take selfies but were actually snapping pictures of him from a distance, he said. He told me he could tell when people were doing it, but it didn't bother him. Without me raising hell at the gall of people who intruded on his every movement, he took the selfies and rolled with the trappings of fame like he always did.

It was almost as if he'd never left New York... Almost like we'd never met.

CHAPTER FOUR

Nikki

THINGS WERE a little different when I returned to work post-vacay. For one thing, I saw my office anew, which was always a good thing. The physical office was designed like a tech campus, with a big, open space in the center, containing a shuffleboard table, a well-stocked kitchen and chairs, and couches arranged into seating areas to encourage idea sharing. I remembered how much I liked working there, if for no other reason than the snack jars of M&M's and pretzels and the dizzying selection of refrigerated drinks.

I also liked the intensity of the work, which kept my mind sharp and challenged me to think of new solutions to problems my publicity clients had. And I liked my colleagues. At least, I'd liked them before my two weeks away.

On my first day back, I felt a palpable shift in energy when I walked into the conference room for our Monday briefing. I expected to feel a little out of sync with everyone because I'd been out of the loop for two weeks, but I'd underestimated the Chris factor. It turned out that everyone knew we were seeing each other, and that fact had unleashed some sort of fervor among my colleagues.

I should have been prepared for it. I worked at a public relations firm, after all. Business depended on knowing news *and* gossip, so of course, everyone at my firm already knew about my time on the red carpet in Cannes with Chris. Still, I figured that after a couple of questions about how we met or what we did in France, the conversation would shift to the regular Monday work imperatives.

It didn't.

"So *he* approached *you*?" asked Jemma, a junior publicist who'd been at the firm for a little under a year. Until then, she'd barely acknowledged we worked for the same company, even though I outranked her, and I'd tried to be friendly on several occasions. Jemma was a cool girl who liked other cool girls—which, until Chris, I was not. Suddenly, she was making plans for us to "grab lunch later."

"Um, sure," I said, watching her finger-comb her blond lob and adjust the tortoiseshell frames of her hipster glasses so they perched higher on her nose. I could actually see her lash extensions brushing against the glass when she blinked. It looked uncomfortable. Maybe I could ask her about them at lunch.

Sure, that's why she wants to have lunch with you. To talk about eyelashes.

As if to prove my point, she stared at the ceiling, as though Chris's face had suddenly appeared there. "I just need to know. What's he *really* like? Is he, like, super nice? He seems super nice but with an edge, you know?" she asked the room. "It's like he has this image of the damaged superhero with the complicated past, but you can tell he actually calls his mom once a week. Have you met his mom? Is she stunning and youthful but without having any work done?" She was no longer talking to me but instead running her theories past everyone in our group. I stared at her and hoped she would keep talking so I didn't have to.

Those dreams were short-lived, because James, whose

accounts included some of the biggest celebrities the firm had as clients, entered the conference room at the tail end of Jemma's diatribe and joined in with his own questions. "Oh, good. We're still talking about this. Is the real Chris Conley an asshole? I hear he's hard to work with and kind of a diva."

It went on like that for the better part of a half hour. I felt like an unenlightened pacifist who'd inadvertently showed up at a tactical shooting range with a powder puff as my defense.

I didn't want to gossip about "the real Chris Conley" and satisfy the idle curiosity of my coworkers, who were acting like breathless superfans instead of responsible purveyors of public relations solutions. Okay, maybe I should have been a little less grandiose about the importance of what was, in essence, spin control designed to make bad situations look better. Maybe none of us was actually a responsible purveyor of anything, and I needed to join the fangirl club, because that was the business we were in.

I looked at our boss, Ben Dwyer, hoping to catch his eye in apology for derailing the meeting, but he was reading something on his phone, seemingly oblivious to the chaos around him. He had a habit of seeming detached and uninvolved, but I knew for a fact that he heard every word that was spoken and enjoyed pretending to be a fly on the wall.

Eventually, the chatter died down after I'd promised enough lunches and "gab sessions" with colleagues to satisfy their curiosity and implied that they would get more dirt later if only they'd shut up for the time being.

Dwyer had seemed oblivious to the kerfuffle and continued our meeting, only to corner me as we all headed back to our desks and let me know that if I were to convince Chris Conley to sign on as a client with our firm, it would "definitely be a coup" for the firm and—hint, hint—my career.

But I didn't plan on sullying our nascent relationship with a hard sell to switch PR firms, so I nodded as though I understood why it was the obvious win-win outcome to get Chris as a client.

Of course, I knew any public relations firm would like to have a megawatt star for a client. What I didn't know was whether switching firms would benefit Chris in any way. He seemed perfectly happy with the team he was using, so switching would be a favor to me. I wasn't prepared to ask him for that kind of favor, at least not yet.

It wasn't that I wasn't ambitious. Clearly, bringing in big clients would lead to a promotion and more clout, higher pay, and a better title at the firm. I wasn't sure I wanted that.

As I walked back to my desk, I paid a little more attention than usual to the chatter of voices around me, all talking to clients and reassuring them that we understood the mission and knew how to strategize for their best interests.

I normally liked my job well enough, but after Chris's baby mama scare, I saw it in a slightly less rosy light. I could imagine his public relations team scrambling to put a better spin on the truth, and it made me feel disingenuous about doing the same for my clients.

My job didn't delight me with inspiring daily moments and mind-bending challenges, but I liked it and was good at it. It had never bothered me much before that I hadn't zeroed in on one career passion. I was a Renaissance woman with many interests, I told myself. How could I be expected to commit to a single path and make it my career? Maybe I wasn't the kind of person who could do that.

But maybe I was. It just wasn't this job.

That thought continued to haunt me. So much so that I wanted to talk it through with Annie, my best friend, when she was in town later that week for a meeting with an expert witness she needed for an upcoming trial.

Annie had always been my sounding board, from the time we were college roommates through the bad boyfriend years, the bad hair years, and at every career crossroads. She'd once insistently argued her case for why I needed to give country music a chance —because it's epically sad but it tells a story—but she also respected that I wasn't going to get a tattoo just because she wanted company when she had the final daisies put on her flower sleeve.

I loved her like the sister I wished I had when, as an only child, I wrote different girls' names on my clothes and pretended they were hand-me-downs from my cool older siblings. Annie made me laugh harder than anyone, often just as I'd taken a sip of something that was sure to come out my nose. I never learned to wait until she stopped talking before I drank. Probably never would.

The timing of her visit couldn't have been better. With Chris back in New York and the jet lag wearing off, I was ready for a night out. And she already knew most of the details about Chris and how we met, so we were free to talk about other things. Or so I thought.

At least she started with the pretense of talking about other things. "You want me to be honest?" she asked. We were in her room at the Waldorf Astoria Hotel, where she was unpacking her overnight bag, putting everything into drawers, and hanging her dress and blazer in the closet.

"You're only here for one night. I can't believe you're unpacking."

"I don't want my dress wrinkled for tomorrow. And not everyone likes to live out of a duffel bag like they're at camp."

"I don't travel like that anymore. I have a roller bag now. And yes, in answer to your question, of course I want you to be honest. Always." I sat in a club chair next to the window, overlooking a view of the mountains to the north of Beverly Hills. I knew Annie had chosen the hotel for the view, even though she was only staying one night. When she first moved to San Francisco, she bragged that on any four-mile run she took, she could get up a hill that would afford a sweeping view of the San Francisco Bay.

I was impressed she could jog four miles uphill. I liked running as long as the road was flat, which was why the beach bike path was the only place I ever jogged.

She continued emptying her bag, and I looked out the window and waited for her to be honest about some part of my life that I probably thought was fine before her scrutiny.

"I never understood why you took the job at the PR firm."

"I took it because there was a learning curve and it involves a lot of writing."

"And on the daily, are you happy there?"

"Happy enough. I don't hate it."

"Ugh. I hate it for you. I've never heard a person less passionate about work."

Annie was nothing if not direct, and suddenly I wasn't in the mood to have my life choices ripped apart.

"Okay, maybe honesty's overrated."

"Too late. Horse has left the barn." I was pretty sure she was mixing metaphors, but why quibble?

"So put the horse back in. I changed my mind. I don't want to talk about work."

"Okay, let's talk about your sexy, hot boyfriend."

"I don't want to talk about that either." I'd just gotten my heart to a place of détente, where it wasn't rioting on me every second, asking for a dose of Chris. I had it bad for him, and I was doing my best to push those feelings down to a manageable place so I could get through each day without sulking.

"So what do you want to talk about?"

"How about the paleo diet?"

"Are you on the paleo diet?"

"No, but maybe I want to be."

She shook her head. "You love carbs too much. You'd cave after a day." Then she patted her stomach and looked sideways at herself in the mirror to see if any errant bulges appeared where they shouldn't. Like the mere mention of carbs might have caused her to gain five pounds. She'd always been worried about her weight, something she attributed to having Eastern European genes.

"Someday, when my swinging bubba arms take out an eye,

you'll see I was telling the truth," she once told me. Right now, with the miles she ran to keep fit and the long hours she spent at work, there was no excess anything swinging anywhere.

"Are carbs not allowed on the paleo diet?" I asked. Maybe I should have proposed a better topic.

"No, they're not. So since you're trying so hard to avoid talking about work, let's start there. Why haven't you quit?" With her usual fastidiousness, she used a travel steamer to take a couple faint wrinkles out of her dress before closing it in the closet.

The truth was, I'd thought long and hard about quitting in the couple months leading up to my vacation. Part of what I hoped to figure out by walking through Europe was whether there was something I was dying to do instead. But I'd come to decide that my job was fine for now. "Because I still enjoy it. My job involves a lot of writing, which I'm good at, and it's not hard, and I basically like the people."

"You basically like them. Exactly." She pointed at me as if she'd just distilled whiskey from a pile of wheat. She also like to point at the jury during her trials. "Your answer tells me everything I need to know about why you should quit."

"Does it tell you how I'll pay my bills if I quit? Or what job I should do instead?"

She shook her head and walked toward the door, signaling me to follow. "I'm done unpacking. Let's go upstairs. There's a rooftop restaurant with a grain bowl that's supposed to be delish." Annie was a foodie, so it didn't surprise me that she knew more about a hotel restaurant in LA than I did. She barely waited for me to extract my body from the chair before she left the room.

"We're eating a grain bowl? I thought we were getting drinks."

"Relax. We're getting whatever you want, as long as you tell me everything." It felt like a deal with the devil, but I followed her to the elevator.

When we exited the elevator, I felt a light breeze and the feeling of being on vacation without leaving my home city. Something about being at a hotel, especially a swanky one with a great view and drinks that cost more than my pants, took me away from the everyday and allowed me to relax more than if I was sitting on my couch at home. I started thinking maybe she'd forget to outline her grand design for my future if I up and quit my job, something I was highly unlikely to do, given that I was risk averse and not unhappy with my job.

Annie insisted on paying for the drinks, which did not bode well for me and the planned interrogation. "Cheers," she said. "Now, let's talk about finding you a better job." The devil never got waylaid from a plan.

"Are you really gonna make me do this? Why can't we talk about your job and what your expert witness had to say?"

"Because he said ordinary expert-witness things and therefore will make a perfectly good expert witness. I probably didn't need to come in person to find that out, but I wanted to visit you, so I boondoggled down here."

"And I love you for that, but I don't need you dissecting my work life and telling me to scrap my job just for sport."

She took a sip of her drink, something with gin, bitters, and a nasturtium floating on the top. Sipping was difficult with the large flower in the way, so she chucked it onto a napkin and sat back in her chair to take a real sip. I stared at my wine, watching the condensation collect on the outside of the glass under the hot afternoon sun. I could never out-argue Annie. She was a litigator, for crying out loud. No one had a chance against her debating skills, and least of all me, when all I wanted was to talk about the weather, and she was encouraging me to make a major life change. I sighed, readying myself for the onslaught of challenging questions that would make me question my motivations and reason for being.

Instead, she changed her tack. "I'm not telling you to scrap your job. I'm just planting a seed. So maybe it will grow, eventually, into a tree that will fall on your place of business and you'll have to flee the building."

"Fine. I'm fine with the seed. But here's the thing: I may not be the kind of person who's passionate about a job. I have other things in life that I'm passionate about. Maybe my job just needs to be good enough to allow me to do those other things." The sun felt nice against my face, and since I'd forestalled the discussion about work, I resumed my faux mini-vacation and looked out at the view over the hills.

"I guess I can't relate to that."

"I know. You're like Chris. Your passion for your work is what drives you. My passion for art and travel—and for my friends—is what drives me to do my job and have energy left over for all those things. It's a different mindset, but that doesn't make it wrong."

"Okay."

"Okay?" I asked. I expected her to put all her litigating skill behind arguing her case."

"Yes. Okay. I hear what you're saying, and I more or less accept it as a life choice."

"Gee, thanks."

"Oh, you know what I mean. I love you. I'm always going to push if I think you're settling, but you've convinced me. For now."

I rolled my eyes. Her qualifying afterthought pretty much ensured we'd be having this conversation again. Fine. As long as I didn't have to examine all my life choices tonight. It wasn't the time.

"So.... Let's talk about your dreamy superhero boyfriend instead."

"Oh my God. You sound just like the people at work. Why does everyone care so much about him?"

"Because he's super hot, and every woman with a pulse would like to be in your shoes."

The view was nice. The conversation was not. "Yeah," I said on a sigh.

"That's not the sound of a woman who's falling hard for a gorgeous actor."

"Maybe that's because of the tree in the forest." I sipped my wine, which reminded me of France.

Annie picked up the flower and twirled it in her fingers. "Now you've lost me."

"Like when the tree falls and no one hears it. Does it make a sound?"

"I'm familiar with that. What does it have to do with your hot boyfriend? Unless you're telling me something about his wood." She winked. I wished she wouldn't do that, but if anyone could get away with it and still be my closest friend, it was my closest friend.

"I mean, if I fall in love with him and the relationship fails, it all feels very public. Everybody hears the tree crashing to the ground. I'm used to failing privately."

"Who says you're gonna fail?"

"Because he's there and I'm here. Because I'm bad at relationships. Because he's a sexy hot superhero, and eventually, I won't be able to keep up. I don't want to let my emotions run wild, only to have to reel them back in when it all falls apart."

"Wow. So you'd just rather cut it off at the knees instead?"

"I just don't want to set myself up for disappointment."

"Yeah, but no great love ever came from calibrating expectations. You need to aim for what you want."

"Maybe I don't know what I want yet."

"If that's true, I respect it. But if you're lying to yourself to avoid putting your heart on the line, I don't."

She was making my brain hurt. I chose to avoid choosing one of those options. Drinking more wine was infinitely more pleasant than continuing the conversation. Hoping she would forget what we were talking about, I changed the subject. "Hey, do you want to go for a hike while you're here? On the other side of those hills, there's a great trail we can access from Mulholland Drive."

Annie flagged down our waiter and ordered a salad and a chicken sandwich for us to share. And being the dogged litigator, she didn't let me change the subject. "Okay, listen. I'm not gonna bug you for details about Chris... right now. The more important thing is that I bug you to deal with your shit."

I couldn't help but smile a little. Her bluntness didn't annoy me as much as the winking. "Didn't we just talk about that? Do I have more shit?" I had a feeling I knew what she meant, but truthfully... not really.

"Can I be honest?"

"Why do you always ask that? Yes, you can be honest. But if I said no, would it stop you?"

She held up her hands like she was weighing the two options on a scale. "I think you do know what you want. Come on, we've known each other forever. You're different about him than with other guys. You feel something profound, and it scares the crap out of you. This could be the real kind of love, the big epic love. But I worry you're too nice. You don't stick up for yourself. You don't ask for what you want."

I was surprised at her assessment. I'd always thought of myself as someone who stuck up for herself. I wasn't a doormat. "I told you. I don't know what I want."

"Of course you don't. Because you're holding everything back, trying to control your heart so it doesn't get crushed. You think you're doing a good thing—the smart thing—because you always see the best in people, even yourself. But you just might be ruining the thing."

Annie never ceased to make me think and see new perspectives when I'd thought I'd covered them all. I had to admit, her view was interesting. I didn't have a ready retort, which seemed to give Annie license to keep going.

"You don't ask for what you want because you don't want to upset people, even if that means you don't get what you want.

You did it with Johnny, convinced you were okay with his live-in-the-moment shit when really you wanted a real relationship. That way, when it failed, you hadn't really ventured out with all of yourself. So you didn't lose as much. And now you're doing it again."

Am I? It was a lot to sort through, and my instinct was to tell Annie she was dead wrong. "You're dead wrong."

"Am I?"

"I don't know."

Annie laughed. "Exactly. You will people-please to the point of contradicting yourself. Or not even understanding yourself. You need to champion how you feel and what you think, because no one else is going to do it for you."

"What if I just don't know what I want?"

"You do know. And by always hedging your bets and holding back out of fear, I'm worried you're dooming it to fail. So at the end of the day, you'll end up being right in your expectation. But only because you caused it."

As if to punctuate her sentence, she picked up her drink and downed about half of it. I didn't know if she was right. It would require some thinking later on, maybe with a paintbrush in my hand and a nature soundtrack in the background. That was how I did my best thinking.

"Do you feel like doing some shopping? We're a stone's throw from some good stores they don't have in my 'hood, and I could use some shoes," she said.

"Shoes?" I immediately perked up at that, not to mention feeling relief now that we were done analyzing my relationship missteps.

"I hear the Beverly Hills stores are open late on summer nights. It's called BOLD or something. Open late days?"

"They are? How do you, who live four hundred miles away, know this, and I've never heard of such a thing?"

She shrugged. "I know stuff. Let's get one more round to go with our food. Then we can walk to the shops."

As if on cue, a beautiful salad and sandwich were placed on our table, along with two plates for sharing. I wouldn't normally have described food as beautiful, but the two plates looked like art pieces, with every vegetable and swirl of aioli styled for a photo shoot. I ordered another glass of wine, and Annie followed by asking for another flowery drink without the offending flower.

Once we'd polished all of that off, we walked to Neiman Marcus to look at all the fabulous shoes. And they were very fabulous. Shoe shopping was my happy place, and that particular store was a golden temple of shoe divinity.

Annie tried on about ten pairs and settled on a pair of loafers she could wear to work or with jeans. At five foot seven, she didn't need shoes with heels and rarely wore them.

I found a pair of navy stilettos with a black-and-white silk wrap tie around the ankle. They were gorgeous. And I knew I wanted them.

CHAPTER FIVE

NEW YORK

Chris

I had to admit, it felt good to be back in New York. As much as I loved Antibes and the beach, I'd been craving the fast pace of the city and feeling a little antsy during the last few days of my vacation.

It was true, what people said. After living in New York, it was hard to live anywhere else. I had to come to terms with leaving, though, if I wanted my time with Nikki to be more than a two-week fling.

Brittney, the barista at the coffee place on my corner, smiled at me when I walked in the door and was already clicking the espresso machine and tamping down the grounds by the time I got to the counter. She'd worked there for as long as I'd been coming to the shop, which was going on three years. I had fifteen minutes to grab a cup before I needed to head home and meet the car picking me up to go to 30 Rock for my late-show gig. Just enough time if I walked quickly.

"Hey, stranger. I wondered if I'd see your face again," she said, tucking a wisp of hair behind her ear. Her hair hung straight down her back, and she wore it in a low clip, which didn't do much to keep it out of her face.

"Are you kidding? I couldn't stay away for long. The flat white here is too good." The place was empty, which was unusual. Or maybe I hadn't been there in the afternoon before.

"I do make a sick flat white," she said, smiling. She had a tiny diamond nose piercing and tattoos on the insides of both arms, bright flowers that were prettier than most tattoos I was used to seeing.

"How've you been?" I asked.

"Chillin'. One more semester at NYU this fall, then I'm done."

"Yeah? That's great. What's next?"

She shrugged, steaming the hot milk for my coffee. "Who knows? But if I'm still posting up here in a year, please kindly kill me."

"You've had enough of making coffee for assholes like me?"

"Especially for assholes like you." She checked the temperature on the steaming milk and poured it into a paper cup, shaking the metal pitcher and drawing a heart shape in the foam. She was quiet when she handed it to me, looking down at the counter instead of at me, which was odd. I took a sip, figuring she wanted some affirmation that I liked her creation, so I sipped and complimented her.

She nodded silently.

"Okay, well... nice to see you." I started to leave, wondering about her abrupt shift in tone, but not too much.

"Um... I guess, congrats?" she said, asking it as a question.

"Thanks," I said. I waited for her to elaborate. Maybe she wanted to talk about the latest *White Serpent* movie, but I had no way to be sure.

She was staring at me as if she was trying to figure something out. "Crazy, right? Parenthood's gotta be a trip."

Oh, here it comes.

Tabloid news traveled quickly, and I was naïve if I thought the paper was above publishing rumor and she was above believing salacious gossip just because I was a regular. At least she was nice enough to try to make lemonade of it.

"I imagine," I said, feeling desperate to leave the coffee.

"So are you gonna raise this kid?"

The last thing I needed was to get into a debate about twenty-first–century parenting.

"I'll keep you posted," I said. I would not. I waved at her and pointed to the coffee. "Thanks, as always. Good stuff." Then I hurried out of the place and called my attorney. "What the hell?" I asked the second his assistant put the call through and I heard him click onto the line.

"Welcome back," intoned Dave Craggs, my lawyer for ten years, speaking smoothly and as though the supposed non-story hadn't already morphed into a real story that the barista down the block took as fact.

"I thought you were handling this pregnancy thing."

"I am handling it. It will go away as soon as they get the paternity results. You took the test, right?"

"Of course I took the test. But that didn't keep a college kid with no horse in the race from asking me if I was going to raise the kid."

Dave sighed. "Chris, will you please relax?" I could tell he was more concerned by my reaction than by the fact that the story had leaked, which meant he already knew but hadn't told me.

"Who ran the story?"

"Page Six."

"Great. Might as well hire a skywriter."

"And again, I urge you to relax. They're not saying you're the baby daddy. They're reporting that she's making an accusation. Big difference. They came to me for comment. I told them you took a paternity test, and there's no story there."

A car honked at me, and the driver yelled a string of profanities because I'd ignored the traffic signal and crossed right through traffic. I couldn't walk through the streets and have that conversation if I didn't want to die. So I wandered toward

Washington Square Park, found a quiet spot under a tree, and sat.

Dave didn't respond, and I heard him typing. He was a multitasker, and I was used to him checking out during our conversations while he read an email or looked something up.

"Dave. Talk to me. Can you get them to chill out? Or take it off the online edition?

He chuckled quietly, and I was annoyed by what I assumed was him paying more attention to something other than my problem. "Their job is to sell papers, and they didn't print anything that isn't true. They're allowed to do that. Quit reading Page Six."

"I don't. I was informed of my paternal options by my neighborhood barista."

"Good times. Seriously, don't worry. Assuming you're not the father, this will go away yesterday. And if you are... We'll deal with that tomorrow."

"I'm not the father. It's impossible. I wasn't even in the country when she got pregnant. And unless her dates are off by a month, Page Six should be worried about looking really stupid for printing that shit."

"Okay, okay. Cool your jets, man. Is there anything else I can do for you?"

"Try to get ahead of this stuff. I'd rather not read about the paternity results before I get them. And I'd really like to avoid having Nikki read about me on Page Six when she's across the country."

"So why are you on the phone with me? Call her."

It was my turn to sigh, because he was right. The truth was, I didn't put any stock in a story on Page Six, any more than I was actually concerned that I was someone's dad. But now that we weren't in the same city, I did worry about what Nikki would do when the detritus from what she called "my world" leaked out of its barrel drum and littered her front lawn. There was only one way to find out. I had to call her.

According to my watch, I was already late to meet the car the show sent to take me to the studio. I knew the driver would wait, but I had to pick up my pace to a jog, and I would still be five minutes late. That meant I had to dump the coffee and hustle. I couldn't do that and have a phone conversation, so I sent a long voice text, hoping it would reach Nikki before the tabloid news did: *Hey. Don't freak, but Page Six got the pregnancy story. They're treating it as an unproven accusation, but still. Please don't let this bug you. I'm on the run, but I'll call you in a bit.* As long as I alerted her, I felt pretty certain we could talk through the details later and she wouldn't freak out.

I felt better. Even if the story made its way to other gossip news sites, at least I'd warned her. I slowed my pace to a fast walk as I approached my block and saw the black car idling in front of my building. Then my phone buzzed with a text from Nikki: *I'm not freaked out. But that's annoying. I'm sorry they ran the story. Try not to let it get to you. Unless of course it's true...*

I'd been feeling good until the last sentence. Damn, texting. It was impossible to detect tone, and I had no idea if she'd tacked that on as a joke or if she was really wondering whether I'd knocked up my ex-girlfriend and was denying it.

Me: *Haha. I think*

Nikki: *Don't worry. I am reserving judgment until there's something to judge*

Me: *Can't stop thinking about you*

Nikki: *Back atcha.*

Me: <3 *call you soon*

Nikki: <3 <3

I exhaled heavily. No wonder I was feeling like my lungs were going to explode while I ran home. I told the driver I'd be down in five then jogged up to my apartment to grab a change of clothes. I wasn't that worried about getting to the studio a few minutes late. They always had me sit in the green room for at least an hour after hair and makeup.

As the driver steered us to the Westside Highway to get us uptown faster, I looked at the Hudson, which had yellow streaks of sunlight dancing in the current. Yeah, its water was a little browner than the Pacific Ocean—okay, a lot browner—and it didn't have a wide, sandy beach, but I really did love living in New York.

I would have lived in an anthill in the freezing tundra to be with Nikki, but the East Coast was home, and it always would be. I did need to find a house to rent in LA, but maybe I could be bicoastal. With the amount of work I always had in New York, it made more sense to keep my place. There was no point in staying in a hotel when I had a great apartment.

Better than great. With its sweeping view of Hudson Bay and proximity to my favorite Village restaurants, it was a good investment property and an awesome place to live. I would just have to buy a second set of clothes and other personal stuff to keep in LA.

I immediately felt better with the knowledge that I didn't have to give up New York for good. I felt certain Nikki would like it in the city when she got a chance to visit. Maybe she could even meet my parents.

Funny, like you'd let that happen.

Okay, so maybe she wouldn't meet them right away. I needed some time to prepare her first, and even then, it seemed best to keep them apart for as long as possible.

CHAPTER SIX

LOS ANGELES

Nikki

Someone had recently refilled the jar of M&M's, which left me in a quandary. The new candies were the peanut variety, and they were currently occupying the top two thirds of the glass jar. I hated the peanut kind, but I didn't see an easy way of scooping down to the regular ones at the bottom.

Therefore, I had a critical choice to make. I could wait until my colleagues ate through the peanutty goodness at the top, which could have taken days or even weeks. Or I could use the metal scooper to dredge through the peanuts in hope of finding the regulars. It seemed unsanitary.

I supposed a third plan could be had if I dumped the upper contents of the jar into a bowl, scooped out the ones I wanted from what remained in the jar, and reintroduced the peanut variety afterward. If I was honest, I had to admit I'd already spent way too much time on the M&M problem.

So I did what any self-respecting chocoholic would do, and I walked away from the rainbow candies and went back to my office by way of the vending machine that sold Twix bars. I bought two.

The candy fix seemed particularly necessary, because my nerves were starting to fray over the ex-girlfriend and the pregnancy. That's how I referred to her, as the ex-girlfriend, as though she was the main character in an eponymous mystery novel like *Nancy Drew and the One Hundred Steps,* only without the threat of death at every turn.

For the most part, I'd done a good job of keeping my wits about me while Chris sorted through the legal and professional implications of his ex-girlfriend's pregnancy, all things considered. Yes, I was referring to it as a pregnancy—not a scam or a scandal or a ruse to bilk him out of an outrageous fortune. Not yet. I had to assume she was pregnant, alone, probably scared, and trying to figure out the best road forward. I also had to avoid unfairly accusing her of intentionally dragging her heels and not getting her blood test done immediately. Maybe she was really busy, not simply avoiding the truth.

Women had to stick together, even women who were involved with the same man and who most definitely didn't share a common objective. As far as I or anyone else knew, she was doing what she thought was right and what she thought was best for her unborn child. I felt strongly about it.

Until I had all the information, I couldn't judge his ex or call her a money-grubbing whore skank who was looking to exploit Chris for money and fame. Not unless the paternity test came back negative and she continued pursuing Chris and the tabloid news. Then, all bets were off.

When Chris called me later that day, I assumed it was to tell me he'd gotten the results. Once his ex had finally taken her blood test, the turnaround time was supposed to be quick.

Unfortunately, he had something else to say. "The goddamned lab lost my sample. I had to go give another one."

Okay, these things happen.

I decided not to get too worked up about the delay or imagine any nefarious plotting.

Maybe that made me open-minded. Maybe that made me a patsy.

"If they can't keep track of this one, I don't know who I'm gonna strangle," Chris said, his hoarse laugh sounding like a lunatic about to go off the reservation.

"I'm sure it will be fine. Are they expediting the testing?" I thought that if I kept repeating the words "it will be fine," either it would become so, or at least I'd start to believe it.

"They bloody well better be," he said, having apparently spent enough time filming in the UK to have picked up some linguistic twists.

"Did they tell you when they'll have results?"

"No, because they're a bunch of wankers who don't know their eyes from their asshole," he said. He was making me laugh, despite my lingering unease about the whole situation. It seemed a little suspicious that the lab lost his sample, given the lawyers breathing fire all over the place and his high profile.

He still didn't seem concerned, and his mind was clearly too occupied with work to think devious thoughts.

I wasn't going to be the one to go there. It was better not to put those thoughts into his head. "Is there any chance they're repeating your test because it came back positive?" I asked. Apparently, I couldn't help but go there.

He was silent for a moment, and I wondered if he was thinking about how to answer or distracted by something else. "I… hadn't thought of that. Do you… wouldn't they have said if that's what they were doing?"

"I have no idea. You have lawyers and people who know how to handle everything, but you know me. I tend to overthink and prepare for the worst."

"Now I really hope the lab is manned by wankers."

"It probably is. I don't know why I asked you that."

He sighed, and I could hear footsteps on the other end of the line, so I knew he was pacing in his trailer. "Look, I know this hasn't been easy, and you've been great… I really hope to put it all behind us soon."

I wanted to reassure him that it was fine. I wanted to promise that it didn't matter either way, but the reality was… it did. If he ended up being the dad of his ex's child, there was no denying it would change things between us. I hadn't wanted to think about the possibility, and with the quick initial paternity test, I didn't give myself time to worry. But it had been a week, and I couldn't keep the errant thoughts at bay. "It'll be okay."

"It's a lot to ask… but *if* the test comes back positive—*if* I'm the dad—will you please give me time to figure everything out? Please don't cut and run."

I didn't know what to say. I didn't like that he was giving voice to the possibility that there might have been truth to his ex's accusation, but he didn't really have a choice. He had to at least consider what life would look like after that. It would look messier. And if I wanted to be with Chris, I would be part of it. "I won't. I won't cut and run. I promise. But can you use your pretty face and celebrity influence to expedite the new test results?"

He chuckled. The sound warmed my heart. "Darling, I will do my best."

I DIDN'T HEAR the news from Chris, because Page Six got to me first. "Can you comment on the news that Chris Conley is the father of his ex-girlfriend's child?" a reporter asked me the next morning. I was at my desk. At work. I was also surprised, because it was the first I'd heard that the paternity test had come back with a positive result.

"I have no comment. Can I return your call in a bit? I'm at work," I said. I tried to sound much calmer than I felt, which was brain-exploding, not-at-all calm. As soon as I hung up, I texted Chris: *WTF? Page Six reporter just called me to comment on your daddy-hood.*

Chris's immediate reply: *WTF!! The test results aren't back yet.*

Me: *U sure?*

Chris: *Hundo P. I would know!!!*

Me: *So why are they calling me?*

Chris: *Dunno. Fishing expedition, prolly. PLEASE don't let it get to you.*

Me: *I love when you use shouty words.*

Chris: *Sorry. I'm not shouting. I miss you. And Page Six can go fuck themselves.*

Me: *Okay. I won't call them back. <3*

I left my desk and went to the kitchen. I found a large paper bowl, put two metal scoopfuls of peanut M&M's into it, and walked back to my desk—that was how unnerved I was. I had tried to keep calm and chalk the pregnancy mess up to normal celebrity fare, but it wasn't at all normal for me.

I was also thinking about what Annie had said—that I felt differently about Chris than anyone she'd seen me with before. I was afraid she was right. I was trying to hold back my tender heart and keep it from hurtling over a cliff where it would thud to its death. Maybe it was the pregnancy issue. Maybe I would feel free to love him—to really fall in love with him—once there was some resolution on that front. Or maybe Annie was right, and I was hedging my bets and holding tightly to my heart because I couldn't bear the thought of loving him and getting crushed.

Do I have to know?

I shoved a handful of M&M's into my mouth and crunched them, making a decision. I wouldn't keep holding my feelings back from Chris. I would tell him as soon as I knew for sure what was up with the ex. That was surely the problem. Knowing the truth would surely open the floodgates of my emotions.

I was so busy talking sense into myself that I didn't notice my phone had vibrated with a missed call from Chris.

I didn't bother listening to the message. I dialed him back, and he answered right away. "Hey, did you hear my message?"

"No, I just called. What's up?"

"Got the test results. It's all good. They're negative."

"Wow, seriously? That's great news. Have you talked to her? Does she have any idea who the father might be?"

"No, I haven't talked to her, and I don't intend to."

"I thought you might be curious."

"Not at all. Not even a little bit. I'd be sympathetic if she hadn't chosen to go to the tabloids before talking to me, but I've got nothing to say to her now. My legal team cautioned me against it anyway."

"Makes sense. I still feel a little sorry for her."

He was silent, and I wondered if he'd heard me or gotten distracted by something else. That was the problem with not being with him in person. "Hey, you still there?" I asked.

I heard him exhale. "You amaze me."

"Why?"

"Because you're such a good person. You've never met Ashley, my ex, even though she's made your life stressful and unpleasant... your first instinct is empathy."

"She's a human. Of course I have empathy."

"Most people wouldn't. You're... you're special. And it's just one of a hundred reasons I'm stupid in love with you. I hope you're okay with that."

I was stunned, but also a little bit elated. "I'm okay with that," I said quietly.

Say it back. You love him. Tell him.

And... fail.

"Good. Because it's a nonnegotiable truth." He was silent for a moment, but when he spoke, I could hear the smile in his voice. It was a welcome change. "Listen, I've gotta run, but I wanted to make sure you knew as soon as I knew."

"Thanks. I wish I was with you so we could celebrate."

"I wish you were too. I miss you. And I love you. I'll talk to you soon."

He didn't wait for me to say it back. Maybe he was in a rush.

Or maybe he knew I still couldn't.

CHAPTER SEVEN

SANTA MONICA - Two Weeks Later
Nikki

MY HEART HAD BEEN DOING somersaults all day in anticipation of Chris's quick LA boondoggle. "This is lunacy. It's such a short trip," I'd said when he confirmed his travel plans.

"Believe it. And get ready. We have a lot to fit in."

My initial thought when he said that was a long seduction in my bedroom, but Chris had other plans. He wanted to go to the beach.

After his plane landed, he had his driver take him to Santa Monica, where we met in front of Shutters Hotel, an all-white sprawling Craftsman bungalow with a roundabout for valet drop-off. I met him in front of the hotel, and we walked due west to the deep beach south of the pier. The driver said he would be available to take us back to my condo whenever we were ready. I started to object and say it wasn't that far and we could walk the mile or so back to where I lived, but I caught the exhausted look in Chris's eye and decided to acquiesce.

As soon as we reached the sand, we took our shoes off and

padded through it until we'd left the more crowded bike path behind us and were nearing the crashing waves. Once we were alone, Chris dropped his shoes and pulled me into his arms. "The whole plane ride, all I could think about was you," he said, kissing me tentatively at first, our lips getting to know each other again. Then, as if he was experiencing the first drops of rain after a drought, he kissed me more urgently, hungrily. It wasn't want. It was need.

I wrapped one arm around him and ran my fingers through the hair at the nape of his neck. My other hand was pressed flat against his back, holding him to me because I didn't want to let go. He took my face in his hands and pulled me to him, angling his lips against mine and pressing a little harder.

I felt it in my bones. A chill ran over my skin as his lips grew more desperate and insistent, and I gave back with my own need and relief at feeling him against me.

Three weeks had been too long. The languid hands of time had hurt me, and I needed to feel his lips and his skin in order to heal. I wasn't going to forgive the unkind slowing of hours into days any time soon.

"I missed you," he said quietly, leaning his cheek against my temple, then kissing me there.

"I missed you too. So much." I wanted him to know that being apart for three weeks wasn't okay with me, even if I wasn't going to come out and say it. I couldn't tell him that. But I still hoped he'd know.

He brought his lips to my cheek, my chin, the tip of my nose. Then I reached for him and insisted on another long kiss. I'd give him his beach time, but I needed my kissing time.

After a few minutes—or an hour; who could tell?—we came up for air. Chris curled a few errant strands of my hair behind my ear, and I watched his eyes take in my face. "It's so hard to be away from you. I'm so happy to see you," he said.

"I'm happy too." I was more than happy. I was a wild streak of emotion filling a desperate heart. I knew I'd missed him, but I was assaulted by how much I needed to see him when he exited the car and I looked at his face. It wasn't normal, at least for me.

I felt a strong, beautiful ache in my chest that I couldn't control. There was no question I was falling in love with him, but I still couldn't put my feelings into words. I was still afraid.

The ocean had a bright sheen across the flat expanse of water, broken only when the waves welled up and crashed in a white churn of salt and sand onto the beach where we walked. Chris had tied his Converse One-Star laces together and was carrying them on his shoulder. My flip flops dangled from one hand while we walked along the shore, Chris's arm around my shoulders, mine around his waist. The bottoms of his pants were getting wet with the occasional waves, but if he noticed, he didn't care.

The waves lapped gently at the sand at high tide, the water reaching an inch farther with each wave, as if hoping to capture a tiny bit more of the beach and a few more grains of sand before the tides reversed and the water receded.

"This is ridiculously pretty," Chris said. "New York City might be the center of everything, but there's no getting around this view."

"It's the one thing New York doesn't have. That and maybe good Mexican food."

"Eh, not sure I agree with the second point, but I'll give you the sandy shores, hands down."

"We try to keep quiet about it so you all stay in your tiny fifth-floor walkups in the snow and don't crowd us out of our beaches."

"Ah, a conspiracy."

"Absolutely."

Chris held my hand as we walked south, with the Santa Monica Pier in our line of sight but still far enough away that we couldn't hear the screams from the roller coaster or feel the crush of people who crowded onto the boardwalk. The sun was dropping lower in the sky, but it was still high and bright enough that it forced me to squint behind my sunglasses when I looked out at the ocean. I didn't mind the inevitable crow's feet I would have someday. The view was worth it.

Even though I had physical evidence of Chris with his fingers laced through mine, I kept stealing glances at him to convince myself—to reassure my moaning heart—he was really with me. We'd talked on the phone every night, but despite our attempt to get my work schedule to jibe with flight schedules and his call times on the set, this was the first time we'd been able to line up enough free hours in a row to make a trip seem worth it. And even then, the brief trip was crazy.

I'd gotten as far as planning to fly out on a Friday night after work and had brought a packed bag to the office when Chris's assistant called to say they'd be shooting late, and he probably wouldn't have the empty block of time he'd thought. Work had been intense that week. She was sorry. I told her it wasn't her fault.

"He feels really bad about it. He wanted me to make sure you know he wishes he could change the shooting schedule, but..."

"I know. It's not up to him." I felt like it was on me to make her feel better about delivering bad news. I hadn't met her yet, but lately, I felt like she and I had more of a relationship than I did with Chris. We certainly talked on the phone nearly as much as Chris and I did.

"Right. Thanks for understanding." She seemed sympathetic, and I got the impression it was a big part of her job to apologize to people for things she couldn't control.

"Sure. It's cool."

"And I have him down to be in LA next Sunday night, so he'll see you then," she said, her voice friendly and soft. She would have been great at reading a bedtime story.

It was strange to think that helping Chris manage our relationship was part of someone's job.

For the moments we stood there, wrapped up in each other, the frustration and longing from the past three weeks ebbed away. I was fully in the present, not thinking about how we got there or where we were headed. I just wanted to drink in the moment, the feeling of being back with Chris for as long as it lasted.

In that case, we had just under twenty-four hours.

~

UNTIL THE MOMENT he boarded the plane, Chris had been working hard, cramming his lines and working on a character study for the role. It wasn't a superhero movie. It was a historical drama, and he was struggling to find ways to identify with the character. "It's not going to be good—hell, it's not even going to be passable—if I can't get this guy down," he'd told me one night when we talked. It was almost two in the morning in New York, and I felt a little guilty that he was talking to me instead of sleeping.

"I know you take your work seriously. You'll get it," I said, trying to be reassuring even though, as usual, I didn't really know what he was going through.

"I know. I'm just worn out, and this whole thing has been a fire drill, pushing up the schedule."

All the time apart meant that our time together needed to encompass a lot—a lot of kissing and sex and sex and kissing, yes, but also a lot of talking and connecting and moving our relationship forward.

But the kissing… I didn't want that to end too soon, either. So we stood on the sand for so long that I lost track of time. I needed to have his face that close to mine. I needed to feel his lips and the heat from his hands on my skin. We only came up for air because of the incessant buzzing of his phone. He extracted it from his pocket without his lips leaving mine, but he had to back away and check the caller ID. Satisfied that it wasn't important enough to answer, he clicked it off and returned it to his pocket, but the spell was broken.

Instead of kissing some more, we walked to the water. Chris draped his arm around my shoulders.

"I can't believe you're here," I said.

We stood in the shallow surf, letting the waves lap at our feet. The big ball of sun shone directly in front of us. Chris ran a hand over his chin, which had the beginnings of stubble after just one day. His hair was a little rumpled, probably from running his fingers through it on the plane while he memorized lines, but his dark eyes were just as mesmerizing as I'd remembered. "I can't really, either. I feel like a wind-up doll. I go wherever they point me and work my ass off. But this direction was true north. I wouldn't want to be anywhere else."

The weekend beach crowds had thinned by late afternoon that Sunday, but the air was warm enough that a few dedicated sunbathers were still lazing on beach towels, catching the last few rays of the day.

Breathing in the salt air and feeling the squish of wet sand between my toes, I could almost convince myself we were back on a French beach. Maybe that was why he'd wanted to come to the water, to try to recapture some of what we'd had on those endless sunny days when nobody controlled our schedules.

A few sandpipers pecked at the soggy sand, their long beaks tapping, searching for tiny crabs. When the water approached, they ran up to drier sand, their skinny legs racing up the beach. "I wonder how much energy it takes to fly," Chris said, watching them.

"You thinking about taking flight?"

"No. I mean them. Why are they running?"

"Why do they run when they have wings?"

"Yeah. They're birds. It seems like they'd just fly when the waves come. So it must be more efficient to run instead."

I hadn't thought of it like that. But once I did, I was pretty certain he was incorrect. "Could it be… maybe it's just a game to them? Maybe they run on the sand because having the ocean chase them is fun."

He looked at me like I was something new to him. "I really missed you. The way you think, talking to you…" His lips twisted into a smile, and I realized how much I'd missed him too. "There's no one on the set like you."

"I missed you too."

I looked at Chris's profile, reminding myself what he looked like in person. I'd stolen a few looks at Internet fan sites with pictures of Chris plastered all over them. I'd marveled at his dedicated fan base and the effort they put into keeping up with all his latest news and sharing their enthusiasm with each other. It seemed crazy that I didn't recognize him when we first met, but then, I wasn't a superhero fangirl and probably never would be.

Chris turned to me and smiled. In some ways, it felt like no time had gone by since I'd seen him. But in other ways, something was different, and I couldn't put my finger on it.

I knew from experience that sometimes it took some time to fall back into a rhythm after not seeing a person for a while. Annie was a case in point. I loved her like a sister, but anytime she visited, we bumped into awkward bouts of conversation and annoyed each other for a couple hours until we found our rhythm again.

I was desperate to spend some time just talking, since our brief phone calls over the past three weeks had mostly consisted of apologies—his—and attempts at figuring out logistics—mine. There had been no wild phone sex or even sexting, and we'd barely had a chance to exchange pleasantries before Chris inevitably had to deal with a last-minute request to run lines or a conference with the director or a wardrobe emergency.

I'd never been on a film set, but the way he talked about it made it sound like he had to be involved in every decision. I knew why. He'd told me in France that he was an executive producer on all his films, but we hadn't talked in detail about what that meant.

So I asked.

"It means I get a say, and I share in profits," he said, taking my hand as we walked barefoot along the shore. We were each carrying our shoes in the other hand. Chris hadn't mentioned that before.

"So what does that mean? A say in what?" I didn't care if everyone he knew understood the jargon of movie making. I still needed basic training in what it all meant, and he never made me feel silly for asking.

"Pretty much anything creatively, but I know my place. I know better than to start tearing apart a script just to exert some power. But since it's my face on the billboard, I reserve the right to speak if I have something to say."

"Which means that even if you don't say anything, you're aware of everything. You care."

"Yes. I care a lot."

"That's all I needed to know. So you're super stressed about everything that goes into making the filming a success, on top of learning your lines and acting."

"Pretty much."

I looked at the creases around his eyes, which normally highlighted a glint when he smiled. Instead, they looked like evidence that he was worn out. I wondered if flying all that way instead of catching up on sleep had been such a good idea.

We stretched out our walk on the beach until the sun had lowered enough to cast orange light on the eastern clouds and the last straggling beachgoers had left the sand. Then we walked up the beach, the area finally empty enough that Chris Conley wasn't immediately recognizable to passersby at every turn. We took the stairway two steps at a time to the bluff overlooking the Pacific Coast Highway and the ocean. The sun was dropping fast, nearing the horizon line. We'd timed it perfectly, and minutes later, we watched the final moments of the sun's performance before it slipped away.

Watching the sunset usually calmed me, but this time I just felt sad. We had only one night together, and the setting sun signaled the beginning of its end. I didn't like the new association with sunsets.

We stood at the railing on the bluff, gazing out at the ocean.

Then we called for the town car and picked up Italian takeout on the way back to my condo.

We split a calzone, linguini with pesto, and a green salad. And we talked. He told me more about the movie and some of the frustrations, and I filled him in on work and showed him a few canvases I'd painted over the past couple weeks. He shook his head like he had the first time he saw my artwork. "You're an artist. You're not a hobbyist. You could do this professionally."

"Thank you," I said. We'd had this same conversation three weeks earlier. I wondered if he remembered.

After a couple of hours, Chris was fighting to keep his heavy eyelids open, so I backed against the side arm of my couch and pulled him in between my legs with his back leaning on me. He tipped his head back against my shoulder, and I wrapped my arms around him. "This might not be a good idea," he said. "I might fall asleep."

"It's okay." I wanted to be there for him. I wanted him to know that it didn't always have to be day sailing on fabulous boats or views of the Mediterranean Sea for me to want to be with him. Though it did require a little adjusting of expectations on my part. I'd been fantasizing about our night together from the moment his assistant gave him the go-ahead to make the trip. I'd even bought a lacy bra that matched the thong that was uncomfortably lodged where it shouldn't have been. I'd been anticipating Chris tearing off my clothes, discovering my lingerie treat, then tearing it off too. He ran his fingers up and down the length of my leg, but when he abruptly stopped, I knew it was because he'd drifted to sleep.

I wasn't angry. I didn't wonder why he hadn't gotten his sleeping out of the way on the six-hour flight. I knew it was the middle of his workday. I knew he worked on flights. I knew.

"I'm sorry, love. I'm wiped out," he said. And right there, with that tiny term of endearment, my heart was whole again.

"You need to sleep." I leaned forward and wrapped my arms more tightly around him.

He hefted himself up from the couch and turned to tug me up by the hand. He pulled me in close, folding me into a warm embrace. With one hand, he smoothed the hair off my forehead and traced the outline of my lips. "I'm not a very good date tonight."

I met his eyes and tried to convey my empathy for his state of exhaustion. "You're always a good date. I'm happy to have you here."

"I'll be a whole new person if I get a few z's."

"I know. C'mon, let's sleep."

He smiled, his eyes half-hooded. Even fatigue did nothing to detract from his gorgeous face and his dimpled smile. As he led me into the bedroom, I felt a strange sensation that I hadn't experienced with him before. There had been no seduction, no emotional words. It was just two people walking toward a bed under a mutually agreed assumption that we would brush our teeth, maybe make out under the covers, and go to bed because it was semi-late and he was exhausted.

It felt ordinary. And in so many ways, the comfort of knowing that every moment between us didn't need to be noteworthy made me feel happy, like we were leaving the fling stage behind and settling into something more real. I wanted to have a normal relationship with Chris—the regular guy, not Chris the movie star—so even though a tiny part of me wanted him to swoop in like a superhero and carry me off to his sex den, this was better.

After three weeks of waiting to see him, I wanted to connect. It struck me as strange but comforting that curling up in bed with the idea of going to sleep gave me the connection I'd been craving.

I *needed* that relationship proof of concept.

It was the only way I could make it through another three weeks—or three months—and believe we were heading toward something. Because despite the proof lying beside me, I was still struggling with believing.

CHAPTER EIGHT

Nikki

I BARELY SLEPT ALL NIGHT.

There was a family of birds in the tree outside my window that seemed to have some confusion between day and night and stayed up singing throughout the night. Usually, their sounds faded into a pleasant background soundtrack, the live version of something from a calming meditation app. But instead of lulling me to sleep, their chirping felt like a call to action for my overactive brain.

Chris had fallen asleep almost instantly, his body curled around mine and his hand flat on my stomach, grasping me to him like a teddy bear. I was hyperaware of his hand there, and after a few minutes, I was also hyperaware of my breathing, moving his hand in and out. I was so busy trying not to disturb him by taking in too much air that I found myself in danger of expiring from lack of oxygen.

Lest I hyperventilate, I shifted so I could take in a little more air and still feel the security of his palm against me.

Sleep was something I rarely struggled with, but we'd gone to bed on the early side, so I wasn't that tired. I'd also worked myself into a keyed-up and breathless state over the course of the day, awaiting his arrival. I was having trouble bringing myself down to the sleep zone.

Beyond all that, I knew we only had mere hours together, and I didn't want to squander them asleep. So I lay there, my eyes open, allowing myself to revel in the feeling of Chris holding me against his hard body and breathing lightly on my shoulder.

I wanted this all the time. My heart swelled with love for him, and I wanted to tell him. Immediately, though, the beautiful ache in my heart turned to panic. I wasn't sure it was good for me to have expanding feelings when he wasn't making good on his proposition that he'd move to LA so we could be together. What if this—this occasional day here or there—was the extent of what we could have, a cross-continental booty call with some nice words thrown in to keep it going? I had to rein in my emotions.

Love isn't predictable. Nothing ventured, nothing gained.

I decided those platitudes were stupid. What did they know about my particular set of circumstances with Chris?

Then I had a series of even worse thoughts: *Maybe I am the common denominator in all my failed relationships—or maybe I'm the catalyst.*

The effect of having deep, happiness-disrupting thoughts in the middle of the night was to amplify their gravity.

During that sleepless night, I noticed new things about my condo that had never been visible to me during other sleepless nights.

I noticed that the single streetlamp that shone through a crack in my slatted blinds cast a shadow on the ceiling that looked like an oblong pumpkin with a terrifying face that was likely mocking me. My bedside table stood at a height that allowed for pulverizing my funny bone on the corner when I lay on my back and put my hands under my head. It was the worst, most significant sleepless night of all time.

Also, my room didn't have sufficient oxygen for me to survive.

I felt certain that would be my undoing. Or maybe it was just that I'd unconsciously held my breath for about six minutes because Chris had shifted and somehow grabbed for my hand. He'd interlaced our fingers and wordlessly kissed the back of my hand before settling into a new position and continuing the quiet breathing of sleep. Suddenly, once I resumed breathing and despite my concerns over lack of air, I felt myself relaxing. The connection, even though it was small, even though it was an unconscious movement by a sleeping Chris, was enough to calm me down. Everything was okay, and I needed to turn off my infernal, overactive brain so I could rest.

I fell asleep briefly and dreamed that Chris was telling me it had been a mistake for us to try to date in the nonvacation world. I woke up in a sweat, saw him sleeping peacefully beside me, and tried to coax myself back into a REM state.

I tossed and turned and eventually ended up flat on my back on one side of the bed, staring at the part of the ceiling that didn't have the creepy pumpkin shadow and playing a game with myself. *Don't sleep,* I told myself. *Stay up the rest of the night. I dare you.* I was betting that some easily influenced part of me would buy into my reverse psychology, and in trying to stay awake, I would drift off. It had worked once when I'd babysat my boss's kid, who refused to accept that he was tired.

I, however, did not buy it. *Fine, I'll stay up,* my brain seemed to say.

Stupid, stubborn brain.

Maybe because it was bordering on morning in New York, Chris began to stir. I felt him reach out for me, and without saying a word, he pulled me in toward him, wrapping his muscular arms around me and spooning me with his comforting, hard body.

He kissed my bare shoulder and my neck. Then he settled there, his breath growing deeper and slower, his hands warm and reassuring against my skin.

And finally, I slept.

~

BY SEVEN IN THE MORNING, I'd rested a bit and reacquainted myself with the blissful feeling of having Chris's body intertwined with mine. For a few moments, I slowly shook off the residual fog of sleep and reveled in all the ways our tangled limbs were seamlessly connected. It felt purposeful, impossible to achieve without being connected in other ways.

My old Krups coffee maker began the daily wheeze and sputter that indicated the pre-programmed brew cycle was finishing. Like a siren song, it pulled me from beneath the covers. I took two mugs out of the cupboard and went to my fridge for some oat milk, which I'd started drinking after Annie raved about how much better it tasted than soy. She'd already given me a scolding for drinking almond milk, claiming I was contributing to planetary demise because almonds were thirsty, resource-greedy seeds, and I shouldn't support the military-industrial complex by consuming them. Or something to that effect.

The oat milk was a little watery but overall not terrible, and I felt better about myself and the planet immediately after the first sip of hot coffee.

"Hi, gorgeous," Chris said, sneaking up behind me and nuzzling the nape of my neck. He put his arms around me and turned me to face him, dropping his lips onto mine in a kiss that was instantly more heated and seductive than anything that had happened between us the night before. It was a kill-me-and-leave-no-witnesses kind of kiss. It was a kiss that held me in the present. I needed that, so I could stop analyzing and let go of all my fears about us. My hands wrapped around his neck, and I kissed him until my heart was satisfied.

"How'd you sleep?" I asked.

"I don't remember a bit, if that tells you something."

"It tells me you were tired. I don't think you moved all night, except when you cuddled me like a blankie. Now I'm officially ruined for all the nights when you're not here."

He exhaled his frustration. "I know. Being here with you like this is exactly what I wanted when I said I'd move. And then I messed it all up." He grabbed a coffee mug and refilled mine before pouring his own.

"You didn't mess it up. You have a job. I have a job. We live in different places. All that messed it up."

"So we need to maximize our waking hours when we're together," Chris said, coming back and bending to kiss my neck. "What time do you get off work?"

Work. No wonder my coffee maker had flipped on at seven. It was Monday, and despite the rippled abs that I was casually running my fingers over, I needed to be at my desk in a couple hours. Unless...

"You know what? I've never taken a personal day. You're only here until tonight. I'm not going to work."

His smile brightened, but he looked tentative. "Is that okay? Will you miss important stuff if you're not there today?"

I shook my head and wrapped my arms around his waist. His skin was hot and smooth, and I couldn't think of a single reason to step away and go to work. "Nothing I can't deal with tomorrow. I'll have my cell if anyone needs me urgently. It's all good. It's decided."

"Well, great. We can pack in a lot of quality today before my flight leaves tonight."

I sighed, resting my head against his hard chest. "I'm starting to hate that word, 'leave,' but I'll try not to think about it."

He pulled me in tighter. "I have a few ideas for how I can make you forget it, and all other vocabulary except maybe my name and the word 'please.'"

"You and your ideas. I'm in favor. I applaud them." I leaned away to face him, sliding my arms up his strong back and appreciating every lat pulldown he'd ever done at the gym. He'd definitely benefited from a good night of sleep. His eyes sparkled, and I let myself fall for his easy, seductive smile all over again.

"What should we do today? If I recall correctly, I owe you a dress," he said, turning to open the fridge and return the oat milk to its shelf.

I looked up at the clock on my microwave. "Ah, the dress to go with my shoe frenzy. Did you see a pair in my closet that would benefit from a companion dress?"

Ordinarily, I'd balk at the idea of him buying me things, because I was employed and self-sufficient and capable of choosing my own clothes. But I knew he enjoyed shopping for me almost as much as he enjoyed ridding me of whatever he'd encouraged me to wear. His enthusiasm made it fun for me, so my independent inclinations bent with his need to shop.

"I didn't check your closet, but we can always find shoes too when we're out."

I wasn't about to turn down shoes, independence be damned. "If you insist. But stores don't open until ten, so whatever will we do until then?" I was wearing a fluffy white bathrobe I'd bought from a spa after being so enchanted with their facilities that I'd wanted to try to create the experience at home. My attempts at turning my bathtub into an oasis of calm had pretty much failed, but the robe was still amazing. I undid the belt and let it drop to the floor, the robe falling open as I took another step closer to Chris.

"Woman, you will be the end of me. I'll soon be unemployed and bent forever to your will."

"I'll take it."

He lifted me, and I wrapped my legs around him and my hands around the back of his head while I bent to kiss him.

Chris carried me back to the bedroom, and just for dramatic effect, he kicked the door closed behind him. "Ah, finally, we're alone," he said, laying me on my yellow-striped duvet, which he'd neatly pulled over the mattress when he'd woken up.

"Yes, the others are all sleeping. They'll never hear us," I whispered, playing along with his game.

"I don't think any of them suspected anything, do you?"

"I feel like we got away with it. We can relax now. It's over."

He flipped me over so quickly, I cried out in surprise. Then he straddled me and dug his fingers into my shoulders, massaging every muscle down my back and slowly working his way back up. The worry and tension transferred from my body to his hands and began to ebb away.

"Oh my god, you have no idea how good that feels," I said. His hands conveyed his desire to make me feel taken care of and also wanted.

"Yeah? Tell me."

"It's amazing. You're amazing," I murmured, giving in to the sensual way he was gently working the tired muscles in my back, my hips. He lifted me up until I was on my hands and knees, continuing to stroke my back. Then he reached around and ran his hands up my thighs. I moaned into the pillow.

"It's hard to throw you off your game. You're always so steady," he said, lightly massaging my inner thigh. He was just inches away from where I suddenly desperately wanted his hand. But he was drawing out each stroke up and down, taking his time. "Always in your head, always worrying about other people. For once, I want you to stop thinking. Just be here. Just... come away with me."

I nodded but I couldn't speak. I heard him though, and his words moved me. No man had ever seen me—really seen me—and wanted to work within the parameters of who I was. They always wanted to change something, make me more spontaneous or less stressed. Chris appreciated who I was, but he also wanted to help me get out of my own way so I could feel something more. The blossoming in my heart at that realization gave me hope that we were going to be okay, even if we couldn't see each other every day.

Or for two whole months.

CHAPTER NINE

Chris

WE MIGHT HAVE PACKED an entire week into a day.

The morning was spent in Nikki's bedroom, her kitchen, her living room couch, then bedroom again. I felt the need to make up for passing out prematurely the night before.

The rest of the day went as follows: we shopped for a dress, I found six I loved on her, she agreed to let me buy two. Then we spent an hour looking at shoes. Each dress demanded its own pair, and she somewhat-reluctantly agreed. Both pairs were tall stiletto heels, and she looked gorgeous in them. Truthfully, no dress was needed.

We had lunch at Shutters on the Beach. There were oysters. There was wine. There was time to walk on the beach and slowly make our way back to Nikki's neighborhood, where we sat outside a tiny coffee place and I was asked for selfies with four different groups of fans. Nikki rolled with it.

Later, we painted. Or rather, she painted and I splattered colors on a canvas with no sense of space and no identifiable objects anywhere, but I loved the freedom of moving paint around with the brush. I felt like a kid who knows he's not being graded, so I didn't censor myself.

"That's the whole point," Nikki said. "It's an outlet, not a stress."

"It's kind of nice to do something creative and know I'm not trying to make a living at it."

"Exactly. That's why I love it so much. The only person I need to satisfy is me, and honestly, even if I don't like what I come up with, it still feels good to slap paint on a board."

"Yes, but you're not just slapping paint. You have talent. People would pay you to create art for them."

She shrugged. "Then they'd have expectations. I don't need that."

I didn't argue with her. She didn't need me to force her in a direction when she seemed to have her time pretty well allocated. "You have a good balance. You work, you make art, you exercise because you like it, not because you're trying to burn calories."

"Well, the calories are a bonus. Then I can eat more pizza and bake pies."

"You bake pies?" This was important information I felt I should have been provided with earlier.

She smiled, keeping her eyes on her canvas. She was painting the sunset we'd seen the night before, complete with the Ferris wheel on the pier in the background and the sandpipers on the beach. "Yes. Only two kinds. Apple and pumpkin."

"Why only those two?"

She shrugged. "Apple because I love it and pumpkin because it's often in demand at thanksgiving. But I'm open to requests."

I thought about it for a moment. I liked fruit pies, but I was more partial to anything involving chocolate. "How about mud pie?"

"I'm not sure that even qualifies as a pie. That's a no-bake crust, and there's no fruit."

"It's called a mud *pie*. It's a pie."

Shaking her head, she put down her brush and came over to

inspect my canvas. I'd been splatter painting in the style of Jackson Pollack for want of a better idea. "We can make a mud pie later. After we hike."

"We're hiking?"

"Yup. An urban hike, in the canyon." Her grin was wide, like she had a trick up her sleeve, and I didn't question it. "Then pie, I promise."

I'd follow her anywhere she wanted to go.

I hadn't spent much time in LA over the years, so I'd never had time to do much sightseeing. On this trip, the only sight I wanted to see was Nikki, so as long as we were together, I let her lead the way. In the afternoon, we walked in Santa Monica Canyon, which was a winding series of streets just east of Pacific Coast Highway that took us into a tree-shaded neighborhood no one would ever find if they didn't know about it.

It felt like a hidden gem in a city of more obvious jewels.

"It kind of seems magical here," Nikki said as we walked down a shady lane marked by a sign hanging over the road saying "Uplifters Ranch." Farther down the block was a park with tennis courts and more tree-shrouded homes that looked like they belonged in the woods. One home was busy with real estate brokers hosting an open house, so we walked through to check it out.

We walked up a staircase to reach the front door, but once inside, we looked out through floor-to-ceiling windows to the tops of trees. Nikki was enthralled. "Oh my God, it's like a tree-house," Nikki said, spinning in a circle in the living room and taking in the cozy couches and fireplace. "Couldn't you imagine sitting here on a rainy day?"

"Does it rain in LA?" I asked.

"Okay, smart-ass, time to go back to New York, where they have 'real weather.'" She air quoted her sarcasm.

"It's a great house."

"Whatever. Who needs this place with its handmade tile and treetop views? I prefer my one-room condo with garbage trucks in the alley," she said, running her hand over the tile. I had no idea how she surmised it was handmade, but she was the artist. I wasn't about to contradict her. We left the house and walked back toward her place. I was antsy, starting to anticipate my meetings the next day. Damn, I hated that we didn't have more time together.

"I'm tempted to say *no* to this movie," I said, a little surprised at the words as I said them. I'd fought to get the role because I'd been wanting to break out of the superhero mold for a while.

"You can't do that. You told me you really wanted to do a historical drama."

"There will be others."

"No, do this one. You'll regret it if you didn't. And on your next visit, we'll go downtown. Not enough people go downtown, and it's awesome." My next trip was supposed to be a five-day press junket for *White Serpent* after I finished shooting in Ireland.

"I'm game."

"It's no New York City, but there's an incredible bookstore, museums, library. We'll go for sure," she said.

I liked that her neighborhood was walkable. I already knew that if I bought a place in LA, it would have to be in an area where I could get around on foot. If I wasn't working, I didn't want to spend my free time driving through canyons to get a cup of coffee.

The one-day trip ended too soon. How could it not? It wasn't nearly enough time to spend together. No amount of days ever would be, if I knew I had to leave at the end of them. That was the problem with this whole arrangement.

So far, Nikki had been patient with my schedule. She had her job and her life in LA, so maybe she didn't mind it too much that I was consumed with work. We'd talked about it in France. She knew work was my Achilles heel, and I loved my job.

There was also another possibility, one I didn't want to mention for fear that it was true. Also, I didn't want to ruin the little time we had with a nagging worry that would probably be resolved in time. But I couldn't help but feel like she wasn't as invested in some kind of future together as I was.

When we were together, I felt her full commitment to being with me. But she didn't love me the way I loved her. Hell, maybe she didn't love me at all.

I thought you weren't going to consider that possibility.

Yeah, well, I needed to accept that it wasn't completely up to me.

I just knew that after spending barely a day together, I wanted more with her. And more was something I just couldn't have when I was about to go off for two months of work. It was the price I had to pay for getting the roles I wanted. I couldn't turn down the work or—as my agent always reminded me—people would stop offering it to me. I'd always believed him.

But damn, I wish he was wrong.

My head was in a tailspin when I boarded the Virgin America flight back to New York at almost midnight. It felt like déjà vu. I'd just been at the airport the day before, landing and anticipating our time together, and it was over already. From my seat at the front of business class, I could see planes taking off and landing, coming and going. Hellos and goodbyes.

It was worth it. Seeing Nikki even for an hour would have been worth it. But I was going to pay miserably for it next week. Even if I slept for the whole flight, it would only be five hours, mercilessly one hour shorter than the westbound flight due to the jet stream. I hoped I would have a chance to catch a nap before the talk show I had to do in the morning… Or maybe I would just be a goddamn basket case all week. It was still worth it.

That was my last thought before I conked out, leaning against the window. The next thing I knew, the plane was taxiing to the gate, and I was back in New York.

LEAVING 30 ROCK, I felt good about the talk show interview, or at least I thought I did. I was still so damned jet lagged that I couldn't recall a single question that was asked or answer I gave. It didn't matter. It was done.

Traffic was light, and the town car dropped me off twenty minutes later in front of my building. The sun was glinting off the glass lobby door, so I didn't immediately notice the two figures standing by the desk. But as soon as I pulled the door open, the slumped bodies of my parents were unmistakable as they stood talking to James at the front desk.

It had always seemed odd to me that a modern loft-style collection of apartments like mine needed a front desk. We all had keys, and there were only six units in the building. But when I saw my parents standing there, it made me want to pay James's entire annual salary, personally.

"I'm sorry. There's no one by that name who lives here," I heard him say when I swung the door open to the lobby. My parents had their backs to me, and I could easily have walked back out and let James do what I'd instructed him to if the day ever arose: tell my parents he knew nothing about me.

But I caught his eye, which made them turn to see where he was looking, and they saw me.

"Chris, tell this man what's what. I said to him that we were just here to visit and couldn't we wait inside," my mother said, coming toward me. She wasn't coming to hug me. She was coming to scold me.

My father said nothing. He stood with his arms crossed.

"Hi, guys. I didn't know you were in town."

"Well, we are."

It was typical. They generally used the ambush approach because they knew if they called, I would tell them I was busy. God only knew how long they'd been stalking my building, waiting for me. I would have to apologize to James later.

"Can I buy you a cup of coffee?" I asked, holding the door open. My mom cast a longing look toward the elevator, but common sense told her I wasn't inviting her up, and she would have just as good of an opportunity to ask for what she wanted at a coffee shop. Plus, there was the free coffee.

They walked outside into the bright sun, my dad holding a hand in front of his eyes and my mom squinting. Neither one of them would ever spring for a pair of sunglasses. "Not when it's only sunny a few months out of the year in Boston," my mom would say.

They were simple people. Some of what people thought they knew about my family was true. My mom was from Spain, and my dad was an accountant. *Was,* as in, he hadn't worked in twenty years, right around the time I got my first big movie role at age sixteen. And my mom… she did have a degree in art history, and she worked from time to time as a substitute art teacher, but her income was not enough to support them. And it shouldn't have been, not when I could afford to support them.

The fit-for-print version of my family life had been embellished by my first publicist. She created a sweet, loving family dynamic, and it became my story, so I continued to tell it. I'd told it to Nikki. The lie had become so much easier than the truth.

Every month, I sent them a generous check, which I knew more than covered their mortgage and everything they needed to have a nice life. But they didn't manage it well, and they wouldn't let me put my business manager on it. "Frivolous," my mom had said with disdain when I told her he could pay their bills and give them a stipend. "Why would you pay someone for that when your father's an accountant?"

The problem with my father the accountant was that he was wasteful. He bought into scams. He tried to invest in quick money-making schemes that always lost. Then they would come to me to bail them out. That was clearly the purpose of their visit. They didn't spend money on things like train rides to New York unless it was a "worthy investment." In other words, what they hoped to gain from me was greater than the time spent on the train and the cost of the tickets. He'd dragged my mom into his way of thinking. She was loyal to him, and he loved her.

I didn't take them to the coffee place I liked. We went to the corner bodega, and I bought us each paper cups of coffee. They both liked theirs regular, with milk and sugar. I knew that. And they always acted surprised when I asked for mine black.

Then I wrote them a check. My dad nodded at me, raising his eyebrows when he read the figure on the check. He showed it to my mom before folding it and putting it in his wallet, which I'd bought for him six Christmases before.

I knew better than to expect them to take interest in my life or even to attempt small talk. I was a means to an end for them. They'd raised me, so I owed them. My father had said as much as soon as I started making money of my own.

"Good to see you guys," I said, taking a step closer to my mom. She allowed me to hug her, but her shame and embarrassment prevented her from hugging me back. My dad looked at me and nodded.

It was a business transaction. They'd gotten what they came for. There was nothing else to say.

"Well, good to see you," my dad finally said, taking my mom's hand. They'd been through so much together, and despite their differences, they always found their way back. There was something sweet and loving about them. It just didn't extend toward me anymore.

CHAPTER TEN

Nikki

I knew two months was going to feel like a long time. Two months *was* a long time. I also knew that Chris and I had been together long enough that we could weather two months away from each other without it dooming our relationship. And lately, I'd been thinking a little bit about FaceTime sex, which I'd learned was a thing.

Chris had been in Ireland for four days, and we'd had a hard time connecting, partly because of the time difference, but mainly because Chris always went into a mental cave for the first couple weeks of a new film and worked himself to the bone, researching his character and spending every waking hour with the director to make sure he had the role down perfectly. During that time, I knew better than to expect to hear much from him. I respected his process and admired that he was so committed to acting that he gave every bit of himself to it.

The movie wasn't an action tentpole. I'd read the script and ended up crying several times, imagining the scenes and feeling the emotion behind the characters' words. The film was a period piece, set in the 1940s, at the beginning of World War II. The war provided the backdrop, but the movie was about the relationship between two characters, both of whom had joined the resistance against the Nazi invasion. At heart, it was a love story. Chris and his costar played star-crossed lovers who were ravaged by the war and ultimately separated. Chris's character would end up dying for the cause and never knowing that had he lived a couple weeks longer, the war would have ended and he would have been reunited with his love.

I knew it would be a beautiful film, and I respected Chris for choosing the role, for which he did a ton of reading and research, over a lighter project about a baseball player with a feisty young niece he ends up coaching.

So I was surprised when Chris made a point of FaceTiming me when he knew I'd just be getting home from work, or two in the morning in Ireland. "Hey," I said, happy to see his face on the screen. I refrained from telling him he looked exhausted. No one wants to hear that. But I could tell he was working hard.

"Hey. Glad I caught you."

"Yes, just barely. I just left my smokejumper seminar with the volunteer fire department, and now I'm headed to a salsa-dancing class. You caught me just in time."

"Haha. How was your day?"

"Lovely. And better now. How about yours?"

"Definitely better now. I'm beat, but I had to hear your voice," he said, his own sounding raspy and tired.

"I'm glad you called. I miss you."

"I miss a lot of things about you. I wish you were here."

Suddenly, a small germ of an idea started bouncing around in my brain. It was small because I'd never allowed an idea like that to grow beyond a passing thought. I'd never really been the instigator of sex-related ideas. I didn't like this fact about myself, but so far in my life, I hadn't been motivated to change. I hadn't cared enough. "What would you do to me if I was there?" I asked, propping my phone against a pillow so I didn't have to hold it. I folded my hands under my chin and stared at Chris's face on the screen. I saw his eyes widen slightly while he sorted through whether I actually meant what he thought I meant.

"You mean…?" He was a smart guy. Not much got by him.

"I mean you can tell me… or show me."

I ran a hand down the center of my chest and over my stomach, scooting down lower on my couch, then brought the hem of my shirt up halfway, baring my midriff and stopping. I didn't take my eyes off his face, and I saw his eyes follow every movement I made.

"I see." He ran his tongue across his bottom lip then bit it, holding it between his teeth. I could almost feel him biting into me. I wanted to feel it. "Well, I wouldn't put up with all that clothing, I'll tell you that much."

"Tell me."

"Your shirt. Lift it higher." I lifted it an inch. I watched his eyes grow hazy, and he shook his head. "Not what I meant. Keep going." Slowly, I drew it up, making sure to trail my fingers across my own skin as I did it, teasing him. Then I pulled it over my head and turned onto my side, facing the screen.

"I have to say, this is much more comfortable. It's really hot here in LA. Clothes are… troublesome."

"You're killing me."

"Yeah? How badly?"

"If you really were a smokejumper, there'd be a blaze for you to put out."

"What would you do if you were here?" I felt emboldened by the barrier between us. I knew I could say or do whatever I wanted, and it sort of wasn't real. At the same time, it was more real, happening on a screen I could see like a mirror.

"I wouldn't be having a conversation. I'll tell you that much."

"Well, this isn't going to be much fun if we don't talk. Do you like it when I talk?" I purposefully made my voice lower and a little more sultry.

I saw him mash his palm to his forehead. "Seriously, you will be my undoing."

"That was my plan. You should take off your shirt."

He didn't hesitate. He used both hands to yank his shirt over his head and threw it across the room. He mirrored my position, and I had a full, glorious view of his Michelangelo-carved abs and his perfect pecs. His current role didn't require him to hit the gym every day to make for a realistic character, but I knew he got up extra early to get in a workout, anyway. He'd done it every morning that we'd been in at his house in Antibes, usually in the early hours before I was awake, because it was like meditation for him. Working out was sometimes the only way he remembered to breathe. The only problem was that when I saw him lying in front of me like that, I forgot to breathe.

"You still with me?" he asked.

I realized I'd gone quiet, staring at him and imagining my hands languidly touching his skin, covering every part of his chest and running lower to his abs, that incredible, rock-hard six-pack. "Yeah. Got distracted by your abs." I shook my head as if to snap myself back to reality.

He let out a quiet laugh. "Now you know how I feel every time I look at you… Speaking of which, I think I need to see more of you."

"Tell me what you'd do. Imagine you were here. Tell me, and I'll do it," I said, not really knowing where the words were coming from. But I knew I meant them. He did that to me.

Chris ran a hand over his chin, massaging his stubble for a moment, then looked back at me with a small smirk. "You know what I'd do. I'd kiss every damn inch of your skin. That gorgeous waist, those luscious breasts. I'd kiss you through your bra, then I'd tear it off you and suck your nipple until it got hard in my mouth." He sighed.

I was speechless and a little unsure what I'd started and whether I could finish it. "I… I can't do any of those things… to myself."

"Yes you can. Run your hands over your stomach. Lightly. I'd be taking my time, going very, very slowly, enjoying every curve of your body. I'd be trying to make you shiver. I'd want to make you arch your back because you couldn't stay still." His words were seductive enough on their own, but I obeyed and tried to imagine my hands were his. It meant I had to close my eyes, but then I was no longer trying to imagine him. I moved my hands the way he told me to. I was feeling him, even though I knew they weren't his hands.

When I opened my eyes, I saw his heavy-lidded stare, and I knew he was feeling his own version of what I felt. "Now you. Unzip your pants. Slowly. Move them down your thighs and take them off."

He did as I instructed.

I watched, seduced by the slow rumpling of the fabric as he pulled his pants down, revealing his black boxer briefs and his hard, muscled thighs. "I wouldn't be able to keep my hands off you if I was there," I said, my voice still an octave lower than usual, huskier and sultrier. I didn't know where the voice was coming from. Maybe she was a function of FaceTime, and I was just a willing pawn.

He leaned back and ran a hand over the obvious swell in his boxer briefs. "No, no. Not just once. Keep going," I said, imagining myself rubbing my hand over his hard length and taking him closer to a point where he was no longer in control. He did as instructed, closing his eyes and clearly taking his time and enjoying the slow buildup.

I could have just watched him. That would have been enough of a turn-on to take me to all kinds of places I didn't normally go. Really, I would have been fine. But he slowed down the movement of his hand and fixed his gaze on me, his almost-black eyes pouring through the lens of the camera into mine.

"Your turn," he said, his voice husky and deep. "The rest of your clothes. Take them off."

I raised an eyebrow at him. "That's a very general, very vague instruction. Is there a way in which you'd like that to happen?"

He growled and shook his head like I was trying his last nerve, but I knew he loved it. "So many ways… just, so many goddamn ways. First, enough with the damn bra. I mean, it's pretty. I like the lace. But I like what's under it more. Take it off."

I reached behind and unfastened the clasp. Then I peeled the straps from my shoulders and let it fall to the floor. I waited, seeing my naked upper body in the tiny square on my phone. I was glad it was small. Anything bigger would have shot my nerve, and I'd have folded.

"Oh my God. I miss you so much," he said, his voice soft and pleading.

I couldn't help but smile at him. His reaction was so genuine, and I knew exactly what he meant. "I miss you too. And not just because you have abs like a freaking marble sculpture."

He smiled but his eyes stayed focused on the screen. "Can you…? I really wish I could touch you…" he said on an exhale, like he was letting go of the last bits of stress from the day. It was exactly what I wanted for him.

I ran a hand over one breast then pushed it toward the center, creating some cleavage. "Like this?" I watched his eyes waver. He bit his lower lip again. The power I had over him in those moments was intoxicating. It made me want to do whatever he wanted.

"Like that. But also… you're still wearing too much clothing."

I cocked an eyebrow. "So are you."

He returned my glance with a smirk. "Fair's fair. I will if you will."

It was funny. We'd seen each other without clothing many times, but somehow with all the lights on and with a video screen at the ready, it felt much more personal. And hot.

Slowly, watching each other, we took off the rest of our clothes. For him, that meant sliding his boxer briefs down. For me, it meant wriggling out of my skinny jeans and rolling my thong down my legs. But we managed to accomplish both with relative ease and impressive speed. Then we were each curled up in front of a cellphone in the buff, watching each other intently.

"Maybe I should have asked you this," I said, realizing I did want to know a vital piece of information. "Have you done this before? Phone sex or video whatever?"

"No. I'm a phone sex virgin."

"Ah, I like that I'm your first."

"I like that too. But I'd like it a lot more if I was the one who could slide my fingers into your soft, wet—"

"Stop! Don't say 'pussy'! I hate that word. I mean, I don't, but I kind of do. It makes me think of a slutty cat, and I'm not into that."

"I can come up with many other words for where I'd like you to slide your fingers."

I held up my hand again. "No, no, no. I don't need other words. No beavers, no tacos... just... no. Not into it."

He laughed. "See, this is good, actually. The distance. I wouldn't have known this about you otherwise."

I covered my face with my hands, slightly embarrassed but really just needing to get the damn camera out of my line of sight. "I know. It's a thing. Don't judge."

"I would never. But I might use it against you at a future date to be determined."

"Oh, well, that wasn't the goal."

"How about this? I won't talk. And maybe you don't talk, but maybe we just... watch each other. Maybe?"

I nodded. "Yes, I think without the narration, that could be good."

He laughed again, but then he grew more serious, because he was looking me over, I could tell. Every inch of me. And as he did it, he began moving his hands over his lower abs. I was transfixed. But at the same time, I knew we'd made a deal, and I needed to give him something good to look at. So I ran a hand over my breasts and down my abdomen, moving it slowly lower until it was where I imagined he'd want his own hand to be. He nodded and wrapped his hand around his hard length, moving it slowly over the surface.

"I would do that for you. I wish I could do that to you," I whispered.

He held up a finger. "No talking."

So instead I moved my hand lower and parted myself, using my fingers to do what I wished he could do. I was already slick and wet for him, but I didn't have him. "I… I don't think I can do this. It's not the same. And with you right there, I just… can't," I said.

"I know," he whispered. "It's making me feel farther away from you instead of closer."

I pulled my hand back and watched as he did the same. His eyes never left mine, and I felt more connected to him by staring into his eyes than I would have if I'd gotten myself all worked up and orgasmed alone. Maybe he felt the same way, or maybe I'd pressured him into trying to take some sort of sexual high road, but in either case, he moved his hand away and sighed. He shifted his phone screen so it was more focused on his face, and we just took in the sight of each other and stayed quiet for a while.

Eventually, he rolled in the other direction and looked at his watch. I knew it was insanely late where he was and long past the time when he should be sleeping.

"You should sleep," I said.

"I really should," he said. And as if to prove it, he yawned. "But I like talking to you. Feels like it's been months instead of weeks."

"I know. But still… I'm sorry I kept you up."

"I'm not."

"I mean, I know you have an early call and all that."

"I know. I don't care. I'm just sorry I have to go."

"Don't be sorry. Let's make a deal with each other. It is what it is. Let's stop apologizing for it. Don't say you're sorry unless there's a real reason."

"I will make that deal. But I really… regret that I have to go." He smiled.

"That might be verbal cheating, but I'll let it go. Call me again when you can."

He kissed the palm of his hand and blew it toward the phone. Then he was gone. I sighed, rolled onto my back, and pulled a blanket off the arm of the couch to drape over myself. I didn't have the energy to put my clothes back on yet, but I wasn't sleepy. It was only seven in the evening, and I had no plans. I didn't feel like calling a friend and meeting for a drink or a walk. But it was way too early to turn in for the night.

Thinking about Chris sleeping peacefully made me feel peaceful, and I wandered into my bedroom and pulled on a pair of old shorts and a sweatshirt I didn't mind getting dirty. I had a few I wore when I did art projects. The strategy to keep most of my clothes paint free had mostly worked. I'd learned from experience that every time I told myself I could paint a little bit and avoid getting dirty, I'd end up with paint all over myself.

I took out my paints and a new package of flat canvases. I could always do art. I needed to set a timer for myself, or I was liable to be up all night. It had happened many times. And I had to work in the morning.

It felt good to lose myself for a few hours in the acrylic colors that could be painted over multiple times, turned from something I liked to some new experiment to something else entirely. I ended up creating three new canvases. I wasn't sure yet whether I would want them on my walls. The colors were brighter than a lot of what I had up there, and lately, I was liking the more muted tones of the watercolors.

There was no question that art was my happy place. I loved the abstract nature of it. I rarely painted portraits or anything as it existed in the world. Picturing things as they could be was much more interesting, even if that meant that reality ran a close second sometimes, and I only got to see the possibilities through art.

CHAPTER ELEVEN

BALLINASCORNEY, Ireland
Chris

THE KNOCK on the door of my trailer was insistent. I knew that knock. "I'll be there in a sec, Nigel," I called. I heard a grunt on the other side of the door.

I knew he wouldn't leave until he saw the whites of my eyes and could be sure I was coming to set. That was his job, and he took it seriously. He would wait and walk two steps behind me, as if he was trying to make sure I didn't escape from his supervision.

Nigel was the production assistant in charge of getting me to the set. The kid had been nothing but surly toward me from the first day of preproduction, and I loved the hell out of him for it. First off, by using the word "kid," I wasn't belittling him. He really was a kid—seventeen years old, if that—and he was one of the hardest-working people on the set. He'd alluded to the fact that he'd foregone going to university to start working in film, so I put him at high-school-graduate age at most.

Because I'd had a dialect coach for years and had mastered a couple of different accents from different regions of the United

Kingdom, I felt fairly certain he hailed from somewhere near Manchester. His vowels were the dead giveaway. But he quickly set me straight. "I'm from Liverpool. Not the same place."

In my mind, it was close enough to have the same accent, but he took exception to my generalization. "Wales is just over the border, and they speak an entirely different language. You fixing to tell me I could be from there with my accent?"

I had to concede he was right, but only on a technicality. "All you blokes from America think you have us figured. But you don't know shit," he'd said. He was amusing and quickly became one of my favorite people on our Irish crew.

It wasn't lost on me that I worked in a business I loved, but I continually gravitated toward people who didn't give a rat's ass about celebrities. Nigel had made that list on the first day because he shook my hand, gave me his cellphone number, and told him I could ask him for whatever I needed during the time we were on set. "But if you goddamn call me after hours, I will either not answer my phone, or if I do answer, I will rain down hell on you for disrupting my nonwork hours. I'm all yours at work, but then I insist you leave me alone."

I tried to imagine what a teenager—I was certain he was under twenty—could be doing in his nonwork hours other than heading down to a pub with his friends, but it didn't matter. His time was his own, and I respected that.

"Works for me," I'd told him. I liked that he had boundaries. I knew a lot of actors who would have taken advantage of a set PA and tried to turn a guy like Nigel into their own personal assistant, running him all over hell's half acre to do errands and other stupid shit they had no business asking him to do. And in his position, he would have had no alternative but to toe the line and do what was asked of him or risk getting a bad reputation and being overlooked for future jobs. That was the lot of assistants. They had no power, and they had to work harder than everyone else for less pay and no complaining in order to earn their way to a better position.

I'd never really ascribed to the punitive nature of the assistant track. Executives and actors generally got away with bad behavior because they had power. The idea of exploiting that made me sick. So I told Nigel we would get along just fine if he did his job. And he did. He never behaved as if it was beneath him or as though someone owed him something because he was assigned the most menial tasks. And I never made him fetch me fast food after hours or yelled at him if my coffee wasn't hot enough.

Since that first day, we'd had a great rapport. Even though he always had an edge of attitude and unnecessary swagger, he struck me more and more like a bear cub with his wisp of facial hair, skinny black jeans, and plaid flannel shirt that he never tucked in.

I opened the door to my trailer and told him I was coming. I started to close the door. I needed a couple more minutes to think about my character and get my brain organized.

"You know I'm meant to stand out here until you're ready."

I did know, but he also knew I was good at my word when I said I would come to set. We'd been doing the same thing for three weeks. "Fine. You stand there. I need a minute."

"Take your time. I've got nowhere to be."

"Actually, can you get a new set of sides for me?" I asked, referring to the scenes I'd be running that day, which were photocopied and stapled in a small packet, separated from the rest of the script. "Mine are soaking wet, and I can see one page through the next."

"Sure, as long as this isn't a ruse to get me to leave watch and let you lollygag for another half hour."

"I'm not stalling. But I need a dry set."

"Sure. How'd they get wet?"

"They were dropped off outside my trailer earlier, and it rained buckets before I got back from set."

"That's fucked up," Nigel said.

"That it rains in Ireland all year long? I agree."

He waved his hand. "Nah. Who left them outside your trailer?"

I shrugged. "I don't know, and I don't care." I needed a dry set, and the longer he wanted to talk about it, the longer it would take me to look them over and get myself to set. "Look, Nigel, I'll leave you alone after we wrap for the night, but right now, I just need the sides. And I kind of need them an hour ago."

"On it," he said, going off at a jog.

The truth was, I did know who left them outside my trailer. It was my costar, Triss. I couldn't get mad at her, because she was going through a divorce and had been alternating between attitude and tears for at least a week.

I felt terrible for her, even though she'd made my waking life miserable since we'd started filming. She'd been moody, demanding, and self-involved. She'd been short with the crew and late to almost every call time.

Still, I had a feeling she was a nice person, in spite of the vituperative scorn of her ex. No one does well with breakups, and even though she hadn't talked about the details, I had a feeling he'd dumped her without much warning.

Nigel came trotting back to my trailer with a dry set of sides, and I felt ready enough to head to set with him. I looked over the scenes one more time on the walk, feeling more prepared purely because I held dry pages in my hands. I only had to mentally prep for the first two scenes. The next two would be after lunch, and I could spend another hour in my trailer, looking them over and getting my character right.

"Is Triss already there?" I asked.

"Hell if I know. I can't get far enough away from her. I don't know how you work with that bitch."

"Nigel, she's going through a rough time."

"So? Does that mean the rest of us have to go through a rough time too? Every fucking day? Fuck that. She has to put on her knickers like a big girl and do her job."

He had a point. I didn't know Triss that well, so I couldn't do that much to defend her. "Let's hope that's what we get today. All we can do is hope, right?"

"Wow, sounds like you're in love with her or some goddamned thing."

That made me laugh. "You got me. It's true love."

The truth was, I didn't even know Triss. We'd met a couple days earlier during prep and rehearsals for the scenes we had together. She'd been pleasant at first, but as the day went on, I could see her frustration building. Every time the director gave her a note, she took it personally, and instead of rolling with it and trying the scene a different way, she folded into herself and gave a worse performance than the first time.

For the first two weeks of shooting, we didn't have a scene together, so I had no idea if she would eventually lighten up. But for the sake of the movie and my personal sanity, I really hoped so.

I'd seen how films could go from well-run productions to outright disaster based on the behavior of a lead actor or a director who clashed with everyone else. I'd only worked on one film that had to be shut down while a new actor was cast, but it had been a nightmare.

As it was, I'd already been overseas for weeks, and I really wanted to get back to California. Any delays caused by Triss and her drama only spelled trouble for me. I hoped that if she was going to bring the whole production down with her antics, it would happen sooner rather than later.

Triss had a reputation that preceded whatever was happening in her marriage. Rumor had it that she was a difficult diva who only respected actors who were more famous than her, and only because of what they could do for her career. That type of person screamed nightmare to me, and ordinarily, I would have steered clear, but we were in every scene together for the next week. So far, she'd been nice to me, so I wanted to give her the benefit of the doubt.

"How's your girlfriend feel about you two-timing her with a

diva bitch?" Nigel asked, lighting a cigarette on the walk between the trailers and the set. The set was strictly nonsmoking, so if Nigel needed to get in a few puffs, that was his opportunity.

I couldn't help coming down on him like a dad. "Nigel, you should cut that shit out."

"Sorry, mate. Which part, calling her a diva bitch or asking about your girlfriend?"

"The smoking. It's terrible for you."

He waved a hand in between us, as if he could dispel the conversation by waving away the smoke. "Nah, it's my birthright. Like telling me not to drink a pint or six with my mates."

"Your parents know you smoke?"

"I lie and tell them I don't. Then I steal 'em from my dad—who also, by the way, swears he doesn't smoke. So what's he gonna do?"

"They live close by, your family?"

"'Bout thirty minutes."

"You should invite them to the set sometime. I'd love to meet them."

He shook his head. "You absolutely would feel many emotions, but none of them love..."

I wanted to hear more, but we were at the set, which was the depleted backyard garden of a farmhouse that had been occupied by Nazis and ravaged by neglect during wartime. The homes in the neighborhood all looked well kept, and I imagined that this farmhouse would have looked similar, if not for the work of the set designer and her crew.

The back pasture had been swept of almost anything blooming and green and replaced with wilted and dying plants, broken farm equipment, and scraps of ratty clothing hanging on a laundry line. It was supposed to be the childhood home of Triss's character, and in the scene we were shooting, she'd just come back and seen the desolation for the first time.

Mark, the director, made a beeline for me as soon as he saw us. And behind him, I saw the scowling face of my costar. She was angry, but I had no idea why. When I walked over to where she sat, glowering in her chair, she practically shouted at me, "Well, it's about fucking time. I'm sitting here under these blazing hot lights, and now I've got to have my makeup touched up for the third time."

"Good morning," I said, not willing to argue but not willing to let her attitude control the tempo of the day. We had work to do, and whatever bullshit she brought with her wasn't helpful, especially if it prevented us from staying on schedule. I looked at my watch and saw I was only about five minutes late. That didn't merit her attitude, so I met her glare with an icy stare but said nothing else.

Her eyes shot daggers at me, as if I'd murdered her goldfish, and I started to feel an inordinate amount of empathy for her ex-husband. Maybe he'd gotten out within an inch of his life.

I nodded at Mark, letting him know I was ready to rehearse the scenes. He waved Triss and me over to a quiet patch of dead grass outside the area where we would be shooting. He talked through what he hoped to accomplish in the scene. "This is the first you've laid eyes on this place. Your reaction is all emotion," he told Triss.

She nodded. He'd given us the same instructions at the table read of our scenes a few days earlier, and I waited for her annoyed reaction, but she said nothing. She was studying her lines and occasionally looking up at me, as though considering how I would respond in the scene.

"And you... it's just about the love story for you. You're responding to what she's laying at your feet. You relent on whatever agenda you might have had, and you give her your last-ditch attempt to win her heart," he said.

I nodded. "Got it."

We rehearsed once, but the scene still felt almost devoid of emotion. Triss was so locked up and stiff, I worried she would never be able to convey what Mark asked. But all I could do was play my role.

Once we stepped on set, it was his show to run. He blocked the action with us and rehearsed a couple more times until he seemed to feel like the emotion of the scene was getting there. Then we took a break while the lighting crew finished up, and the hair and makeup team put final touches on us.

After another nearly sleepless night, thinking about my character and what I wanted to convey in the scenes, we took our marks, settled, and heard the words that would never get old for as long as I worked as an actor.

The set fell into silence, and Mark settled behind the monitor. "And, action."

THE DAY WENT PRETTY WELL, all told. I'd been the most stressed about the scenes we had to crank out because they were the emotional crux of the whole film. I had to sell an audience on the fact that I was heartbroken because my love interest had chosen to stay in Germany, and my character had had the chance to escape the horrors of the Nazi camps. Triss's character had to explain why she wouldn't leave. She had a calling and a mission. She would stay until the end, even if it meant death.

Scenes were always filmed out of order, so we didn't have the luxury of playing our previous scenes together to ramp up our connection to each other or our chemistry. We just had to hit the emotional resonance at the outset. Later, we would film the rest on a different set in a different location.

In the film, the trip back to her family home was the one chance my character had to draw her away from the war and back to me, to tempt her to live without the risk she faced if she went back to the frontlines.

Unfortunately, some of my fears about Triss's ability to focus on her part bore themselves out. She just couldn't get her head into the scenes. At first, I'd wondered if her histrionics off set were all for show. Some people thrived on drama. I could deal with it if she found her character once the set went silent and we were left to work through the scene together. But after seven takes on the same scene, I saw she couldn't do it. Mark told us to take a break.

"Fuck this," Triss said, walking toward her trailer. "I don't need to keep running the same scene only to be told I'm doing it wrong."

I jogged to catch up to her. She was a fast walker, and her anger had her throwing her arms into pushing her stride along.

"Hey. Triss. Wait up," I called, slowing to a walk because she halted at the sound of my voice. She didn't turn around, but when I reached her, I saw her arms folded across her chest and tears in her eyes. I put my hand on her shoulder in sympathy.

"I can't fucking do it. I can't internalize this character. She's not speaking to me at all." She spat the words out like the taste offended her. "Not to mention my divorce papers arrived this morning."

It was no wonder she couldn't access what she needed. Triss's vision was clouded by whatever baggage her busted marriage had left here to carry.

"Let's not call time of death on it yet. We've got an hour break. Should we try to work through it?"

Her gaze was sharp when she met my eyes. "You keep saying "we." I'm the one with the problem." She was wrong about that. If she didn't find her mojo, we were in for a painful week of filming.

"We both have a problem if you're struggling with this. Let me try to help."

She snorted her disdain. "I don't need a quick fuck."

"I wasn't offering."

Her expression softened, as though that fact really was news to her. "Oh. Well, still. It's not just a question of relaxing or focusing. I don't understand this character. At all. I don't know what motivates her. I'm not prepared. You think you can help with *that*?"

It took every fiber of my being to remain calm and not take her bait. "Maybe I can."

"I don't know why you'd want to." She shook her head, her eyes still stony, her expression unyielding. "I'm so fucked."

I had a choice. I could let her spiral into self-loathing, or I could try to pull her back from the abyss. "Can we work on it? Will you try to let me help you?"

Her sigh sounded like the last fizzle of air leaving a balloon. "Sure. What the hell. It can't hurt."

We walked back to the set, but I waved at Mark to make sure the crew kept away so we could have some space to work without an audience. The set designer had positioned a fallen log in the yard, and I motioned for Triss to sit on it with me. "How about if I tell you how I see your character in this scene? Maybe that will open up something for you."

She shrugged, already defeated. "Sure. Shoot."

"The way I look at it, your character is in a struggle of heart over mind. You want to defend your beliefs, and that means staying in Berlin and being part of the resistance, wherever that fight leads you, even death."

"Sure. I know that. I'm choosing to take part in a war effort instead of coming back to the man I love. I don't get that. Who would choose war and a good chance of dying over being with her great love?"

"Because sacrificing that great love for the work makes you feel like the work matters. Your love makes the sacrifice mean something. The pain when you leave is what makes you believe you're doing something important."

It wasn't lost on me that I could have been speaking about myself and how I felt toward Nikki. Each time I left her was more painful than the last, but the pain made me love her more, because committing to my job amplified the need to be with her. I rationalized that being away was good for our relationship.

Spoken like a workaholic.

Triss nodded. "I see what you're saying. I mean, it's completely misguided. A person who manufactures relevance by leaving the person she loves in order to make her work more important is only kidding herself," she said, looking pointedly at me. "If you love a person, you make the sacrifice, plain and simple. But I love that she's flawed like that. I hadn't looked at the character that way."

She popped up from the log, a lost sparkle returning to her eyes. She extended her hand to me. "I think I'm good now. I've found something I can run with. Thank you."

"Anytime," I said, still digesting her dismissal of my reasoning. If she felt ready to tackle the scene, I had to keep my focus on my character, but her words hung in the back of my mind as unfinished business.

We signaled to Mark that we were ready to resume, and he went about calling back the crew and setting up the shot.

We got it right in one take.

I felt her emotional connection to the material and to me while we were in character as war-torn lovers.

I could tell our on-screen chemistry was there, even though I suddenly felt wobbly with my own performance.

I'd spent so much time thinking about the scene, about what it meant to love a person but not be willing to sacrifice for that person. I'd convinced myself that being in love made the sacrifice bigger, but I'd only been thinking about love being the actual sacrifice, love taking a backseat to the importance of war. Or the importance of work.

What if I had it backwards? What if the better version was sacrificing the work for the sake of enduring love?

I'd never sacrificed work for anything. And I knew Nikki would never ask me to do it. I'd told her about my devotion to my career, and she'd understood. She'd let me continue in my same pattern. But what if… for the first time in my life… I wanted to make the sacrifice?

"And… action." Mark's words spurred me into the next scene, and my brain was temporarily relieved of the obligation to analyze my own possible missteps and misguided ideas about commitment. I put it aside and worked.

I poured every bit of emotion and energy I had into the emotion of the scene, and by the end of the day, I was spent. We wrapped for the day at around nine at night. Twelve hours of filming—with a break for some kind of potato stew for lunch—had flown by. But I was drained.

The film's emotion seemed to have dulled the spite and ire of the real world for Triss. She was the calmest I'd seen her at the end of our final scene. It was almost alarming to see her without icepicks poised to murder anyone within a mile, which was why it surprised the hell out of me when she suggested we go out for a drink after we wrapped for the night.

After the emotional toll of the day's scenes, it sounded like heaven. Even with her.

CHAPTER TWELVE

Chris

IF I'D HAD to defend myself, I guess I would have said I was lonely.

I know that's not a great excuse. Lots of people work out of town for weeks or months at a time, away from their homes or their routines or the people they love.

I used to be one of those people. Or I used to be a person who could do that—be on the road, shooting on location, and not feel lonely. It was just work, wherever the work happened to be. But something had changed within me, and I knew it had everything to do with Nikki. She'd pushed me to want to have a stronger connection to another person. To her. She hadn't done it intentionally. She'd just been herself. It didn't matter. Once I knew her and fell in love with her, I couldn't go back.

Being on location in a foreign country and sleeping in hotel beds for months at a time had a way of making me feel unmoored from myself. I knew I couldn't complain. Being put up in five-star hotels and having pretty much every meal catered—even though I did have a bit of a bone to pick about corned beef and cabbage at a few too many meals—was certainly not a hard life. It wasn't that.

I was a homebody. I liked waking up in my own bed. I missed New York. I even missed LA. But mostly, I missed Nikki. She'd become an anchor, even when I was happy at home in New York. It was different being there without her once I'd been there with her.

I felt my life changing. I felt myself changing.

I'd always been self-sufficient, and I liked that I didn't need anyone. My parents didn't live close by, and I didn't grow up with any siblings. So the peripatetic existence I'd kept for the past decade worked just fine for my psyche. But suddenly, it didn't.

That was my semi–self-aware explanation for how I ended up where I did at the end of the night. I was not making exceptions to justify what happened but merely trying to offer an explanation. And like I said, I know it's no excuse, but what happened happened.

It had been a long, emotional day—emotional because the scene required it, and we couldn't finish until we got it right. The scene required long, emotional embraces and kisses, longing stares, and a heart-wrenching goodbye. Triss and I were tangled up in each other, emotionally and physically, all day and into the night.

But it was acting. It wasn't real, and I knew the difference.

Nevertheless, it felt appropriate to head to the pub down the street from our hotel and treat ourselves to a pint or two to unwind from the intensity.

The pub was about half full of locals, most of them sitting and drinking at the long, polished wood bar. I took a slow look around the place to assess the vibe. It didn't seem like the kind of place where armchair paparazzi would be looking for a chance to cash in on a stolen-moment photo of me with my costar. No one seemed at all aware of our celebrity. Or if they knew, they didn't care.

We chose a table instead because it was easier to talk sitting across from each other. I ordered a pint of Harp, and Triss wanted a cider, so I brought both over to our table, along with a plate of fries.

It didn't take more than five minutes before her attitude was back. "I don't know why an entire country can't make a decent fried potato."

"Maybe this is how they like them. I don't think the barrier to other french fry recipes is high."

She threw a half-eaten fry back onto the plate. I made a mental note of which one it was and where it sat on the plate, in case I still wanted to eat some. Her transition from talented, level-headed actor to sour human was quick. If I'd known she was headed back there, I would have declined her drink offer and made a beeline for my hotel room.

"Sorry," she said. "I don't mean to be a pain in the ass. I'm just… life's been a bit rough lately."

"Well, you killed it today. You worked through it."

"Thank you. And thank you for your help with the scene. I was really… flailing." Her lips barely lifted into a smile, as if she was reluctant to smile all the way. She took a sip of her cider, and I braced myself for a likely diatribe about how the Irish had failed at cider making, but she put the glass down and didn't say anything for a moment.

I sipped—no, gulped—my beer and thought that if I could just drink half of it, I could make my excuses and go back to the hotel. I was in no mood to spend extra time with someone who just wanted to complain.

"Anyway, I imagine you've heard the rumors…" She looked at the table and picked up another fry. She didn't eat it, though.

Unsure what she was referring to but sort of assuming she meant her marriage, I decided to answer vaguely. "I don't really listen to rumors."

She huffed a laugh, and even though it sounded sarcastic and harsh, I still felt that her laughter was a good sign. "That's a good one. I wish I could do that," she said.

"Can't you? I mean, why do you have to listen to what gossip rags or people who don't know you have to say?"

She nodded but still wasn't looking up from the table, and her expression was sad. "The problem is, it's not gossip when it's true."

I could make a dismissive comment and try to keep the conversation light. Or I could get into it with her, whatever it was. She was still being too vague for me to know. The problem with being flippant in the face of her clear desire to talk about whatever was bothering her was that it would have made me a dick. Knowing she was hinting at a conversation and walking the other way was not cool.

On the other hand, I was already starting to feel guilty about sitting in a bar across from an attractive woman, even though I knew my intentions were aboveboard. It just didn't look good. Nikki was still getting used to me coming and going—mostly going—and I'd promised I would call her before she left work. She had plans with a friend after work, so I needed to reach her before then. That meant I needed to call within the next two hours.

"Do you want to talk about it?" I offered. There was still a chance she would say no.

But she looked up from the table suddenly, and I saw the vulnerability in her eyes. She did want to talk about it. She nodded and put her hand over mine. "I could really use a male perspective."

I told myself that it was okay for her hand to be there. We were colleagues, friends. A friend could touch another friend's hand in a reassuring way and not have it mean anything. "Sure," I said.

"It's just… my husband… he recently left. And I probably should have seen it coming, because I'd pretty much left him behind, but I thought he was okay with that."

"What do you mean, you left him behind?"

"My fame. My career. I outshone him, and I don't think he

could handle it. So he left me, and now he's 'figuring out what he wants.'" She put the last part in air quotes.

I didn't know her, and I didn't know her husband, so it was hard for me to analyze their relationship. I wasn't sure she wanted me to do that, so I took another long swig of my beer.

"So what do you think? Do you believe him?"

"I… I don't know him. I have no reason to think he's lying. Do you? Is there something else going on?"

"I don't know. I have no idea. Could he be gay? Is figuring out what he wants code for that?"

"Not that I'm aware of." But I understood. She was casting about, looking for anything she could latch onto that would explain why he'd left, anything that allowed her to avoid looking in the mirror and believing he might just not love her. I turned my hand to grasp hers.

Her fingers clung to mine like a lifeline.

"Listen, maybe you need to look at it differently. What was it like over the past year between the two of you? Was he jealous? Did you spend time together? What was the relationship like? The only way you're really going to understand what happened is to be honest with yourself."

She took a deep breath and shook her head. Then she took another sip of her cider, draining about half of it. "You're totally right. I haven't wanted to do that. I've just wanted to blame him because he hurt me by leaving. But it wasn't all his fault."

"Okay. Okay, that's good. Seeing another side to it is good."

"Yeah. I mean, I still don't totally see his side, but I see why he got upset."

"That's still something."

She took another swig. The glass was nearly empty, and she was looking longingly at the bartender.

He filled up a fresh pint glass for each of us and brought them over. "On the house," he said. "I'm a fan."

"Oh, thank you, sweetie. You're lovely," Triss said, suddenly morphing into a third person I hadn't yet seen, one who was cooing and sweet and happy to have the attention of a fifty-year-old pub owner with a wispy gray beard and a gap between his teeth. I wondered how many other personae she had in her vault.

She took another large sip of the new pint and grinned at me. I wondered if she was already a little tipsy. "I'm gonna tell you the gory details…"

Unsure what details she meant and not wanting to derail the conversation into something even more uncomfortable, I just sat silently.

"I cheated on him," she said, looking a little triumphant. "No one knows. Except him, obviously. And the guy I cheated with."

"I'll… I won't tell anyone."

She waved a hand at me like it didn't matter. "It'll all come out. In the divorce papers, in the rumor magazines. It's fine."

"You're saying you cheated on your husband. So that's why he left?"

"In theory, yes. But… I mean, he knew what he signed up for. So really… WTF?" she actually said the letters. I guess that was better than swearing like a sailor.

It was the night from hell with a woman who was getting drunker by the minute. She'd chugged down half the second glass of cider, and I was still finishing the dregs of my first beer. I was still tightly wound, having a hard time internalizing the fact that the emotional scene was behind us. I still felt overwrought.

I'd been so focused on getting the role right, I'd barely had a moment that wasn't focused on work. I'd barely even spoken to Nikki because I was worried I would let off some of my emotional steam and not have any left for the scene.

So there I was, with the person I was least interested in spending time with, hearing about how she cheated on her husband. But I had to admit, she was entertaining. I was glad to be out. It was stupid. I could have grabbed a beer with any of the people on our crew. Or the director. Or even underaged Nigel.

The point was, I'd already passed the point where judgement should have reined me in and sent me back to my hotel room. The beer tasted good, and the second one was colder. So I drank it while Triss finished her second and asked for a third.

Good judgement would have been letting the conversation fade or changing the subject. But I was interested in her story. "So your husband... what are you saying he signed up for? An open relationship?"

She twirled her hair and leaned back against her chair, shaking her head. "It wasn't like that. It was... look. I was the celebrity. I made more money than him. I worked hard. So there were certain... things... I thought I should have."

"Things like... a piece of jewelry?"

She play-swatted me. "No. I mean, yes... Of course that. But more like extra perks..."

"So... affairs."

"I deserved to be able to do that. I made more money than he did."

"Is that the permission slip for having an affair?"

She leveled her eyes at mine. "Isn't it? We're celebrities. People want us. Are you telling me you've never thought it made you deserving of something extra?"

I thought about it, because she made me want to say no so desperately. I didn't want to be like her. I wanted to be able to say I'd never felt deserving of anything special because of my celebrity. But I couldn't say that for a fact. Not without thinking about it first.

She threw her hands up at my lack of response. "Anyway. That's why he left. It made no sense. We could've gotten past it. We had in the past. I don't know what crawled up his ass and died this time, but good riddance, I guess."

"Maybe he didn't want to come in second place to other men," I said. I knew I wouldn't. I couldn't imagine most guys would be okay with their wives stepping out on them, no matter their level of celebrity, but what did I know?

She laughed dismissively. "He didn't mind it when it bought us our house in East Hampton."

"You're equating the money you earn from work to a carte blanche permission slip to do whatever—or whoever—you want?"

"It's what he signed up for."

"You told him this? At the outset of your marriage?" I wasn't trying to be dense or belabor her points, but it didn't make sense. She was saying he'd been okay with cheating at one point but then changed his mind. I wanted to know what changed. I couldn't have explained why I wanted to know so badly, but it seemed important.

She took another long sip of her drink, nearly draining it. Then she threw up her hands. "Of course I didn't tell him. Who comes out and says, 'I make the money, I have the power, and I plan to do whatever the hell I want'? But it was implied."

"And you think he always knew."

"Why? You think it was news to him this time around? Please. He's not stupid. But I'm starting to think you are."

Maybe she was right. Maybe I was.

With some difficulty, she pushed herself out of her chair and tottered off. "I'm gonna find the loo. I don't even need to pee that badly. But I love calling it the loo." She looked up at the pub owner, who still had a smile for her. "Excuse me, where's the loo?"

Yup, she was drunk. And I was pensive. She'd opened up something I hadn't thought about in a long time.

When I did start to think about it, I didn't love what I saw. Granted, most of my bad behavior was years before, when I was a young, dumb pretty boy in New York who was just getting used to the amount of money being thrown at me to make one superhero movie. There were girlfriends I cheated on and friends I didn't call back. I thought I was better than them. I deserved better. I didn't feel that way anymore—far from it. I went out of my way not to be that kind of asshole. But part of the reason I tried so hard was because I knew I'd been exactly the kind of asshole I'd grown to hate.

When she returned from the loo, Triss watched me as if she could see confirmation in my lack of a response. The thing was, I didn't want to run through my list of past misdeeds with her. It had nothing to do with trusting her or not. It had nothing to do with worrying about what she would think of me.

I didn't want to bond with her over the shitty way I'd treated people in the past. I didn't want to talk to her about any of it. But I did want to talk about it with Nikki. I needed her to know. She'd asked about my darker secrets, and I'd hedged, letting her think that being a workaholic was the worst thing about me. She needed to know the rest.

I needed to get back to my hotel room to call her.

Triss was listing to the side in her chair, which meant I had to make sure she got back to her hotel room safely as well. I paid the tab and extended a hand to her, which she took gratefully. When I pulled her up from the chair, she kind of fell into me. The uncoordinated crash made her laugh, and she put her hands on my chest to ready herself.

It was reminiscent of a scene we'd shot earlier in the day, what would be our final on-screen scene together in the film, the end of our love story. Maybe it was the repetition of playing that moment throughout the workday, or maybe she was just tipsy and feeling sad about her broken marriage, but Triss looked up at me, suddenly vulnerable. She rose on her tiptoes, brought her face to mine, and pressed soft lips against my mouth. It wasn't accidental, and she wasn't falling or off balance. But I was, at least momentarily, because it was the last thing I was expecting. Which was why it took me a few seconds to get my wits about me and pull away.

"Hold on," I said, aware of her vulnerability but also a little angry that she'd presumed I would be interested. "Let's just take it easy." I took a scan of the room, paranoid that someone had seen—or worse, snapped a picture or taken a goddamned video. That was the last thing either one of us needed. But no one seemed to be looking our way. Thankfully, we were in a tiny local joint, where people mostly sat at the bar and had their backs to the door.

I untangled her arms from my neck and swiftly nudged her toward the door with my hand on the small of her back, hating that the gesture seemed at all personal. She reached back and hung an arm around my neck as we walked out of the pub, and I glanced behind us once more for the sign of an errant phone camera. I saw nothing.

Her arm stayed there, and I did my best to guide her down the street, because she was having some trouble walking. She had on high heels for some reason, and that wasn't helping. "Thank you for being you," she cooed.

I was in no mood. "Listen, we both had an emotional day, and I know you've got a lot on your mind, but I'm not in an open relationship."

She turned her head and peeked at me through her bangs, which covered her eyes and part of her face. "When in Ireland…"

"No. Not in Ireland. Not anywhere."

"Wow, who knew Chris Conley was so uptight?"

Looking ahead, I noted that there were still three more buildings in front of us before we got to the front of the hotel. I couldn't get us there fast enough. "Yeah, I guess that's it. I'm just uptight," I said, wanting to close the door on the subject.

The doorman held the front door to the hotel open for us, and I steered Triss to the elevators. I knew our rooms were on the same floor, but I didn't know which one was hers. I assumed she had the wherewithal to find it.

"Do you have your keycard?" I asked.

She dug around in her purse and eventually fished out a tube of lip gloss, which she applied on our way up in the elevator. She handed the purse to me, and I gingerly looked through it until I found the card. "Got it. What's your room number?"

She looked down at the key, which had no number on it because small pieces of plastic issued by hotels never have room numbers on them. "I don't remember, but it's the first one next to the ice." Skeptical of her directional sense, I led her toward the ice machines, where there were rooms on either side. She pointed, and I helped her swipe her key.

The door opened, and I heaved a sigh of relief that the day—and the night—was over.

She lingered in the doorway. "You wanna come in for a bit?"

Not even a little bit. I shook my head. "Get some sleep. We have a nine thirty call." I handed her the purse, and she turned her back on me, walked unsteadily toward the bed, and let the door swing back and nearly hit me in the face.

On my way to my own room, I looked down at my phone, knowing I needed to call Nikki before she left for her dinner meeting. I had a missed call from her and three texts.

Nikki: *You around?*

Nikki: *I've gotta run in a few*

Nikki: *You must be running over. Hope today went well. Call me tomorrow. xox*

I felt like shit.

CHAPTER THIRTEEN

LOS ANGELES
Nikki

I COULDN'T GET past the sickening, heavy feeling of being punched in the gut.

Chris's message and text had reached me before I'd seen anything online or faced my colleagues at work. At first, I thought he was just being overprotective. He knew I tended to freak out over stuff related to crowds and the trappings of celebrity. And honestly, crowds only freaked me out when they were armed with cameras.

It was probably no big deal, just Chris looking gorgeous and eligible in a foreign country and baiting the single women who loved his movies.

Then I saw the pictures.

The nausea set in immediately. Even though I knew there was probably a context that would take the sting out of what I was seeing, I couldn't help my visceral response. I felt as if I'd been kicked hard enough to knock the wind out of my lungs. I needed to sit. I thought I might throw up. I felt so incredibly betrayed and so stupid for thinking something could possibly work between Chris—who was world famous and had women throwing themselves at his feet—and me, who was average.

The worst thing was that a part of me was relieved. I'd been waiting for the other shoe to drop, for him to get tired of my average and return to the glamorous life that suited him.

Waiting—and worrying—had been stressful and more exhausting than being apart for more time than we were together. So after I recovered from feeling sucker-punched, I felt oddly calm.

I could hear Chris's words echoing in my head: "I never look at those."

But that was him. He didn't like seeing stolen moments captured by lurking paparazzi, a grimace as he took a sip of a too-hot latte or a stern expression while he waited for the elevator because no one acts smiley and photo-ready while waiting for an elevator. I didn't blame him. I wouldn't want to see myself that way, caught accidentally in daily life, not ready for my closeup.

Yes, I'd promised Chris I would ignore the tabloids. That had been easy to do when the worst thing in them was some troll hypothesizing about whether Chris Conley and "his LA arm candy" were still an item while he was off in Ireland filming for two months.

I knew the truth, and I didn't much care what someone printed in order to get tongues wagging and sell magazines.

But what I saw in the photos was another thing entirely. The rational purveyor of spin control in me knew how things could be taken out of context. There was a context that was being misconstrued. But the emotional girlfriend was having trouble seeing anything but Chris kissing his costar.

How else could it be explained? He's kissing her.

First of all, there was no avoiding the tabloids. The pictures were everywhere on Instagram and on the *Daily Mail* home screen. I didn't count that as a tabloid, so I continued to read it, even though I was at work and should have been working. Big mistake.

The bigger mistake was that Chris made the situation worse by (a) forgetting to call me the night before when he was clearly occupied with his tongue down the throat of his costar and (b) he'd left me a voicemail that made it sound like I would be the one overreacting to something that meant nothing. I found it hard to understand how being caught kissing his costar meant nothing, even if there was some alternate truth behind it.

How many truths are there? Two? Ten?

It felt like the classic apology from a thief. He wasn't sorry he stole, but he was very sorry he got caught.

Then again, I owed it to him to hear what he had to say. Sort of. Maybe. It would have been one thing if there were rumors swirling around and he explained away their source. But he'd been caught on camera. There was no mistaking that kiss. He couldn't pretend he was whispering in her ear when it looked like he was kissing her cheek. They were lip to lip. In another picture, it looked like he was pulling her into his arms, which was also hard to explain away.

Isn't a photo irrefutable proof? In a court of law, wouldn't that be enough to convict?

My phone rang. I knew it was Annie before I even looked at the caller ID. She was talking before I had a chance to say hello. "Is there a chance you still live in a superhero blackout?"

"Unfortunately, no."

"Are you okay?"

"Unfortunately… no." I was glad she'd called my cellphone, so I could leave my desk and walk out into the hallway for our conversation.

"Oh, sweetie, I'm so sorry. What did he say?"

"I haven't talked to him."

"Why not?"

"Because I'm really, really mad." I expected her to tell me to calm down until I spoke to him, but she surprised me when she said, "Good."

"Why good?"

"Because you're standing up for yourself, even though you might be wrong."

I shrugged even though I knew she couldn't hear that over the phone. "What's he gonna say? Whatever happened, happened. I don't see a need to hear about it."

"But you are going to—right?—hear what he has to say?"

I sighed. When I'd first seen the photos, I'd felt betrayed, but that moved quickly into just feeling sad. I'd already moved through at least one stage of grief, and it surprised me how quickly I was coming to terms with moving on. "Of course. Even though I don't see the point. Maybe this is normal for him when he's working."

"I don't think you believe that. He probably feels terrible. If you love him, you can't just not talk to him."

"For sure I can just not talk to him. I feel like it would be easier for us both to just let it go. There's no need to get all maudlin and dramatic over this."

Even without seeing her face, I could tell Annie was exasperated by her harsh exhale. "Here you go again."

"Just… please stop with the tirade about how I don't ask for what I want."

"I don't think I need the tirade. You know what I'm going to say."

"I do."

"Okay, then. Tell him what you want. If that's an apology, great. If it's a break from the relationship, fine. But please promise me you'll ask for what you need. You owe it to yourself to be honest with him. Then, maybe you'll get what you want."

I felt an unwelcome welling of tears. I hadn't cried at all when I saw the pictures. I'd been shocked and betrayed and angry, but I hadn't felt the kind of sadness that would lead me to break down and cry. "That's the problem," I said. "I thought I wanted this. I thought I wanted him. And now… I'm not sure."

Hearing myself say those words made me realize what had been holding me back the whole time. "I can't ask for what I want if I still don't know what that is."

~

IN PERHAPS A FURTHER sign of not knowing what I wanted, I found myself walking down the block outside our office with Jemma for the first time since she'd started at our firm.

I'd finally agreed to her suggestion to have lunch together, even though I had no appetite and didn't know what we were going to talk about for an hour. Actually, I had a good feeling. She'd been the first to come over to my desk after seeing the pictures of Chris and asked if I was okay. And even though I knew part of her interest came from hoping I would give her some inside scoop, she also seemed to genuinely care.

"We've all been there," she'd said, which almost made me laugh, because they were such sage counseling words coming from someone barely old enough to drink in a bar.

"I'm not so sure about that. But thanks."

So what if she's a little young and a lot starstruck? So what if I kinda know the reason behind her interest in me is her interest in Chris and the salacious details she hopes to glean from me over a slice of pizza and a Caesar salad at the Crow's Nest, a crummy fast-food Italian place down the block?

I didn't go out to lunch that often. Generally, I preferred to eat something quickly from the vending machine and leave a little early at the end of the day. Taking an hour break in the middle seemed like a waste of time. But I needed the break, so I was willing to trade a couple movie-star details because I didn't feel like eating alone at my desk.

"Maybe it's a sign he's serious about you," Jemma said, jumping right into her thoughts about why I should feel flattered by the photos everyone else at the office had seen and no one else at the office had mentioned

As enlightened as I felt I was about relationships, her armchair psychology about why Chris had been kissing his costar didn't make a lot of sense. And that was even after I admitted to myself that I was not at all enlightened about relationships. "How do you figure? I thought being serious about a person was a reason *not* to go around kissing other people."

"Well, yeah, yeah, when you put it that way, sure, It makes sense."

I still didn't understand what other ways there were to put it, so I waited while Jemma composed a thought in her head. When she didn't elaborate, I had to poke her. "Explain your thinking, please."

"I guess… I just meant it in that FOMO way."

"Again, explain?"

"You know, when you start thinking seriously about one person, you get that panicked feeling about everyone else out there. What if I could do better? Am I missing something?"

We were walking down the block, and I couldn't help but tilt my head back and feel the glorious rays of the sun hitting my face. I hadn't been outside at all that week because I'd been working hard and hadn't made it home while it was still light out. "So you think he's making some kind of last-stand kissing effort?"

"I mean, he's your boyfriend. What do you think?" she asked.

I wanted to strangle her. She'd put out some semi-believable theory that sounded like it was maybe the kind of thing all the kids were doing. Maybe I needed to get with the program. But then she started equivocating, and I didn't know what to think. "Generally, I think he's a good guy. But…"

"Pictures are kind of damning."

"Maybe there's another side to it." Jesus, she had a way of making me doubt everything about myself and my relationship. "I think I need to talk to him before I go off the reservation and assume he's an unrepentant cheater."

"Yeah... no. I'd be organizing a murder plot." *Is that what the kids these days are doing?* Lunch was going to be interesting. And probably painful.

~

ONE CAESAR SALAD, two pieces of pizza, and a brownie later—I decided to stress eat, and carb-loading seemed like a sure way to get me there—I didn't feel any better about Chris, but I had succeeded in veering most of the conversation away from him by relentlessly carpet-bombing Jemma with questions, so she couldn't ask me much of anything.

"When did your parents move to California?" I asked. It turned out she lived with her parents, and the job at our firm was her first one after college. And really, unless we were counting sweeping the leaves off her uncle's tennis court, it was her first job. For the record, I counted leaf-sweeping as a job, but not when the employer was a relative. I lived by a unique code of principles.

"It'll be two years in December."

"So they moved while you were in college?"

"Yes. So when you were in France—"

"And where did you go to college?"

"University of Oregon."

"What did you study?" I asked.

"Communications. Anyway, so how did you guys meet—"

I'd just taken a bite of food. Rookie move. It allowed her to get most of her question out before I could wave my hand in front of her, because I wasn't done asking about her fascinating choice of major. "Communications as a general major? Or did you specialize? Mass communications? Something related to public relations? How did you learn about the open position at the firm?"

There. I'd asked her enough questions that I would have time to take one, if not two, bites and chew them while she answered.

I could tell she was starting to understand the futility of trying to lunch-buddy me out of celebrity information, because her face fell a bit and took on the resigned look of a person who knew she'd been beaten at her own game. She methodically answered all my questions.

I respected her work ethic. And I decided she wasn't the celebrity stalker I'd initially feared she was. She just liked her *People Magazine* and her tabloid gossip—and there I was, a living, breathing tabloid story, sitting with her at lunch. She was so genuine about her guileless interest in celebrity gossip that I started to see she just liked the stories. She wasn't looking to turn around and call TMZ with her own unauthorized behind-the-scenes account of what I told her. She just wanted to know because she liked celebrity culture.

And she'd answered all my intrusive and sometimes zany questions for the better part of an hour. It seemed like that deserved a little return favor on my part.

"Okay, since you asked. I'll give you the basics of how we met." I told her about the grocery store meet cute and my ill-fated attempt to buy peaches. Then I gave her the broad strokes of our two-week vacation. I made it sound like it was the most normal thing in the world to meet an international megawatt actor in a grocery store and end up dating him several months later. Because to me, it was.

And that, I realized, was my problem.

CHAPTER FOURTEEN

BALLINASCORNEY, Ireland

Chris

Apparently, even a kindly bar owner from a small Irish town knew there was money to be made by selling photographs to a gossip rag.

The *Daily Mail* had not one, not two, but three pictures of Triss and me in the bar. In one, we were clearly mid-kiss, and it looked far steamier than it was. In the second, she'd just fallen into me, and my expression looked elated rather than the shock I was feeling. And in the third, taken from behind, I had my hand on her back, and she had just wrapped her arm around my neck. All three looked bad.

My publicist, Natalie, called me the minute the story hit the wires, which was at around eight a.m. in Ireland and the middle of the night in California. Natalie had her phone set to send her alerts from all the media outlets when they featured her clients. She was used to being awakened with such things.

"What's going on there across the pond?" she asked with more amusement than concern in her voice. She knew Triss's reputation for being difficult, and she knew me. "You're the last two I'd expect to start up an on-set romance."

"What the hell are you talking about?" It was my standard response where Natalie was concerned. She would call me with some sort of image emergency, and I would be clueless, because I didn't have alerts set on my phone to tell me what the tabloids were writing. I considered it sanity insurance.

"You and Triss Marshawn. There are pictures. They won't be easy to explain unless you tell me what's up."

I didn't need her to tell me more to deduce that someone must have snapped pictures of us at the pub. Sitting across the table and holding hands would have been bad enough. It would have been too much to hope no one had caught the kiss on camera. "Shit."

"Yeah, that's what I'm thinking. So are you and Nikki over?"

"No! Not at all. And I can only hope she took my advice not to read the swill that passes for news in the *Daily Mail* and she doesn't know."

"Does she live in an underground bunker and write on stone tablets? Because that's the only scenario that will keep her in the dark. The pictures are everywhere, not just the *Mail*."

"Okay, I need to call her. I'll call you back."

"Nope, nope. You can call her in five minutes. Right now, you need to tell me what actually happened." I'd put my phone on speaker so I could scroll through the pictures, and I couldn't believe what I saw. *How had someone captured the exact worst moments?*

"Shit," I said again. I flipped to my text app and fired off a couple quick texts to Nikki. *Hey. Need to talk to you. U up? Call me.*

"Yes, I'm aware. Talk to me."

"She kissed me. She was wasted and sad about her marriage and an overall nightmare. I was trying to get her out of her chair, which was when she fell against me, and out the door, which is why I put my hand on her back. I know how it looks, but trust me, I couldn't get away from her fast enough. The woman is relationship kryptonite."

"Uh huh. That may be, but you two had your hands all over

each other. So we have a choice. We either say nothing and let this die with tomorrow's news, or we comment and risk it turning into a bigger story. Denial tells people there's something to deny, as you know."

"I do know. So say nothing. Ignore it like it was nothing. Because it was nothing."

"Fine by me. As long as you assure me you're not going back for round two tonight."

"I don't even want to see her on the set. There will be no tonight."

"Okay, then. Done. I've gotta run. Moving on to the next catastrophe. One of my other clients was caught soliciting a prostitute in a sting operation. Much harder to ignore or explain away."

"Jesus." I could never have done her job, which made me think again of Nikki, who did a version of Natalie's job, and I felt nauseous at the idea of her seeing the pictures before I talked to her.

"It's no biggie. I can handle it. That's why I always tell you, you're my easiest client. Now all you have to do is explain it to Nikki, and you're golden."

"Shit," I said for the third time in ten minutes.

"Yes. You're in deep shit. Work it out, because I don't want to put out a press release saying you've decided to consciously uncouple. If you two can't make it, I don't know who can."

"On it. Thanks, Nat."

"No prob."

"Oh, hey. Any advice for what I can do for Nikki? Should I send flowers or something?"

"Ugh. Please don't be that guy. Be better. Do something better. Flowers have guilt written all over them. Like I said, I expect more from you because you're one of the good guys. Just tell her the truth."

"Okay, will do. No flowers."

"Eh, but what the hell do I know? I've been divorced three times, and none of my ex-husbands ever sent me flowers." Natalie had been my publicist for eight years, and in that time, she'd been with two of her three husbands. Oh, and she was younger than I was. She always had a good attitude about her relationships, even when they were ending. "Happy to see them come, happy to see them go," was how she'd described her exes.

"Thanks, Nat."

"See ya."

Nikki hadn't returned the texts. I hadn't expected that she would, but it felt like torture knowing that whatever the thing was—that piece of information, complete with damning photos—hung out there with nothing I could do to explain it to her first. Times like those made the difference in time zones particularly difficult.

What am I saying? There shouldn't be times like these.

So far, there hadn't been. I'd kept my head down and focused on my work during the times we couldn't be together. It wasn't ideal, but it was something. It made me feel like we were moving toward a future.

But now…

I tried calling her, but the call went to voicemail. Of course it did. It was the middle of the night in LA, Nikki was a sound sleeper, and she kept her cell on vibrate. There was no way to reach her, and I didn't love the idea of waking her up to tell her I'd been caught kissing another woman.

If I lived in the same city, I would have gone to see her in person. The distance was already hard on us, but Ireland was a ten-hour plane flight away, and I had to be back on the set in an hour. The photos and the gossip had the power to ignite into a firestorm before she even woke up.

I called her again and left a long message on her voicemail. "Hey, it's me. Hope you slept well. I'm really sorry I missed you last night. Things ran late," I said, feeling even more like an asshole, because the only thing that had run late was my time at the pub. Not only had I missed our phone call, but I'd been with Triss instead of calling. I continued with my message. "Anyway, there are some pictures printed in one of the tabloids, and I wanted to explain before you saw them. They're out of context, and you shouldn't worry about them. I promise. They're nothing. I love you."

Feeling like my rambling message had done nothing but make the situation sound even worse than it was, I went back to my texting app and fired off one more text. *Hey. Just don't look at the tabloids. I promise, there's nothing to worry about. Okay? Please? ILY.*

I stared at my phone, willing the three thinking dots to appear, a sign that she was responding. But my message sat there like a fat turd on the green grass of my life. Or maybe I was the fat turd.

I'd thought I could handle a relationship, work, and the long-distance thing. But I was blowing it big-time, just as I'd always feared I would.

CHAPTER FIFTEEN

LOS ANGELES

Nikki

From the time I saw the photos and heard Chris's message that morning, I was certain of three things.

First, I knew Chris was going to call me again. His schedule was more or less predictable when he was on location. They generally started at eight in the morning and finished at eight or nine at night. They aimed for eight because that gave them a twelve-hour turnaround, which was required by the unions for all the people who worked on the lighting, sound, hair and makeup, and the grips and gaffers, whose jobs I didn't really understand. But I knew they couldn't report back to the set before they'd been given a twelve-hour break.

I also knew that there was ample standing-around time every day. For as much as Chris got into character and worked with the hair and makeup departments before his scenes, I'd witnessed firsthand when I was in New York that he had a lot of downtime in each day. That meant he had plenty of time to pick up the phone if he wanted to talk.

The third thing I knew was that Chris respected my time at

work and wouldn't have wanted to put me in an awkward position on a call with him during my workday.

But by four in the afternoon, I still hadn't heard from him, and I was struck with a new feeling. In some ways, it was similar to the nausea I'd felt when I saw the photos, except that it was joined by a new emotion: certainty.

He wasn't waiting to call me because he cared about my workday or because he was composing his thoughts. He wasn't waiting at all. He just wasn't calling.

He'd taken the time to leave a vague voicemail and some texts, but clearly since then, he'd copped to what everyone who'd seen the photos seemed to know—there was no explaining away the pictures because he was falling for his costar. And while he needed to apologize for the way I found out about it all, it didn't change the fact that we were over. He wasn't calling me because there was nothing left to say. Nothing that a photograph didn't say a thousand times better or more clearly. We were done.

I also was done. Even though I'd taken a lunch break and therefore probably owed the company a couple more hours of work time, I suddenly really needed to leave. I didn't want to talk to anyone else. I didn't want to feel anyone's eyes on me or be aware of people tiptoeing around me, wondering if I was okay.

I wasn't okay. But I would be. I just needed to leave and clear my head.

My desk was a mess of file folders and half-finished press releases, but I didn't care. I walked away from the mess and out of the office. It wasn't until I exited the elevator on the lobby level and started to walk toward the detached parking structure behind the building that I heard someone call my name. *Crap. Maybe I should have told my boss I was leaving.*

I turned around, ready to throw myself at his mercy and tell him I needed the rest of the day for personal time but that I would be back in the morning, ready to give him one hundred and ten percent.

But it wasn't my boss.

It was Chris.

~

WE LOOKED at each other warily. In part, my shock came from the fact that he was in Ireland—or he was supposed to be in Ireland.

How is he standing in the lobby of my building?

For his part, he looked a little afraid, like I might yell at him or throw something. Yelling wasn't an option because I was stunned speechless, but I would have happily hurled a heavy object at his head if I'd had one handy.

He came closer, and I froze, unsure I wanted him near me. He seemed to sense my hesitance and stopped about three feet away. "Hey," he said. He didn't flash me his pretty Hollywood smile. He looked exhausted, but I couldn't bring myself to feel sorry for him, especially if his lack of sleep came from staying up all night, banging his costar.

He held his arms out to hug me.

A hug? A breakup hug?

"Just... no." I crossed my arms and glared at him, because I had no additional words handy.

"Can we... can we go somewhere and talk? Please?"

It was the "please" that got me. Any time someone asked for something nicely, the acquiescent part of me wanted to oblige. At that moment, I hated that part of myself. She was the part who didn't break up with Johnny because he looked cute and said cute things, and those two factors erased all the not-cute things he did and said.

As much as I wanted to pound that side of myself into the ground and take off at a sprint, curiosity got the better of me. I did want to know how Chris planned to explain himself. I wasn't planning on letting him off the hook with a cute explanation, but I was intrigued enough by what he might come up with that I nodded at him and gestured to the glass doors at the back of my building. He followed me out.

In between the low-slung office and the parking structure was an outdoor patio with some grassy knolls between winding pathways, as if to give the impression of a tiny park-like oasis in which to escape the work environment. The reality was that people rarely enjoyed the oasis. There was too much work to do and not enough time for escaping. But the well-positioned small benches seemed designed to suit our particular needs perfectly.

"Nik," he said, reaching for my hand. Reluctantly, I put mine in his, but there was no warmth. "There's absolutely nothing going on with my costar."

"Okay." I didn't want to meet his gaze. He'd caught me off guard, so I hadn't organized my thoughts.

"Nikki, look at me." I turned. He looked wrecked. I felt bad for him, but I knew I had to stand up for myself. "I am so sorry. I never. Ever. Want to hurt you."

I nodded. I believed him. He wasn't callous and I knew it.

He gestured for us to sit, and I moved far to the edge of the bench.

"I don't have a disease," he said, his smile entirely gone.

"I know. I just want to be able to look at you while we talk. I can't see you if I'm sitting closer." As if to demonstrate my point, I turned my back against the armrest of the bench and leaned on it. He moved to his side and did the same, but he didn't speak for a long time—so long, in fact, that I started to imagine that maybe I was the one who'd suggested we go somewhere and talk. Maybe I was the one who had something to say. So I said it. "You didn't have to fly all the way here, you know. I get it. You feel bad about the pictures, and you didn't intend to hurt me. I get it. Let's just call it what it is. We're far away from each other, and we're living different lives. Maybe we can't do the long-distance thing."

He shook his head. "Goddammit. See, I knew this. I knew it. This is why I had to come see you in person. I knew where your mind was."

"What, that after you kissed someone else—or slept with her, or whatever you two are doing—I wouldn't want to date you across an ocean anymore? Gee, you're a genius."

"No. I knew you'd see it as some kind of proof that we're bound to fail. And I don't want to see that happen, so I'm here, telling you I'm sorry and pleading with you to trust me."

I was so shocked by his nerve that an unintended laugh erupted. It came out sounding like a quack. "Wait, your issue is that I don't trust you? Are you kidding me? You, who just proved why I never should have trusted in the first place, are faulting me for that?"

"You really don't get it, do you?"

"Don't get what? What is there to get?" I was feeling myself get angrier, effectively moving through another stage of grief, all in one day. At least I was efficient. "Why are we even doing this? Why are you here? Don't you have a movie to make and a costar to make out with? They have phones, you know. Oh right, you forgot how to use them." It felt good to be surly and mad. I tried so hard all the time to control my feelings and react rationally. I tried to be nice, and this was what I got for it.

"Will you please stop? Just let me talk. Please." He was raising his voice. I'd never heard him raise his voice. Maybe I'd never seen him angry.

I'd made him angry. Good. That made two of us. "Fine. Talk." I'd said my piece. So I sat back against the arm of the bench and looked at him. When he didn't meet my gaze or start talking right away, I looked around that the park, wondering who came to mow the tiny mounds of grass. It seemed like a waste of resources to have a gardening crew come out just to mow six blades of grass.

Chris got up and walked a few paces away from me. Then he came back and sat on the bench, closer to me that time. He didn't look at me, and at that proximity, I could only see part of his face. He blinked heavily. "I'm going to tell you what happened last night. Which was nothing, by the way, despite what it looked like in the pictures, but then I'm going to address the elephant that's destroying the goddamn room."

I shrugged. "Okay." It was his story to tell.

"My costar, Triss, and I went out for a beer after we finished yesterday. The scenes were hard and emotional, and it felt good to go out with a colleague who could relate."

"So that's what you were doing? Relating? With your tongue?"

"No. Oh my God, no. She's… a piece of work. And not particularly kind. Good actor, but kind of a train wreck as soon as the cameras stop." He ran a hand through his hair as though just thinking about her was stressful.

I didn't say anything. He hadn't convinced me of anything yet.

"She drank a lot, and when I went to help her up from her chair, she fell against me. That was the first picture. She's going through a divorce, and her emotions are all over the place, so she tried to kiss me, which I quickly rejected. That was the second picture. And because she was drunk, I needed to halfway hold her up to get her out of the bar and back to the hotel. She grabbed my neck. The third picture."

I relented a little bit. His story made sense. And I felt a little bit bad that I hadn't waited to hear all this from him before judging. But he hadn't picked up the phone. "Chris…"

He held up a hand. "Now, here's the troubling part. You don't trust me. And I don't mean that you don't trust me not to cheat on you. I think that despite the photos, a big part of you knew there was more to the story, and you know I wouldn't do that."

I nodded. "I don't think you'd do that."

"But it doesn't matter. Because you're waiting for something to end us. You're trying to fast-forward to our breakup because you're so certain that it will happen eventually that you want to get it over with now."

Hearing him say it out loud, I realized how messed up it was. "I know. I know, you're right. I'm an insane person. It's just that I'm feeling all these feelings for you, and the higher I go, the farther I have to fall, and I'm trying to stop myself before I get hurt."

He closed his eyes and didn't say anything, but he shook his head slowly, sadly.

"You know, Chris, it's not even about the pictures. I know stuff gets misconstrued. It's that you're there and I'm here and it's just… too much. I don't want to have a long-distance relationship. I'm sick of missing you all the time. I hate it."

"I know. I hate it too. You're right… we can't do this." His voice cracked when he said it.

And in that moment, I heard him say we were done. I heard it that way because he was right—I didn't have faith. I didn't believe in us. All I could hear was the other shoe falling hard and hurting me. I could see no other outcome even as I hated myself for being that way.

"Did you really fly all the way here to break up with me?" I asked. I steeled myself for his answer. I wouldn't be happy if we broke up—in fact, I'd be miserable—but I wouldn't be surprised.

"No," he said, his voice riddled with such disbelief that the word sounded almost like a laugh. "No. Not at all. I wanted to make sure you knew that even though I have a job that's forcing me to stay away, I'd rather be with you. I wanted to assure you—because I suspected you might be freaking out—that the only person I think about every day is you. And I'm sorry about all the long distance. It was not my plan."

I reached out and put my hand on his leg. He picked it up and brought it to his heart, where he held it for a moment, and I tipped my head to rest it on his shoulder.

"This is all just… it's harder than I thought it would be."

"I know. And I'm sorry. I didn't think it would be this way." He tipped his head down and leaned it against mine before shifting and pulling me into his arms.

When I looked into his dark eyes, I saw the kind, handsome guy I wanted so badly to trust with my heart. He covered my mouth with his. It wasn't a tentative, searching kiss. It was a commanding, assuring, devouring kiss. He pushed one hand into the hair at my temple and wrapped the other around my back to pull me closer. His tongue sought mine, sweeping dreamily across the inside of my mouth until a tiny moan escaped from the back of my throat.

It was a kiss that communicated feeling and connection. I needed it more than I realized, and my lips and my body melted into his with the force of all my emotional turmoil.

He absorbed it. He met it with reassurance, and he calmed it.

Even though my heart was pounding when we finally broke the kiss, I felt as if I'd been relieved of a burden. I felt better.

Nothing else had been explained. But everything had been communicated in that kiss. I didn't know what to say. Maybe he didn't, either, because neither of us spoke right away. It suddenly seemed that words were insufficient to communicate with the kind of precision delivered through a kiss like that.

Chris focused his eyes on mine again, questioning and waiting for my response.

"I can't believe you came all this way. I… don't know what to say."

"Say that you'll stop waiting for the end of us. Say that you understand the way I feel about you. There's no distance I wouldn't fly to tell you that. I only want one person, and she's here on this bench."

I let out a breath. "I do understand. And it's not your fault that trust doesn't come easily to me. It's a learned behavior. I know I need to work on it."

"*We* need to work on it. So we will."

I was annoyed with myself and my inability to evolve. I wanted to get past my issues, but some of them were deeply rooted in old relationships and ingrained fears. I ran my hands through my hair, which pulled some wisps free from the clip. I could see them dancing in a halo around my shadow on the ground.

Chris reached up and tucked a few of the errant wisps behind my ear. He looked at me tentatively, tilting his head and gazing at me with his penetrating brown eyes. The anticipation and wonder felt like the moment before a first kiss.

His fingers dragged along my cheek and cupped my chin lightly. "I have to be back at the airport in forty-five minutes. Will you ride with me in the car? The driver can drop you home after."

I nodded. "I'm not ready to say goodbye yet."

In one graceful motion, he was on his feet, and he'd scooped me up into his arms. He planted kisses on my forehead and cheeks and lips as he carried me to the waiting town car. "I hope there's a lot of traffic between here and the airport."

"It's LA. There's always a lot of traffic." For once, I was thrilled by that fact. I buried my face in his neck and held tight while he carried me to the car.

CHAPTER SIXTEEN

LOS ANGELES
Chris

THE OUTDOOR STAIRCASE on the tarmac rolled away as soon as I stepped onto the plane.

"Everything good, lovebird?" I heard the words before my eyes adjusted to the darker interior. Then I saw her, sitting cross-legged on the couch, blond hair tossed around her shoulders, her expression more smirk than smile. If anyone had walked onto that plane and seen her sitting there, reclined in a lazy, inviting position, they would have gotten the wrong idea for sure.

Nikki had wanted to walk me to the plane. The only thing that prevented it was her lack of a passport, since my flight would be leaving the US and required a special security check. It would not have been a good situation, all things considered.

Triss's voice had the effect of a knife gutting me without doing me the courtesy of killing me first. The mere tenor of it was painful, and I steeled myself for another long flight in close proximity.

"Everything's fine," I answered, tight-lipped and disinterested in having a conversation with her.

Triss had jumped at the opportunity to share my last-minute ride to Los Angeles because she wanted to pick up the Maltipoo that she and her ex had been co-parenting. They'd decided she would keep the dog, though I suspected that the urgency in retrieving him had more to do with pissing off her soon-to-be ex than with necessity. But I couldn't really say no—I'd already disrupted our shooting schedule, and she would have to work part of the weekend to make up for the lost day. If she was willing to do that, I couldn't begrudge her one of the seats on the plane.

I thought better than to tell Nikki we'd flown together, especially once our conversation had grown tense, but not saying anything felt the same as a lie. Once again, I'd been asking her to trust me and be honest, and I couldn't get there myself.

What the hell is wrong with me?

I felt like shit. And I was leaving yet again. And I was exhausted.

The dog—Marley, named after either Bob or Ziggy, but I didn't bother to ask—slept in its Louis Vuitton carrier at Triss's feet. I wondered if she'd given him a sedative. It would bother me to know she'd drugged an animal, and it was one time when I decided that not knowing was the better call.

I dropped into one of the white leather club chairs on the plane and cracked open a water bottle from the side console.

"Good. I'd hate to think we flew all this way and you didn't resolve things." She was smiling at me through layers of eyelashes I assumed were fake and twirling her hair around her finger. She sat cross-legged in yoga pants and a sleeveless tank.

I huffed a laugh at that. "Okay."

"What's that supposed to mean?" she asked, blinking as if her eyes stung with tears.

Actors…

"I just said okay."

"But you didn't mean it."

"How can a person not mean the word 'okay'?"

"You said it like you think I'm being insincere. You know I only have your best interests at heart. I didn't mean to have pictures end up in a magazine so your girlfriend would find out about us."

I closed my eyes in some small hope she would disappear when I opened them. A long flight with her was going to work my last nerve. "Triss, there's no us. She didn't find out about us. She saw the tabloid photos, which never should've happened because you never should've kissed me." I'd said this to her several times already, but it clearly hadn't sunk in.

"I didn't kiss you. You kissed me."

"What?!"

"I'm just kidding," she said, giving me a playful punch in the arm. "God, you're so easy to mess with. I'm just trying to get you to have a sense of humor."

"Triss, why do I get the impression you find humor in other people's problems?" As soon as I'd said it, I wished I hadn't. It was a dick thing to say.

She shrugged, twirling a strand of her hair. "I do like drama," she said, not offended. "Too bad you don't. It's gonna be an awfully long plane ride if we're just sitting here like a couple of nuns. We could have some fun." She reached over and punched me in the leg, raising an eyebrow and pursing her lips in a seductive pout.

"Then I guess it'll be a long plane ride." I turned away from her and picked up my sides for the next day's shoot.

"Oh, don't be so dramatic. I'm just teasing you 'cause you flew six thousand miles to explain a photo. Who does that? Couldn't you have just had a phone conversation with your girlfriend? What's her name again?"

I held up a hand to stop the conversation. "Just... never mind."

Triss picked up her phone and tapped on the screen. A couple seconds later, she said, "Nikki." She squinted at the screen of her phone, then moved her fingers to blow up what seemed to be a photo. "She's cute. I didn't know you liked the granola type."

"She's not granola," I said, falling right into her trap, realizing it, then pressing my lips together to keep from saying more.

Triss laughed. "You're so easy to rile. I urge you, lighten up. Does she like this side of you? Is she into brooding?" As if to show her nonbrooding side, she walked to the mini-fridge at the front of the plane, grabbed a can of pink wine, and popped the top. "Is it uncouth if I drink this from the can?" she asked, slurping off the rim.

It amused me that she even thought about it. "Do what you want. There's no one else here." I looked around to make sure I was correct. Nope, no one was there. Just us for hours and hours.

She took a big swig then another. After placing the can on the table between our white leather armchairs, she wiped her mouth with the back of her hand. "Well, hallelujah for that. I don't need to be followed around and photographed every minute of my life."

"Seriously? I thought you lived for that shit."

"You thought wrong. I don't like the media in my business any more than you do. You really think you know me so well?" She glared at me as though I'd said I was going to throw her dog off the plane.

I shrugged. "Okay, my bad. I apologize." God, her moods were all over the place. And she was difficult. If not for her acting ability, which was impressive when she committed herself, I might have pushed to get her replaced on the film. I'd never used my clout in a film to get another actor fired, but she begged me to make an exception. Daily.

"I'm just saying, what's the point of getting upset about it? They're gonna do what they're gonna do. Haters gonna hate, right?"

From underneath us, I felt a rumble as the engines fired up. The pilot closed the door dividing us from the cockpit, and the plane started rolling toward the runway. I fought the feeling of sadness over leaving—again—after only a couple hours with Nikki. It was never enough. It would never be enough.

So fix it, asshole. Or enjoy stewing in your own stubborn stupidity.

Ignoring my outspoken conscience, I looked out the window and watched the last place I'd been with Nikki—the last place I'd gotten to kiss her and hold her before reluctantly letting go—fade into the distance. I knew our current situation was my fault but had no idea how to fix it.

"I guess we're both in a bad way," I heard Triss say. When I turned back to look at her, I saw sympathy that had generally been absent when the cameras weren't rolling. "I mean, I'll get my shit together about my marriage eventually—mostly by talking about it. I'm an extrovert, as you've learned. But you seem like you need an intervention."

"I'm fine."

"Really? Are you a climate change denier too? You're not fine. You have it bad for her. You can't keep jetting around the world on some kind of apology tour. So whatever you're doing wrong, do it different. That's free advice from me to you."

It wasn't a conversation I really wanted to have, and especially not with Triss. I was still pretty pissed off at her about many things, so I said nothing and looked out the window again. Maybe she would drink her wine and fall asleep for two hours—or nine.

She reached out her toe and nudged my leg. "Hey. I'm sorry. I know I've been a pain in the ass. I have… a special talent for it."

To save my sanity, I either had to get her to stop talking or get over my annoyance and engage with her. Both seemed like insurmountable obstacles. "It's okay," I said, not choosing either one.

She nudged me again. "Really. I'm sorry. I'll try to be more of a human being."

That made me laugh a little. "Sounds good."

She was quiet for a while. Eventually, I looked over and saw that she was reading a book that had dragons on the cover. That made me relax, because if she was occupied, I could work a little. The hardest scenes were behind us, and I felt pretty good about what we had to do in the upcoming week, but there was still the project I'd agreed to do after this one.

I was in a bit of denial about the fact that I would barely have any time off between when this movie wrapped and when preproduction began on the next one. I still kept thinking I could finesse the dates so I would have some time in LA with Nikki, but the calendar wasn't going to budge.

I was used to the pace, but I couldn't blame Nikki for not liking my schedule.

Regardless, I needed to read through the script again. My role was a professor with special needs who falls in love with his caregiver and doesn't want her to know how he feels. He wants to save her the embarrassment of rejecting him. The concept was sweet, but the character was pretty far outside my action-hero comfort zone. I needed to do some research and put in the work in order to play the character with the sensitivity the part deserved.

I pulled the script out of my bag and flipped it open. The dialogue drew me in immediately—it was so beautifully written, I felt the emotion through the pages. I'd read about thirty pages before I looked up and realized Triss was staring at me. "What's up?" I asked.

"Is that our movie?" she asked.

"Oh, no. It's my next project. It starts prep pretty much right after this one."

At first, I thought she was annoyed that I was looking at a new project when we were in the middle of filming ours. "Does it shoot in LA?" she asked.

"It was supposed to, but they changed it. Budget issues or some crap. A few of the locations are still in LA, but most of it will be in Atlanta, actually."

"So you're gonna be away from her for, what, another month or two? And she's okay with this?"

"We had other stuff to talk about. I didn't want to bring it up."

"But you're doing the film."

"I'm supposed to." I wished she'd go back to her book.

"And she doesn't know."

"No," I said, getting annoyed. Why was she carping on this? I'd tell Nikki when I wasn't busy apologizing for something else.

Triss shook her head. "You. Are. Fucking. This. Up."

I still thought she was talking about our movie and worrying that I'd lose focus if my mind was on another project. "Triss, I'm set for our next set of scenes. I've been working on them for weeks. Trust me, I'm able to multitask and not lose the thread of what we're doing."

"You are also an idiot."

"Awesome. Thanks. It's good to hear," I said, the sarcasm thick. I'd worked hard to get my character right, and I felt good about the job I'd done so far. "Do you really think my work on our movie has been subpar?"

"I'm not talking about our movie, you thick-headed dumb lug. I'm talking about Nikki. You're blowing it."

And… she had my attention. I was going on twenty-four hours without sleep, and I'd flown across an ocean to try to fix things. So I really hoped she was wrong. "Stick to what you know. We're all good."

"Exactly. You're great because she doesn't know you're leaving again. Men are so clueless. Actually, that's not fair. Not all men are clueless, but you… you are clueless. I'm sorry to have to be the one to set you straight, but you, Chris, are a brilliant actor, but you're dumb as a rock when it comes to relationships."

I put the script down and closed it in my lap. My eyes hurt from fatigue. "Please don't make me guess. Just tell me what the hell you're talking about, Triss, so I can understand what you want."

"See? There. That. If you just said that to Nikki, I'll bet you'd be taking the next four months off after our film and spending time being in love."

I shook my head. "Being in love isn't an activity. It's a state of being that can exist with a full-time job."

"Not in the beginning, it can't. If you don't put in the time, you're going to blow it. You and I will be done in a couple weeks, so I won't be here to set you straight. You need to figure this shit out now, while I can still tell you you're doing it wrong. Make a mental list of your priorities. And if she's at the top of that list, don't blow it by flying off to another city. Now … sit in your chair and think about it, you silly, unevolved, pretty-faced man."

Triss cracked another can of wine and went back to her book. I considered ignoring her and going back to the script, but I quickly found that my concentration was shot.

What if she's right?

The idea that I was doing *anything* wrong didn't sit well with me. I'd had acting success at a young age, and my career had only soared from there. With it came women and directors and more women clamoring for my attention. That was my baseline. It all looked pretty damn good. And now I was off on the wrong track, I guessed, but I had no preparation for it.

Shocker. You know squat about how to have a relationship, and that's why you avoid them.

That thought did not fill me with optimism. I talked myself down, something I was pretty good at doing because it saved me from actually having to analyze my behavior. And why should I? My career was on fire. I was good at the work. I just needed to focus on that. I was a goddamned superhero, for God's sake.

Holy shit, you've actually drunk the Kool-Aid.

I really was stupid. Even the superhero doesn't get the girl if he's busy rescuing people twenty-four-seven. How could he get her if they were never in the same city?

CHAPTER SEVENTEEN

SAN DIEGO
Nikki

WORK WAS nuts for the next couple weeks, which was a good thing, because it kept my mind off of Chris. More specifically, it kept me blissfully free from self-examination. I loved Chris, but I was over the long-distance relationship.

You love him. You want to be with him. So ask for it.

That was another problem, and I was pretty sure it went hand in hand with the first one. I was afraid I couldn't have what I wanted. At the same time, I was falling harder and more fully in love with him, even at a distance. It scared the wits out of me—not only was I powerless to control it, but I was worried we'd never live in the same place. I would be stuck in a sad rut, completely in love with a man I couldn't have.

Until I could see past that day and find some convincing hint about our future that would sustain me, I would still have one cautious foot out the door... even though I'd promised to trust him.

Even when I'd said it, I knew it was wrong. I wasn't ready. I didn't want to get hurt. I also didn't want to hurt him. He was working his tail off on his movie, and I didn't want him to be distracted by worry. I wanted him to believe we were going to be okay, even as I feared that we weren't.

I thought about all of those things on the two-hour drive south of LA, where I was headed for a meeting with the CEO of Aventria, a biotech and pharmaceuticals company. I didn't mind the drive, and normally, I would have listened to a podcast and zoned out, but I kept the radio silent so I could think.

Because I didn't want to deal with my fear of love and loss, I'd been pouring myself into my job and my art projects. That had worked out well for me at work because I'd been able to pick up two new accounts, both of which were in a public relations tailspin and needed my intervention. Corporate crises were my specialty, and I liked being the calm in their bad-publicity storm.

One of the new clients, Aventria, was trying to manage the fallout from the CEO speaking out of turn about a new drug and the certainty that it would get FDA approval. In fact, he'd gotten no assurances from the FDA, and even if he had, he shouldn't have said anything publicly.

I drove down to Torrey Pines, a wooded area near San Diego, where its labs and offices were located, so I could have a meeting with the chief executive who'd misspoken.

I parked in the spacious outdoor lot and noted that the San Diego area was more spread out than what I was used to in the heart of LA. His assistant walked me from the bright, austere lobby to the corner office of the chief executive, chatting the whole way about different beverage options I could have during my meeting. I told her that coffee sounded great, and she deposited me in her boss's office. "Be right back with the coffee. Cream and sugar?"

"Just cream. Thanks."

By the time she returned with two cups, which she deposited on coasters on the desk, Donald Leaf was looking very contrite but also unsure exactly what he'd done wrong. I had no problem explaining it to him.

"You know, you can't make promises that will affect the stock price. But you and I both know it happens all the time, so we just need to manage investor expectations and put out a few well-worded statements explaining the exact state of your research and potential FDA approval," I told Donald Leaf, who was sitting across his desk from me and typing on his computer while we talked. I could tell I only had his partial attention. It was the first time we'd met in person, despite the fact that he'd hired me to be his representative at the firm two weeks earlier. His colleague at another biotech company was also a client of mine, and he'd hired me on blind faith. I wanted to live up to his expectations.

He looked up from his computer when I stopped talking. "I trust you."

Ha. He had no trust issues whatsoever, and he didn't even know me. People were not all alike.

"You shouldn't, not without thinking through what I'm saying."

His fingers were poised over his keyboard, and he was ready to tune me out again, but some of my words must have penetrated. He moved his hands away from the keyboard and folded them on his desk. "Okay, here's the problem with what you're suggesting. I can't say much about our research at all. My tease about potential FDA approval was meant to allow me to avoid talking about specific research."

"Well, now you get to talk about it. I'm not saying you break protocols. But there's a way we can word the statements to make it clear that what you *meant* by your comment about FDA approval was really a reference to fascinating developments industrywide that will allow a lot of players—including your company—to push through products in the coming years that will meet with FDA approval and change the game."

Donald Leaf was a serious man who spent serious time thinking about science. But the grin that spread across his face told me I'd opened his mind to the beauty of spin control. "That's brilliant. So in essence, I'm not saying anything specific about my company that will get me in trouble."

"Exactly. We're controlling the narrative and telling people only what they need to know to understand that your company is doing great things and will continue to do great things that will make your investors a lot of money. We're not saying when, and we're not saying what. But when you accomplish it, you'll look brilliant, because you told people to expect it a long time ago."

"So it's lying, somewhat. Taking advantage of people's lack of sophistication with respect to the science and then telling them we've been saying everything all along. And this works? People will believe this? This lying?"

"We're not lying. We're molding the facts to fit the scenario."

He let out a hollow laugh. "That sounds like dirty pool, but since it will help me stay out of hot water, I'm giving you free rein to pursue it." I loved his string of metaphors, none of which would be allowed when he made his official statement.

Molding facts was what I did all day long. I'd gotten so good at finding the conclusion I wanted to extract from the end of the machine that it almost didn't matter what facts I put into the front end. Kind of the way I was deciding where Chris and I would end without regard to the facts. I had to stop. And I would. I'd save all my fact-molding for Donald Leaf.

"Perfect. First, we'll do a download—in confidence—on the state of your research and your FDA approvals, so I know what's really happening. Then we can talk about what's safe to say publicly. I'll craft a few statements for you to look over, and once you approve, we'll put out the press releases. You'll make yourself available for interviews with the bigger news outlets, and we'll consider this crisis solved. Sound good?"

"Sounds perfect. And I owe Jeff Pettit lunch for recommending you to me. I can already tell this will be a fruitful relationship."

"I'm here to help. But let's not go looking for opportunities for me to bail you out. We should have a sit-down and go over things you should never say in a public forum. Or on Twitter. Please, God, never on Twitter."

We shook hands and set up our sit-down. Within two hours of arriving, I was back in the car, driving north. I wasn't expected back at the office until late afternoon, so I took a little detour to a lookout point by the coast. The tall pines were so dense in places that it was hard to believe they'd yield to a view of the beach, but after a few minutes of winding along a westbound road, I could see the misty marine layer over the still blue water.

Water down there was a different color than the more polluted Santa Monica Bay, despite cleanup efforts to make it better. There were just too many people in LA and too many dirty storm drains emptying into the ocean. I parked and walked down a scrubby path to the lookout point, which was marked with a bench and a coin-operated telescope.

I didn't need the long view. Sitting and taking in the wide landscape of beach and ocean was enough to bring a little peace.

When I took my phone out to snap a photo, I saw a string of missed texts from Chris.

Chris: *Thinking about you.*

Chris: *Okay, that's a lie. I'm not thinking. I'm fantasizing about your gorgeous body. And your beautiful face.*

Chris: *And your lips.*

Chris: *And your tongue.*

Chris: *And… other things. Not necessarily in that order.*

Chris: *Missing you. A lot.*

Chris: *Okay, gonna stop now before I ask for naked pics.*

Chris: *P.S. send naked pics*

Before typing my reply, I thought about what I wanted to say. So much. Too much for a text. I missed him. I beyond missed him. Missing him had become such a persistent state of affairs that a permanent ache had taken up residence in my chest. My breathing always labored under a weight of sadness. I never felt whole.

And yet, I wasn't sure that having him fly in for another

quickie could fix that. Seeing him for twenty-four hours here and there was almost harder than not seeing him at all. And as much as he kept saying that it was an unfortunate collision of projects and it wasn't always going to be that way, I wasn't sure I believed him. He'd been honest from the start. He'd told me he was a workaholic.

At the time, I'd thought that his dark side seemed pretty lily white. But he was more than a workaholic. He was someone who never stopped working, even when it meant letting other parts of his life suffer. He had no work–life balance. He just had work. There was no room for me in the equation unless he made room.

But I couldn't say all those things, at least not in a text. They would have to wait until the next time we saw each other. So I responded as though everything was fine.

Nikki: *I miss you too. A lot.*

Nikki: *And there will be no pics.*

Nikki: *Kidding. There will be pics. And if you're lucky, I'll send them to you.*

CHAPTER EIGHTEEN

SANTA MONICA - Two weeks later

Nikki

AT SIX IN THE MORNING, it was still early enough to be light out, but the bright-yellow sun hadn't risen high enough above the horizon line to be visible above the low-rise buildings in my neighborhood. That made it the perfect time of day for jogging, because it wasn't so glary that I needed a hat or sunglasses. I preferred to run unencumbered.

I passed a few fellow joggers, and we nodded to each other, acknowledging the same love of getting up before most other humans to pound the pavement. Runners were a specific breed. I couldn't count the number of times someone at work had said to me, "I don't know how you can enjoy running. It's just... not my thing."

When something isn't one's thing, it is hard to understand how someone else can love it—or need it. I'd do my best to explain that it was about the breathing, the rhythm of my feet hitting the pavement, the clearing of my head. To me, it was a contact sport. When my feet landed hard with each step, I felt relief from whatever pent-up thoughts or worries were plaguing me that day. The list was always long.

But by the time I came back to my block and walked the last couple hundred yards as a cool down, I felt good. There was time for a shower before my daily call with Chris, and I wanted to make a pot of coffee and go over a client's file from work. My brain had started shuffling through those tasks and pulling me out of my runner's endorphin fog, so I almost didn't see the person sitting on the steps in front of my building until I was too close to do an about-face and run the other way, which would have been an excellent plan. Because the guy sitting there was Johnny.

As in ex-boyfriend Johnny.

Bad-breakup Johnny.

Don't-call, don't-write, don't-show-up-on-my-doorstep Johnny.

I did a double-take. I did the thing where a person rubs her eyes to see if the guy she thinks is her ex-boyfriend standing in front of her apartment is really just a telephone pole or a bush. I expected him to vanish and be replaced by tall, mocking foliage.

"Hey," he said, standing as soon as he saw me.

"Um, hi." After that, I was out of words. I had thoughts, but they were of the variety I didn't want to say out loud.

Why are you here?

What the fuck are you doing here?

How dare you fucking come here now, when you're the last person in the world I want to see?

So I said nothing and waited for him to explain why he'd parked himself outside my building at seven in the morning. I doubted he was just passing by.

"Um… I was hoping we could talk," he said, his expression serious. I wasn't used to it. In fact, in the time we'd dated, I'd almost never seen him without a guilty grin or an open, inviting smile. Johnny loved to have a good time, and if he couldn't have fun, he didn't bother. It was a sort of life choice, and I'd finally come to terms with understanding that he never took anything seriously.

His difficulty with being serious, at least occasionally, might not have been an issue for some people, but it was for me.

Meanwhile, we were standing outside my building, and I really wanted to get out of my sweaty workout clothes and wait for Chris's phone call. But I didn't voice those thoughts, because I knew he'd come to find me for a reason. He could have called. But he showed up, knowing I was a creature of habit and would be out for a run. He'd thought it through, which was maybe the first time I'd known him to do that since we'd met.

"Is everything okay?" I asked, hoping he would say yes and go.

He didn't answer, and the awkwardness in his expression didn't change. Maybe he was dying. Maybe he missed me and wanted to beg me to date him again. It had to have been something rather monumental, and I really wished he'd come out with it.

"Everything's okay. I just... I really need to talk."

"You mean... right now?"

"Yeah. Could we? Can you spare the time?"

I couldn't leave him hanging, even though the last time we'd spoken, he'd been spiteful and mean. And he'd cheated. He was still a human who was asking me for something, though, and I decided I could give him that something. So I said okay.

Johnny stayed on the front steps of my building while I went inside. I didn't invite him in but agreed to come back in fifteen minutes, after I'd showered and texted Chris to let him know I had an early meeting and he could call me at work when he got a break, and I'd make time to talk.

When I returned downstairs, Johnny hadn't moved. He wasn't checking his phone or amusing himself with some found object that caught his attention. Something was different, and it unnerved me a little bit to see him that way.

"Should we walk to a coffee place?" I asked.

He nodded, and we headed up the block to where there was a Starbucks, a Peets, and two independently owned cafes. I always picked the nonchain places when I could, and he knew this, so he steered us into the Bread Company without asking if I wanted to go there.

He also ordered me a coconut latte, which used to be my favorite, and asked for an iced tea for himself. We sat. He looked at me as if I was the one who'd called the meeting. As much as I wanted to hear what he had to say, I also had to be at work in an hour and a half. I couldn't just sit and trade glances. "Johnny, what's going on? Just tell me."

He nodded. "Okay, I'm just gonna say it… I'm sober. Newly sober. It's been two months."

Of all the things I might have expected him to say, that was at the very bottom of the list. Not because I didn't think he had a problem with alcohol—he definitely drank what I considered too much, and he'd always denied there was a downside to his behavior.

"That's… so great. Congratulations."

He looked sheepish. "Thanks. So, anyway… as part of my twelve steps, I need to make amends with people I've… hurt… with my behavior."

It all made sense. He needed me to forgive him so he could forgive himself. After a year with him—despite the fact that he'd gotten a blow job at his high school reunion from someone other than me—I knew he wasn't a bad person. I had some fond memories. And despite his easy laugh, I could tell this was hard for him. It didn't need to be. "We're good, Johnny. Water under the bridge."

He seemed surprised. "That's it?"

"What did you expect me to say. That I'm surprised you're in a twelve-step program? I am. That I can never forgive you? No, I'm not gonna say that. It doesn't help anyone."

"Okay…" He didn't seem to know what to do next. He also seemed shocked that I wasn't arguing.

"Have people not been open to making amends with you?"

"Truthfully, you're the first person I've reached out to. You were the one I think I hurt the most, so I started with you."

"Oh."

I don't know why, but it surprised me that he even realized I'd been hurt. At the time, I never got that impression. He'd seemed blasé about our fight and our breakup. He seemed to roll with it like he did everything else.

"So... I'm really not sure how this is supposed to go."

I waved a hand at him and tried to put him at ease. He really seemed to be suffering through the conversation. "Don't worry about it. Tell me what happened. What made you start a twelve-step program?"

He sipped his iced tea through the straw. I wanted to tell him that straws were terrible for the environment and he shouldn't use them, but I decided it was not the time. For the first time since he'd shown up at my door, his mouth pulled into a small smile. "Well, you know I never met a beer—or twelve—I didn't like."

"I recall. It never seemed to occur to you that it was a problem. Your high metabolism and all that," I reminded him. He always had an excuse for why he could put more beer away than seemed humanly possible. Or healthy.

"Yeah. I'm pretty sure you told me." He still seemed tense, but the tentative smile stayed on his face.

"Listen... you weren't ready to think about it or deal with it before. I'm just glad you're dealing with it now. Please don't beat yourself up over what happened when we were together."

"Yeah... that. I'm sorry I couldn't be what you wanted. I know you needed plans and structure and a future, and I was just looking for a beach with a good wave. And hell, I didn't need to hurt you on top of it. I'm sorry I got together with Caitlin the night of the reunion. I was out of my head and didn't know what I was doing. Whatever I said that night... I didn't mean it."

I nodded. "I'm not gonna lie. It sucked. But it also woke me up. So maybe it was a good thing." It was hard to think of it quite so magnanimously, but I wanted to try.

He reached over and gave me a playful punch. "I don't know if I'd necessarily say it was good. Just inevitable." He drained the last of his iced tea and got up for a refill. I watched him saunter up to the counter—Johnny always sauntered—and made the barista laugh at some joke he made. He always did that too. It was what had initially drawn me to him—his mile-wide smile, his easy attitude, and his confident swagger.

I took a moment to think through how absolutely bizarre it was that I was sitting there, watching him laugh and smile. I never expected to see Johnny again, and I really never expected him to apologize.

While the barista was refilling Johnny's glass with fresh ice, he indicated with his thumb that he was making a pitstop in the restroom. I nodded.

While he was up, I checked my phone and saw that Chris had texted me back.

Chris: *Sorry I missed you. Will call later.*

Me: *Can't wait.*

I hated that I'd missed my call with Chris, partly because it was so hard to coordinate time when we could talk, and I didn't like backing out of our plans. I also felt a little bit guilty for saying I had a meeting instead of telling him I was canceling so I could have coffee with Johnny. It felt like a transgression, even though I knew it wasn't. More like a lie of omission, which was a little bit like him declining to tell me about his public kiss with Triss until it was front and center in the *Daily Mail.*

I wondered if I was holding back my truth because he'd done the same.

Chris might not have thought coffee with Johnny was a big deal at all. And it wasn't. I hadn't told him much about our relationship, other than the fact that it had ended badly. But now I'd made it a bigger deal by not telling him.

Is it a big deal? Do I have unresolved feelings?

The truth was, I did have unresolved feelings, but not because I still wanted to be with Johnny. I lacked resolution. I still didn't understand why we didn't work, why I couldn't get what I wanted from him. Maybe understanding it would help me learn how to ask for what I wanted from Chris.

We're always supposed to be learning and evolving, right?

I thought back to the night Johnny and I got together for the first time. I'd been sitting at the bar at Moby's, the pub where he worked. I'd gone in alone, something I'd never done before, because I'd seen him working there a few times I'd gone in with friends, and I wanted to see if my hunch about him was correct—that his wicked smile was a sign he was up for anything. Because I wanted to be the kind of person who was up for anything too.

He'd kissed me that night like it was just part of our conversation. He never left his barstool. He kept his elbow on the bar and rested his chin in his hand, asking questions and looking into my eyes like he really cared about the answers. That night, I told him whatever he wanted to know.

I drank a little more of my coffee, oddly comforted by the fading memory of our first night and the possibilities that never played out later on. I'd eventually accepted that we'd never have anything long term. I'd basically had a yearlong hookup without realizing it.

When Johnny came back, he picked up his iced tea from the counter and jumped right back into the conversation. "So, you asked me why I sobered up. I'm sure you know it has a lot to do with you." He grinned widely in the way that used to bend my emotions to his will. He always knew the right thing to say.

It really pissed me off.

To some people, his pronouncement might have sounded like a compliment, as though I'd been an angelic presence who had led him to a happier place. But it wasn't like that. Being with him when he was drinking a lot had been painful. He'd never acknowledged it when we were together. On the contrary. He'd blamed me for bringing him down.

I wasn't in the mood for a platitude. "Why would I know that?" I was having trouble with the new Johnny, who seemed to be sweeping away all the hurt and wrongness of how things ended with us by using his newfound clarity. I still didn't have clarity. It annoyed me that I'd somehow helped him find his, while he was doing nothing to deliver mine. If anything, he was confusing me more. "You hated when I got on you about drinking, and you used it as a reason to cheat on me." It felt better to be angry. Maybe I wasn't ready to make amends.

Getting sober and apologizing to the people he'd wronged was supposed to be hard and painful. He was approaching it like he did everything else, as if a cute smile and a few nice words could take the place of hard work.

"I did hate it. I didn't understand that you saw something I didn't."

"So what changed?"

"I guess… after we broke up, I was sad. It was… an unfamiliar feeling."

I looked at him out of the corner of my eye. What he was saying didn't make sense. First of all, he hadn't seemed all that sad that we'd broken up. He'd grabbed the things he'd left behind at my apartment and hopped on his bike. Second, sadness was not a novel feeling. I'd felt it most of the time while we were dating. It made no sense. He'd let me go without a fight. He'd cheated on me. There was no reason for him to care what I thought about his drinking.

"How do you mean?"

"I realized a few things after we broke up. I realized that my drinking—my poor judgment when I was drinking—led to what happened at the party. And as a result, I lost something—someone—I cared about."

I nodded. He was right about that.

"But what I realized after you were gone was that no one else cared about whether I drank myself under the table or not. I missed having someone who cared about me enough to worry. I guess when I realized that no one around me cared, I started to care. And I realized that drinking had become a crutch… or a self-destructive vice."

He'd said he stopped drinking two months ago. I did a quick calendar check in my head and calculated that was right around the time we were supposed to be in France together. "Why didn't you say something at the time?"

Although, what if he had? What if he'd told me he was sobering up and came to France with me?

I never would have met Chris. My life would have been completely different. And for the first time since I'd started coming to terms with my trust issues, I realized my life would not have been better. I wasn't supposed to be with Johnny.

He was the reason I always expected to get hurt. He stomped on my trust, and it hadn't recovered. He *should* make amends for that.

He shook his head. "I was never going to be able to give you what you wanted. I knew I had work to do on myself—and believe me, there's still work to be done, even though I know you think I'm perfect the way I am." The grin was back, but I wasn't drawn in by it anymore.

"You're perfectly you. You always know how to have fun. I used to envy that so much because I didn't think I could have fun without someone pushing me."

He looked surprised. "That's a silly thing to say. You were fun. We had a great time." As usual, he didn't really understand me. He never would.

So I had to be grateful that he'd set me free. It was strange. I didn't feel the need to finish my coffee in order to feel awake and alive. I just needed clarity. "Thank you," I said, "for telling me all this. I'm really glad to know you're doing well."

His smile faded a little. I knew him well enough to understand there was still something he wasn't telling me. I really hoped he wasn't going to say he wanted to get back together. "What? There's something else. What is it?"

He took a deep breath then exhaled in such a forceful way, I had to bite my lip to avoid smiling at him. "I'm getting married."

I had to laugh. "Wait, what?"

"Yeah… married."

"How?"

"We met at a coffeeshop where I was hanging before my AA meeting."

"Is she recovering too?"

"No. That's discouraged, for obvious co-dependency reasons."

My jaw grazed the floor tiles at the evidence of Johnny's evolved self. Also, meeting before an AA meeting meant that whoever he planned to marry had known him for two months or less. He saw nothing wrong with that. He had no problem promising a future to a person he barely knew, because he didn't overthink things the way a lot of people did. If it felt right, he did it.

In some ways, I envied him. I wished I could be as open to trusting in my own happiness. "How do you do that? How do you just decide to get married and believe everything is going to work out? How do you know you're going to be happy?"

He looked at me like my question made no sense. "Why would anyone not want to be happy?"

I looked at him like he was being dense. "That's not what I meant."

He leveled his warm, puppyish eyes at me, reached out a hand, and gripped my arm. "I know what you meant. And the way I go through my life is a one-eighty from how you approach yours. I know that. I'm not super deep, and I'm okay with that."

"Don't say that. You're—"

He held up a hand to stop me. "I'm decently smart. I'm not talking about that. I'm saying I make a choice to live my life without thinking too hard. I know you're not built that way, and I'm not saying you should change. But I do think you should get out of your own way. Trust that what you want—whatever it is—is the right thing. And that will make you happy."

I stared at him, a little dumbfounded that this guy who seemed to live always in the present without much concern about anything besides hedonistic pursuits had just distilled my issues down to a single directive.

I had to trust that the karmic life rulebook wouldn't penalize me for asking for what I wanted.

My phone buzzed with an alarm I'd set so I wouldn't be late for work. "Johnny, I've gotta go. But it was good seeing you. And congrats on your engagement."

He smiled. "So, am I forgiven? We've done the amending?"

I kissed him on the cheek. "Consider us amended."

CHAPTER NINETEEN

BALLINASCORNEY, Ireland
Chris

WHEN I CALLED Nikki after we wrapped for the day, the last thing I expected her to say was that she'd just had coffee with her ex-boyfriend. I mean, I was glad she told me, but at the same time, it was information I could have lived without.

No, that wasn't true. I wanted to know. It was just that her being so honest and open made me feel shitty about not telling her that Triss had tagged along on my apology junket to LA. I saw not telling her as protecting her feelings, but her immediate honesty about seeing her ex only made me realize I was just protecting myself.

It was a learned behavior, borne of self-preservation. I needed to keep my walls high in order to guard the pieces of myself that I didn't want to leave open to public consumption.

"It's a learned behavior." Her words came back to me. She and I were no different, really, both guarding parts of ourselves for different reasons. Or maybe the same reason—fear. If I wanted her to trust me, I had to be trustworthy.

Our day of filming had gone pretty well, and the only thing I knew for sure was that I was going to Nigel's parents' house for dinner before heading back to my hotel to watch movies until I fell asleep. I'd gone to my trailer to call Nikki for our daily conversation, which was always the best part of my day... but not that day.

We weren't more than a few words into the conversation before I started picturing the two of them together, even though I didn't know what he looked like. It wasn't a problem. I just pictured him from behind, looking at Nikki, who of course was lovely, talented, and brilliant. He would have been an idiot not to want her back.

It turned a decent filming day into a pile of shit. Even before she started telling me why he'd come by and what they'd discussed, I felt an unwelcome burning pain in my gut at the possibility that I'd already blown it with her, like Triss had said, and that she was losing patience with my career.

I couldn't control anything when I was far away on a movie set, letting local bar owners do away with my credibility. If they were getting back together, I deserved it.

My mind had been visiting jealous places it hadn't been to lately while she said things I didn't even hear.

Is she really telling me what beverage he ordered her? Does she think I care when I'm busy calculating all the ways I've blown our relationship?

"...and Johnny really wanted to talk, so..." she said.

I'd heard none of it. Instead, I was scrambling to recall what I knew about the guy. When we'd been in France, she'd mentioned that she was just getting out of a relationship, but she hadn't seemed interested in talking about it, and I hadn't pressed. I didn't need to know. I didn't especially want to know. She'd been with me, and that was enough proof that the other guy—whose name I'd just learned was Johnny—was a distant memory.

But is he really? I hadn't pressed her for information because I'd assumed she was over him. She hadn't seemed inclined to elaborate. We were in Antibes. It was beautiful and relaxing. There was no reason for me to ask for details about her breakup. I'd been cocky enough to consider her interest in me proof that she wasn't looking backward.

As we were talking, however, I wanted to know everything. *Who is he, and why did he take her to coffee? What had their relationship been like? Why did they break up? Why did he want to see her?*

So I asked. "Who is this guy? And why did he take you to coffee? And why did you break up, anyhow? Is there a reason he wants to see you now?"

At first, she laughed, and that put me at ease because it seemed like anything that was a laughing matter couldn't be that serious. Then I realized she was laughing at me. "Chris, that's a lot. It's a conversation for another time. I'm at work."

"So why did you tell me you had coffee? You can't open a can of worms like that and just put the lid back on."

"I'm telling you because I want to be up front with you. But I can't go into details about all the reasons our relationship tanked on a ten-minute break. That isn't the point."

I paced in a circle in my trailer. *What is the point? If she didn't call to tell me he's old news, why do it at all?* "I'm not sure why I needed to know about this."

She was silent again, and when she spoke, she wasn't laughing at me. "You needed to know because it happened. I thought we were being honest with each other. Or is it just me?"

"Is this some kind of dig about the pictures with Triss?"

Her voice was stiff and labored. "It's not a dig. But since you mentioned it... Would you have told me she kissed you if no one had taken a picture?"

I guessed I didn't answer quickly enough. I took a moment to think, and it was a moment too long. *Thinking? You really want to sabotage your relationship by thinking?*

"You wouldn't have, would you?" Her voice had gone an octave higher, and I could tell I needed to do damage control.

"No. Of course, I'd have said something."

"Really? Because..." I heard the muffled sound of someone talking to her in the background. Her response was also muffled. Then she returned. "Hey. Sorry. How late will you be up? Can I call you when I'm done with work? I think we really need to talk. About a lot of things."

I closed my eyes and wondered how we had gotten from coffee with her ex to needing to talk about a lot of things. "You can call me whenever you want. I'm not going to bed until we talk."

"Okay, perfect. I'll call you as soon as I'm done. Okay? Talk to you soon." She hung up without any pleasantries, and I threw a water bottle against the door of my trailer, where it cracked and splashed water everywhere. It felt good to throw something.

I'd gone two days without getting my morning workout in, which was always a mistake. If I hustled, maybe I could get on the treadmill for half an hour before heading to dinner. Just the thought of sweating out my aggravation made me feel slightly better.

I looked at my phone and saw that I had a good eight hours before I would be able to talk to Nikki.

And then I felt like shit again.

CHAPTER TWENTY

GLENCREE, Ireland
Chris

DINNER AT NIGEL'S PARENTS' house went about as well as could be expected, considering I was in a foul mood. I hadn't had time for the treadmill, and on the way over, Nigel had told me to expect an inquisition from his mother. "She likes to pry. Prides herself on prying, really. And she'll tell you what's what if she sees fit."

I needed that like I needed a lobotomy. "Ah, looking forward to that," I said with moderate sarcasm that didn't seem to trouble Nigel one bit.

Despite my inner glowering, the dinner had the effect of pulling me out of my head for long enough to enjoy the evening outdoors in the yard.

His mother, Nora, could only be described as a delight. When the two of us arrived—me with a bottle of wine tucked under my arm and a box of milk chocolates one of our craft services people had given me—his mother punched Nigel in the arm and embraced me in a giant hug. Then she hugged him.

"The fist was for only giving me a moment's notice he was bringing company," Nora said.

Nigel looked guilty.

"When did you tell her I was coming?" I asked him. He'd invited me to dinner three days before.

"Just about an hour earlier," Nora said, giving him another solid punch.

"Oh, I hope you didn't go to any trouble," I said. I immediately felt badly that she'd felt pressured to cook something special at a moment's notice.

"Not a bit of trouble. My cooking's the same as always, but I'd have made a better dessert. You'll see why later on," she said in a loud whisper. She winked at me and led us both to the kitchen, where I saw an enormous pot of stew on the stove, a freshly baked tin of buns, and six small mince pies. It was enough food for ten people, and unless she'd invited people I didn't know about, there'd only be four of us at the table.

"Mum's a proper chef. You'll thank me later." Nigel's admiration was clear in the way he looked over the kitchen and everything she'd prepared.

"Okay, okay, enough blowing smoke up my bum. Take your friend out back, and I'll tell you if I need you."

Nigel herded me through the house—which was modest and cluttered with ceramic collectibles ranging from bunnies to teacups—without pointing out anything in particular. I hesitated before following him through the back door. He turned back and looked at me. "What?"

"You live here, right?"

"I do. Why, you keen to see my bedroom or something?"

"I don't need to see it, but if you wanted to give me a tour or something, I wouldn't object."

"You wouldn't object. And they say the British are proper. Just say what you bloody want, Christopher. You want a tour, ask for a tour." Yeah, he insisted on calling me Christopher. He'd explained on our first day working together that given our age difference, it would make him feel like he had slightly more authority if he could call me Christopher. "Like when your mum uses your full name right before she whacks you upside the head for taking the Lord's name in vain."

I'd agreed to let him call me whatever he felt like, but now that I'd met his mom, I had a whole new visual.

"Fine. Show me around your house a bit."

It was as if I'd asked him to recite a poem he'd memorized for school. He walked slowly from room to room, intoning in a bored voice, "This is my mum's sewing area. She's a quilter. You can see the piles of fabric and the machine. Here's where me pop keeps his books…" He demonstrated by waving a hand in front of a bookshelf. We made it to his childhood bedroom, where he still set up camp.

There were some photos of him with friends on a dresser and a blank wall painted red. He had no evidence of hobbies and no artwork on the walls, ruining my vision that all kids in the UK had British invasion posters and old guitars they played in their spare time. Nigel told me he was into rap, much to the dismay of his father, who I met a few minutes later when we went out back.

"Out back" was a sprawling field of tall grasses which got their verdant color and health from the prodigious amount of rainfall that seemed to be a constant there. I'd read the average rainfall was forty to fifty inches a year. There was no need for a carefully watered central park in a country where every direction looked like an endless painted landscape.

"It's nice out here." I inhaled a deeper breath than I'd taken in days. Even when I'd made it to the treadmill, I'd felt like my lungs were stifled.

Something was happening, and I didn't like the way it felt. Lately, my heart wasn't in my work the way it always had been. I needed to turn that around. My work was my life. *Your life? Really? Sounds healthy.*

"Get you a beer?" Nigel asked, leading me to a cooler packed with bottles of Nut Brown Ale and Irish lager.

"I do. Yes." *If it will shut up my brain, yes.*

Nigel's dad introduced himself as Tom and shook my hand. "Always enjoy it when Nigel brings his mates by the house."

"We work together, Pop. It's different."

"What, you're telling me I can't be friends with the blokes from work? We're supposed to stand on ceremony or something?"

"No, but…" Nigel, who always had a swagger and confidence at work, suddenly seemed unsettled in front of his father, as if he didn't want me to think he was trying to elevate his importance at work.

"Nigel's one of the best PAs we've got. And despite that, I consider him a friend," I said.

Nigel rolled his eyes, reached for two beers from the cooler, and handed one to me. Tom was already halfway finished with his own and had two empties on the table in front of him. I had no delusions about trying to keep up with him.

Tom indicated a couple of lawn chairs across from him, and we sat. "You're not gonna pepper him with a bunch of questions, are you?" Nigel asked suspiciously.

His father laughed and ran a hand over his stomach, which strained the buttons on his oxford shirt. "Nah, I'll leave the interrogating to your mother. I just want to sit and drink in peace."

Almost on cue, Nora came out of the house with a tray of meat pies, which she placed on the metal table with a pile of napkins. "These are my mother's recipe," she told me, fanning the steam that emanated from the tops of the pies. "So if you don't like them, don't worry about offending me. Or her, for that matter, because she's dead, may she rest in peace." Then she turned and walked back into the house.

"See what I mean? She's not shy, my wife. She'll be so clever at telling you stories, you won't realize she's really asking you questions until you've sold her half your livelihood."

"Pop, leave it," Nigel said. I looked from father to son, noticing the strong resemblance. Nigel had his father's build, his auburn hair, and his square jaw but none of his ruddy pallor. His freckles and pale skin were all Nora.

Settling into my chair with a cold beer and a hot meat pie, I felt pretty good—not entirely content, because the brewing conversation I'd yet to have with Nikki weighed heavily on my mind, but damn near close. Nigel's parents were the dose of fresh air I needed.

I loved that they were so normal. And just as soon as I thought it, I started feeling exceptionally sick of myself and my constant search for people who I could describe that way. *Is it because they remind me of something I'm trying to recapture? Something that used to exist in my life? Or something I've never had?*

"Nigel, do you have any siblings?" I asked. I felt a little guilty that in weeks of working with him, I'd never asked before.

"I have six. Three brothers, three sisters."

I almost choked on my beer. "Six? Do they all live locally?"

"Most of them do. My oldest brother and one sister live in London, but the rest are local. Three are married with kids. I'm the second to youngest." He shrugged like a family of seven kids was an everyday thing. Maybe it was.

"Wow." I shook my head. "No wonder your mom cooks for an army. She's used to it."

Tom laughed. "You noticed that? Yeah, she still hasn't gotten over the fact they've moved out—even the ones who are married. So she'll be bringing care packages to them all tomorrow with whatever's left over."

"That's sweet."

Nigel studied me and nodded. "You don't get along with your family." He said it as a statement. I'd gotten used to his directness, but it still struck me as odd that he didn't have any question in his voice when he said it.

I shrugged. "We get along great but don't live in the same city, so we don't see each other that often." I didn't feel like bullshitting them with the made-for-print version of my life, and since they didn't seem to know it already, I went with a vague, harmless version of the truth. I assumed that would end the conversation.

But I hadn't seen Nora, who'd just arrived behind me, pushing a rolling cart with her entire dinner on top. "Who doesn't see each other that often?"

The smell hit me immediately. A fragrant steam from the stew combined with the scent of warm bread, and I felt embraced by a childhood I'd never known I was missing. "Oh wow, that smells amazing."

"Yes it does. These are my own recipes, not my mother's, may she rest in peace. And thank you for noticing. I'm glad all your senses are primed, because my food will delight you."

"It already does," I said. "Can I help with anything?"

"No, just grab yourself a plate and help yourself," she said, gesturing to the shelf on the trolley she'd wheeled out, where a stack of plates and utensils were neatly laid out, along with cloth napkins and filled water glasses. As I bent to grab a plate, she leaned in and whispered, "And don't you think we're done with the topic of not seeing your family that often." Then she winked.

We scooped stew and sliced bread and plated pieces of mince pie. Then we ate. "Oh my God, this is delicious," I told Nora, salivating with each bite of home cooking.

"I'm chuffed to bits you like it. But if you take the Lord's name in vain again in my house, I'll give you a proper beating."

Even though Nigel's yard looked nothing like Tribeca, being there reminded me how much I missed being at home.

What the hell is happening to me? I used to be able to go from project to project and work nonstop without thinking about it. I loved the cleanliness of hotels and the fast pace of working on projects that were constantly different.

But I wasn't feeling it anymore.

After dinner, Nora leaned toward me while Nigel and Tom took the dishes into the house. I started to get up to help them, but she gently pushed me back into my chair. She cracked the top on a beer, took a healthy pull, then clinked it against my bottle on the table before putting hers down. "Now, tell me why you don't see your family, and don't try to pull punches. I'll know if you're lying," she said.

The sun had set somewhere behind us, but the sky was pale blue, and bright shadows still danced on the stand of trees at the far end of the grassy field. I liked that time of day. It felt calm, because the bulk of daytime was over, but there was still plenty of light to enjoy before night took over.

I didn't want to lie to her, but I also had a decent idea that I wouldn't see her much, if ever, after that night, so I didn't feel like I had to spill all the details of my life. I'd given enough interviews that I knew how to dance around a subject I didn't want to touch. "We don't live close, but I see them when I can. I travel a lot for work."

"You part of the crew? Nigel has aspirations of working on lighting. He tell you that?"

He hadn't, actually, and I wondered why not. Maybe because I hadn't asked. "I'll talk to him about it. Maybe I can help with it."

"So you work in lighting, then?"

"No, I'm an actor, but I know a lot of people on crews. They're always looking for good people."

"Ah, you're the talent, then? Isn't that what they call it? Nigel didn't mention your role at his work."

I wasn't surprised. Nigel wasn't at all starstruck, and he'd barely remembered to tell his parents he'd invited me to dinner. I sipped my beer, which had gotten warm in the hour since I'd opened it.

"That must taste like swill by now," Nora said, plucking it from my hand and using it to water the grass. She popped the cap on a fresh one and handed it to me.

"Thank you."

"You're very polite," she said, "for an actor."

I didn't know what to make of that.

Her face widened into a grin. "I'm just teasing you. But I

suspect you think people treat you differently because you're an actor. Are you famous?"

"In some places, people know who I am."

"That why you're not close to your family? Because you're more famous than they are?"

"No."

"Well, that's a relief to hear. I was worried you'd outgrown them. It can happen when a child lives on a different social tier than the rest of the family. But if it's not that, then why?" Her questions were matter-of-fact, as though she was interested in getting to the bottom of something puzzling. As if to prove that, she added, "I'm not judging."

I shook my head, but I didn't have a ready answer. No one had ever asked me the question. Partly, that was by design. My public story about my family background reduced the need for explanation because it was sweet. "I don't know the reason, actually. We just kind of drifted apart."

She shook her head. Then she punched me in the same way she'd decked Nigel earlier. "I feel that we're friends now, so if I feel like someone needs sense knocked into 'em, I'm gonna come out and do it. And you need sense."

I couldn't help smiling at her. "Why's that?"

"Any boy who isn't close to his parents… well, there has to be a reason, doesn't there? A good one. Do you have one?"

I ran a hand through my hair, wondering how my life had brought me to that moment, feeling like I was suddenly on a therapist's couch at my PA's parents' house in Ireland, while the back of my mind couldn't let go of Nikki's "a lot of things" that needed discussing. It was a lot to take in at the end of a long workday. I almost felt like drunk Triss might be preferable to an inquisition about the one part of my life I'd never discussed. Yet there we were.

I had a choice. I could tell her what I told everyone and leave it at that. Or I could tell her the truth. Two months ago, it wouldn't have been a debate. But the status quo I'd always clung to felt tired.

So I took another big swig of my beer for confidence, and I told her what she wanted to know. "My mother's from Spain, and my dad's from the States. Boston. They met when my mom was a professor at a school where my dad was earning his accounting degree. She loves to cook, and he's terrible at it." I paused. That part of the story was easy. I'd told it a hundred times.

"That sounds lovely. Do they get along?"

I could have lied some more about my family. It would have been easy. As an actor, I could make anything sound convincing. But it felt wrong to lie to Nigel's mom after she'd cooked me dinner and told me not to take the Lord's name in vain. "My mother cheats on him. She's done it for years. He pretends he doesn't know, but he does. And it eats him up. That's partly why I don't see them very often. It's hard to watch them pretending."

She reached a comforting hand out and patted me on the knee but said nothing.

So I told her the rest. "Plus, my dad is terrible with money. He makes bad investments, and he's always one car repair way from going broke. But my mom puts up with it because she feels guilty about her infidelity, and he beats himself up because he thinks he's failed her. He resents her, he resents me, he's depressed, and he blames himself, but she's the only thing he knows, so he stays. And I give them money, so I suppose I enable the whole thing."

I hadn't expected to say all of that, but once I got rolling, the words took over.

When I finally stopped talking, I took another sip of my beer. It tasted much better than I remembered from a few minutes earlier. Colder and crisper, as if there was a new clarity to my senses. I looked at Nora, wondering what the kind, committed parent of seven children would think about my mess of a family.

She nodded at me and patted my knee again, as if I'd done a good job reciting my alphabet lesson. "I reckon… carrying all that around must make you well annoyed."

I laughed. Her directness, the way she summed up ten years of frustration and inertia in our attempts at a relationship, cracked something open.

"It does. I guess you could say it does," I said.

"Is there hope?"

I'd avoided thinking about it, because in the back of my mind, I knew that if I admitted to being hopeful about something better with my parents, I was opening myself up to disappointment. "Truthfully, I'm not sure. They seem to have accepted the way things are."

"Have you?"

Damn this woman. I knew I wasn't lassoed to the lawn chair, but I might as well have been. Sitting under her sharp gaze, I didn't dare lie, and I knew I couldn't leave without satisfying her questions with real answers. "I'm… not sure. Maybe I can help them and fix things."

She reached out and smacked me again. She had a decent right hook.

"With seven kids, did you use that arm a lot?" I asked.

"Every bloody day. Every time they said something wrong. Which was every bloody day."

"What did I say wrong?"

Her expression changed, and instead of looking at me with her sharp-eyed gaze, her face softened with the love of a mother who sees her youngest duckling wandering off and has to shoo him back in line with the others so he doesn't get lost.

"Now I understand why you look so hopeless. You're trying to fix things. Why do you think you need to do that? Just accept the situation. Even if it's messy. It's what life is—messy. Maybe that seems strange to you since you're an actor, and you're forgetting we don't all look like they do in the movies. And we don't get a script with a happy ending. We're all just people. If you try to keep something perfect in a box, you're only going to be disappointed when you take it out and it doesn't look the way you remembered it. The messy stuff is what lasts. Do you like brownies?"

The non sequitur confused me, but I nodded. "Sure."

"Well then you know. It's not the perfect squares from around the edges that taste good. It's the mushy, undercooked stuff in the middle. And the scraps." She tilted back in her chair like her work for the night was done.

All I could do was nod. It was a lot to take in.

Nigel and Tom appeared from the house, carrying a berry crumble cobbler and steaming cups of coffee. They'd dispensed with the trolley cart and carried everything on a twin set of trays. Nigel leaned over and picked up a couple of beer bottles from the table near me. "Sorry I left you to the wolves, mate. Hope she didn't rip you a new one."

"It was fine," I said. Because it was. I hadn't experienced that kind of mothering in a long time, and I didn't mind.

"My pop and me, we know better than to venture out when she's on a tear, so we cleaned up the kitchen. Twice."

I couldn't help laughing, which made Nora turn toward us suspiciously. Nigel held up the empties he'd just picked up as evidence he was just doing some innocent straightening.

"We did the dishes, Mum," Nigel said. I found it amusing to see that mom-whipped side of his, which wouldn't dare give her the surly attitude he gave me at work.

"Good boy," she said. Then, she turned to me and whispered, "The cobbler is Tom's mother's recipe. She dropped it off earlier. You don't have to say you like it. Or even eat it."

Tom pretended to glare at her but then leaned in and kissed her cheek. "Thank you for dinner, love. Brilliant as usual. Especially the mince pie."

"You do love your mince pie."

"I do. And I heard what you said about my mum's cooking. Tsk tsk, Nora."

"You heard nothing. Now if you'll all excuse me, all the cooking and chatting has me knackered. I think I oughtta skip dessert and get some sleep." She leaned in and kissed me on the cheek before whispering, "That was my excuse. You're meant to conjure your own reason to skip the dessert."

Then she was gone. I looked at Nigel and had a new appreciation for him. "So. Six siblings, huh? Are you the runt of the litter?"

"You really want to get into that with me, mate?" he challenged, puffing his chest and stretching to his full height, with was easily five inches shorter than me.

Tom spooned a heaping plate of cobbler and alternated bites of it with sips of beer, which must have had the effect of washing down each bite so that the flavors mixed. When he caught me looking, Nigel said, "Yeah, that's how he gets through it. But it's his mum, so he had to learn a technique."

We stayed a little longer, but by ten, I wanted to get back to my hotel. I said goodbye to Nigel and Tom and left them drinking together out back.

On my cab ride, I started thinking about Nikki and our impending conversation. I had a feeling it might be messy.

For once, I was cautiously eager to see what that looked like.

CHAPTER TWENTY-ONE

BALLINASCORNEY, Ireland
Chris

IT TURNED out I still had three hours to kill before Nikki would be done with work and we could talk, so I flipped channels and eventually decided to order something on pay-per-view. There was the usual—new releases, action and adventure, comedy, family entertainment.

The problem with new releases was that watching recent work of colleagues sometimes stressed me out when I was in the middle of shooting a movie. Watching the movies that had done best at the recent box office made me second-guess acting choices I was making on my current project, and I didn't need that kind of self-editing when I was already overthinking my motivation and my take on the character.

Action and adventure, despite being my bread and butter, didn't appeal to me. I'd seen so many over the years that I didn't need to watch more in my downtime. Comedies were usually my go-to, because I was always in the mood for something light that would make me laugh. But between recent flights and other late nights in hotel rooms, I'd already watched everything that I was remotely interested in seeing.

That left hotel-room porn or histories and arthouse films, most of which were foreign-language picks with subtitles. I didn't feel like reading a movie. But maybe there was something decent in the bunch. I scrolled, remembering how Nikki had told me she only watched smaller art films.

It felt somehow appropriate to try to lose myself in one while I waited to talk to her. I wouldn't tell her that the kinds of movies she liked ran a distant second to jerking off. I would just watch the damn thing.

Two hours later, I was more depressed than I'd been all day. *Why would a normal person watch these movies?* I could see that the touching portrait of suffering and humanity was cinematically pretty, but it packed such an emotional wallop that I wasn't sure I could even jerk off. Ever. Let alone have a phone conversation.

The movie, while well done and beautiful, may have ruined my chances at ever seeing the world as a happy place, which I found borderline unforgivable. So I launched directly into an excoriating review of the shitty movie as soon as Nikki called.

"She knew he was sleeping with her sister. She knew he didn't love her, and yet she stayed with him and had children with him, and meanwhile, her sister fell in love with him but he didn't want her either. So then you had the two sisters, with no man at all, raising the kids and deciding their bond was so strong because of him that they'd never marry and would just be with each other until they died. But they were so young, and they just gave up. And then the older one died before her thirtieth birthday, and the younger sister raised her sister's kids? What kind of fucked-up person thinks of a story like this? Why do you watch these movies?"

I stopped talking because I'd finished asking questions and awaited Nikki's answer, but she said nothing. We were on a video chat, so at least I could see her expression, which was somewhere between amused and confused.

"You watched an arthouse film?" she said finally.

"Um, yeah. In the room here, while I was waiting for you."

"And this is your first one?"

"I don't know. I've seen a few. But not like this one. This one came straight from the lost-and-found bin at the post office or something."

She rolled her lips between her teeth in what I figured out was an attempt to keep a straight face while I ranted. "So you didn't like it."

"I wouldn't say that. The cinematography was excellent. The acting was great. But the story… it was awful. I want to go to a movie and feel uplifted or entertained. Not pummeled and suicidal."

"You should definitely stick to action movies and comedies."

"I think I might have to. Otherwise, I'll end up tying a rock to my ankle and taking a night swim."

"Please stick to action movies and comedies, then."

Finally, I stopped ranting. I felt exhausted. I was already losing it from lack of sleep and working myself to the bone. I really didn't need that black cloud of a movie to finish me off. "Can you just explain to me why you like them? I think I need to understand this about you. Are you a dark, disturbed person who feeds on human suffering?"

She was laughing. "No. Not at all. You're missing the point. I like these movies because they make me feel something. It's the reason I seek out this particular kind of art, for when I want to be surprised by my emotions and I want someone else to put in the work of getting me there. Does that make sense?"

"I mean, I guess. But it was hard to watch, and now I feel drained."

"It's supposed to be. Because it's art. It's real. It shows the sides of us that we don't always want to see, the messy stuff. It's not always pretty, but I want to see it. Otherwise, it's too easy to pretend it doesn't exist. And when I do that, I feel like I'm looking at the world in monotone and missing all the other colors."

Is it a coincidence that for the second time in one night, the conversation is turning back toward the messiness of life? Probably. I didn't really believe in cosmic, karmic life forces on a united mission. I believed coincidences happened, and that was probably one of them. But still… maybe it was worth investigating. I was starting to understand that maybe messiness was something other people accepted about life, even if it was new to me.

"Can we talk about that? About how life is messy?" I asked. I'd been sitting at the desk, which meant my back was ramrod straight against the back of the chair, and that seemed like a terrible choice for what I hoped would evolve into pillow talk. I moved to the bed but did not take off any clothing. Despite laughing at me, I knew she felt that we needed to have a serious conversation, and I wasn't about to derail that by trying to turn it into a booty call. Yet.

"Sure. Do you have thoughts?"

"Actually, I do. I've had a conversation earlier that made me think about us and some of my assumptions that might not be true."

"Oh yeah? I'm intrigued. Who did you talk to?"

The truth was, the conversation with Triss on the plane had gotten me thinking, and my talk with Nora had solidified all the ways I was approaching things wrong. My instinct was to tell her about Nora and leave out the part about Triss. I didn't want to stir the pot.

And… that kind of thinking was what had eroded Nikki's trust in the first place. I had to be honest, even if lying by omission kept things clean. I'd just told her I was embracing messy, so I grabbed it in a big bear hug. "Triss gave me a talking-to and made me realize I was being selfish with my schedule and not being fair to you."

Nikki looked surprised and a little touched. "She said that?"

"Yes, and she's right. Then, tonight I had dinner with the parents of my set PA. They live nearby. His mom raised seven kids, had a killer right hook, and somehow intuitively knew the story I tell everyone about my parents was a bald-faced lie. She had some… thoughts about how to be a better son."

"I'll bet."

"Her thoughts made me have thoughts. About being a better person. For you."

Her smile was lazy. And even though it was way earlier there, it looked like she was tired. "You're already a good person."

I rolled onto my side, leaning my cheek on my hand. I was exhausted. No. I was spent. If I put myself into any more of a reclined position, I risked falling asleep mid-conversation. "Not always. Not in the way it matters. And what I realized was that I've been pretending that this long-distance thing is going well and thinking that as long as our relationship looks fine on paper, it must be fine, according to some wrong idea I had about how things should be."

She looked confused. "So what are you saying? That you're not happy?"

"I guess I'm not really happy, when I think about it. Because you're right. I want to know you better. I want you to know me. Even if that means the things we learn about each other are messy."

I saw her exhale, but I couldn't tell if it was relief or frustration. Not knowing was one more bit of proof that we weren't equipped yet to have a long-distance relationship. I wanted to know what she was thinking just by looking at her. I wanted to trust us without worrying.

How had I missed learning all the critical steps in having a relationship?

I'd been dating women who I didn't really care about. So none of the rest mattered.

I looked at her on my laptop screen, which I preferred to my phone because of the bigger view, and noted the small things about her that I'd loved since the first night we met: her deep, soulful eyes, her plush lips, which she kept pressed together unless she had something to say or unless I kissed her, and the way she rested her chin on her fist and tilted her head to the side when she was listening to me. She listened like she was really considering what I had to say because it was important to me, which made it important to her.

"Hang on," I said, adjusting the tilt of my screen so the angle was better against the overhead light. "Can I just… can I just look at you for a minute?"

Her eyes, normally so sharply focused, found mine. They relented and softened. Her lips pulled into a faint smile. "Yeah."

For a couple minutes, neither one of us spoke. At one point, I felt myself reaching for the computer screen and wanting to connect. If I could touch the image of her face, maybe I could feel her with me when I closed my eyes.

She was correct that having these kinds of conversations over the phone was difficult. It amplified the distance between us.

"This is harder than I thought it would be," I said. "I thought… we could keep things going even with the distance, but I feel like you're slipping away." I hadn't realized I felt that way until I said it, but once I said it, I knew the words were right. That had been the problem from the beginning. Each time I left, and each time we tried to bridge the distance, it felt like we were drifting farther apart instead of tethering ourselves together.

She nodded. "That's why I thought we should talk."

"Is that how you feel too?" I asked.

"Yes. In some ways it's harder," she said. "But in other ways, it's no different from before we met. And that's what makes me sad."

I wanted her to say I was wrong, that everything was fine, and I needed to relax about the ex-boyfriend. Everything was fine. It was fine. Because if it wasn't fine, I wasn't sure what it meant, and I didn't know how to fix it.

She moved her fist out from under her chin and wrapped her other hand around it. Then she put both hands under her chin and removed them again. "Sorry. I never know what to do with my hands on FaceTime. I should just sit on them, but then I feel like a newscaster."

"Put them wherever you'd like. It's just me."

She wrapped them around one knee, which she pulled into her chest. Then she decided against that and crossed her arms in front of her. She shook her head and went back to resting her chin on her hand. "So here's the thing… I feel like we're doing everything backwards. We've made this big commitment based on feelings we didn't want to end, but the fact of the matter is that we're trying really hard to keep things going, but we don't have a foundation yet. Because we don't really know each other that well."

"I disagree."

"About which part? All of it?"

"No, the last part. I know you."

"You know part of me, and I know part of you."

"That's how it is with everyone when they're first starting out."

"Exactly! It's how people are when they've been on a couple of dates and have decided they're up for more. Then, maybe it builds into what they'd hoped it would. Maybe they connect. And then—and in my experience, only then—do they decide to say things like 'I'll move across a country for you.' We did this all so fast because we wanted it to last. But maybe it wasn't based on enough. We don't really know each other."

I didn't like what she was saying, and a part of me wondered if she'd had a change of heart about me after seeing her ex. I had to know. "Does this have anything to do with your ex-boyfriend?"

She was silent for a moment. And in that time, I realized I didn't expect her to give credence to my insecure line of thought. I expected a quick denial. Instead, in her moment of silence that seemed to stretch into several minutes, I was feeling that painful surge of bile in my chest again that made me want to tear a hole through my own ribs to get it out.

"Actually, it does. But not in the way you think."

"What way is that? How do I think?"

"You think… I don't know, that I'm not over him? That I have second thoughts about breaking up with him?"

"I have more confidence in myself than that."

"Okay, good."

"But do you? Regret breaking up with him?"

She pressed her lips together. I could tell she was trying to be kind to my jealous heart and not laugh. "No. Not at all. Definitely not."

"So what, then?"

She was walking through her apartment, and I could see the background moving with her as she went, but I didn't know which room she was in until she stopped. When I heard the whoosh of the door and a twittering of birds, I knew she'd pulled open the patio door, and then I could see she was sitting outside. "I hate that we're having this conversation over the phone," she said. "We're so disconnected. We're nowhere near each other."

"Well… yeah… I'm across a continent and an ocean, but that—"

"No. I don't mean physical distance. I mean… we're having all-out experiences and aha moments separately, with other people. Instead of growing together."

I had fully reclined against the pillow on my bed. Even though we were deep into the conversation, it was coming on two in the morning, and I was feeling the effects of my day, the beer from earlier, the emotionally taxing movie, and the strain of being on two separate continents. I just wanted it all to go away until I had a chance to sleep and recharge my brain.

"Can I explain what I meant earlier when I said that seeing Johnny made things more clear for me? I think it will make you understand that we're kind of on the same page here," she said.

"Sure."

"And please don't feel jealous. I promise you, I'm way over him."

"I'll do my level best. Talk to me."

Another big inhale and exhale. Either she was nervous, or she was just using her breathing time to think and make sure she said what she meant. The birds were chirping at a furious pace, like they were trying to outdo each other, but I didn't want to interrupt her by asking her to go back inside.

"The long and short was, he made me realize that it's not me. When he and I were dating, he challenged me all the time for not being spontaneous or carefree. And he wasn't the first boyfriend in my life who said I was too serious because I like to have a plan. He only wanted to live in the present, and he convinced me that I was the one with the problem because I couldn't be that chill. And then he went looking for someone who was more easygoing than me. He eroded my trust and make me believe it was my fault."

I couldn't stand this fucking guy, and I didn't even know him. I hated him for cheating on her, and I hated him even more for fucking with her trust. She didn't deserve that.

"I hope he paid for the coffee, at least," I grumbled. She was good and sweet and wouldn't tell him to shove off, but he had no claim on her now, and hearing that he'd made her doubt anything about herself made me crazy. "And I hope he told you that he was the one with the problem and set you free from that burden."

She huffed a small laugh. "Not exactly. I realized that the relationship didn't end because of my personality defects. It ended because of his. And that did set me free. So I have to be myself with you."

"I never asked you to be different."

"I know. It wasn't something you asked for, but because I'd grown accustomed to thinking I needed to be more carefree, I tried to give you that version."

She got up from her chair on the porch, moved inside, and shut the balcony door behind her. The sudden quiet was a relief.

"Sorry. Birds were disrupting my train of thought," she said, settling on the couch. "Anyway, I've been trying to be this chill version of myself that was cool with you working in New York or leaving for two months at a time. But I'm not that chill. I'm serious, and I think about the future, and I want what I want. Which is why I need to stop being a chickenshit and ask you for it."

I couldn't help but laugh a little. "Sweetheart, I hate to break it to you—you never convinced me you were easygoing and chill. And I love you for every freaked-out, methodically organized thought in your head. And for so much more."

Nikki smiled at that and met my eyes on the screen, her own eyes round and a little dewy.My heart started racing. Here was my opportunity, my chance to listen and really hear what she needed from me.

I didn't care what it was—I would give her anything. I would give her everything.

"Tell me what you want."

I watched her eyes, waiting for an indication of what she was thinking, but her expression betrayed nothing. It hurt to see her on a screen and not be able to touch her. I hated it. I thought she knew, because the corner of her mouth edged up into a smile.

"I want us to be together in the same place. For more than a day at a time here and there. I want to be *with* you. Do you want to be with me?"

I didn't have to hesitate. Being away from her had confirmed it even more. "Yes. So much. Yes."

"Then we need time. Together."

"I want that too."

"Okay... well, it's not just gonna happen. We have to make it happen. I still feel like a temporary houseguest in your life. I want to know you better. I want to be sure of you. I want to feel like we're on a path together, and right now... I don't."

"Then we have to fix that. I want you to know."

"I want me to know too."

My mind scrambled to come up with a plan to get her onto my path. Gone were the scenes I had to shoot in the morning. My only thoughts revolved around when we could see each other in person for as long as it took to convince her to take a chance on me. "Can you come to New York? Two weeks from now? I'll be there for a week after we wrap the movie. Can you take time off?"

Her eyes looked glassy and tired, but she nodded. "If that's when you're free, I'll try to work that out. But only if you have time to spend with me while I'm there. I only want to do this if we can really be together."

"I'm all yours, I promise. I'll bite the head off anyone who suggests I lift a finger unless it's to bring you breakfast in bed."

"You don't have to wait on me. You have to be with me. You have to get to know me."

The weight that had been sitting on my chest, compressing my breathing and making me miserable for weeks, seemed to shift because for once, I saw a way forward. She lifted the weight away, and I felt only relief.

One week. One week to get her to fall so deeply in love with me that she would never want to leave.

CHAPTER TWENTY-TWO

NEW YORK CITY - Two weeks later
Nikki

I RUSHED OUT of Eataly with my recycled canvas bag over my shoulder and a paper cup of coffee in my hand. I had Earth guilt for not bringing a reusable cup, but it was not the kind of day that had started with the organized sense of planning and purpose that would have meant knowing I would need a double espresso at three in the afternoon—I'd hopped off the redeye at the crack of dawn.

Leaning down to slurp the hot coffee through the small lid hole, I acknowledged that the cup was just a manifestation of my entire day, which had been a whirlwind of anticipation as I wrapped up my half day of work and met Chris at his apartment.

The door to the upscale grocery closed behind me with a vacuum of air that made my skirt flutter behind me, but not in a good way. Anyone following me out the door would have gotten a nice show of the thong that sliced between my butt cheeks in a way that was not altogether comfortable. I tried to believe no one was behind me and chose not to confirm or deny it by looking back. There was no point.

Walking down Fifth Avenue in the Flatiron District, I marveled at how I'd just spent seventy-three dollars on two panini sandwiches, two wedges of French cheese, a basket of raspberries, and a package of Italian flatbread. Surely, there were grocery stores in New York that charged less money—and had fewer tourists—than the gourmet market once owned by Mario Batali, celebrity chef who'd given up his stake in his restaurant empire after sexual misconduct allegations derailed his career.

"You have to see it. Just the way everything's displayed… it's a work of art," Chris had told me that morning, talking about the market as if it housed the crown jewels. I'd agreed to venture over there after a morning spent at the Met, where I'd looked at the permanent collection for three hours before making my way through Central Park to Eataly in Midtown.

It wasn't that I wasn't impressed by the rows of perfect produce, the polished plums displayed by the dozen in wooden crates, or the tiny boxes of perfect berries, which looked like they'd been plucked that morning and driven over in a bike basket from a country farm stand. The cheese display was especially entrancing, rivaling anything I'd ever seen in France and containing cheeses that were hard and semi-soft, ripe, blue, and flecked with herbs, all procured from sheep, goats, and cows of the best breeding. I didn't dare ask to sample any of them, but I did look carefully at each one, considering what I knew about cheese—not much—and price—anything over five dollars seemed expensive.

"Are you looking for something in particular?" Eataly's cheesemonger asked. His pale-green eyes looked clairvoyant, as if he was about to tell me about the next ten years of my life after divining my cheese preferences.

He wore a starched white chef's apron over a faded blue chambray shirt, and his friendly smile made me feel like I belonged there and like I knew what I was looking for as I considered cheese priced at over twenty bucks a pound. "I know I like brie," I said, aware that I sounded like I had only the most basic cheese knowledge. "And I remember having something called Comté that was good."

Rather than looking down his nose at me, the man nodded and leaned over the cheese display, picking up a couple different slabs cut from wheels of cheese before carefully slicing the thinnest wafer from the side of one. "This is a thirty-six-month-old Comté. See what you think," he said, handing me the tiny slice of cheese on a slip of parchment paper.

Even from the small bite, I could taste how delicious it was. "Great. I'll take that."

The cheese guy laughed. "You've only tried one. I've got half a dozen variations you might want to taste." Before I could object, he handed me another tiny slice.

According to my indelicate palate, it was equally good. I nodded, unsure whether to choose that one or the first, and saw that he was handing me a third. That one tasted a little different, almost acrid and definitely not as good as the other two. I had no idea what that meant in regard to the cheese-making process, but something had gone terribly wrong, as far as I was concerned.

"Okay, that's not my favorite."

"See, you do know what you like. That's why we try them. Care for another one?" He reached for another buttery slab of cheese then sliced it while I debated whether or not to eat my next six meals at the cheese counter. "This one has a little more of a nutty taste." He handed it to me and waited while I let the flavors gather on my tongue.

"I can see that. I never really thought of cheese as tasting nutty, but I like this one. And I'm officially confused. You probably need to choose for me." Two other customers stood to the sides of me, but he seemed focused only on the cheese-education course he was conducting for me.

"You're getting overloaded. Here, this will cleanse your

palate," he said, handing me a slice of cucumber in a small paper cup.

I munched on that and decided on a different approach. There were easily over a hundred different cheeses in the case, and at the rate I was going, I wouldn't have enough of an appetite left to actually enjoy whatever cheese I ended up buying.

"How about a piece of the first one I tried and a piece of the last one?" I figured I couldn't go wrong with those.

But the cheese guy didn't seem satisfied. "You mentioned brie before…"

"That was just a thought. These are good, though."

"Don't rush yourself. I have a delicious washed-rind cheese you might like and a smooth sheep's milk cheese that falls somewhere between a creamy brie and the Comté."

My head felt stuffed with information. I didn't know nearly enough about cheese to be having such a detailed conversation. I was only one small step beyond basic cheddar. That was when I looked down into the case and noticed the last Comté I tried was over thirty dollars a pound. Even a tiny slice would have cost me a fortune.

"I don't know, whatever you think is good," I said. I looked around at the artfully stacked packages of flatbread and water crackers, trying to distract myself with another set of choices. I reached for a package of artisan cracker crisps while the cheese guy wrestled with what combination of cheeses to send home with me.

"Let's go with a Brillat-Savarin to hit your brie craving. It's so creamy, you'll need to keep it refrigerated until right before you eat it, or it will melt. I'll pack it in a cooler bag for you. And the last Comté. Come back tomorrow and let me know what you think, and we can add to your repertoire."

I nodded, willing to do whatever he told me, partly so he could move on and help the other customers, who were still watching what was starting to feel like a cheese courtship between us. Cradling the cellophane-wrapped crackers, I took a step back from the counter, encouraging them to move up and take their turns.

"Enjoy!" the cheesemonger said, handing me two paper-wrapped jewels and an insulated paper bag to preserve them until I could get them into the fridge. I thanked him and browsed around the rest of the store, my faith in humanity ratcheted up a notch.

~

A FEW MINUTES LATER, with the wind at my back and coffee half empty, I walked up Fifth, trying to determine the time just by looking at the angle of the sun. I guessed it was close to four.

Chris had been in meetings for much of the day. I'd arrived early that morning, after a Thursday-night redeye flight. My boss had agreed to give me a full week off, provided that I put in a half day of work in the firm's New York office each day.

It was only a week, and we both had to work for part of each day, but it would be our official dry run as a real couple living in the same city, kissing each other goodbye each morning after wake-up sex and coffee over a shared newspaper. It would be free afternoons and every night together, putting in the real work of getting to know each other in the same time zone, in the same city, in the same apartment.

And what an apartment it was.

I should have anticipated as much after seeing his beach house in Antibes, which had five bedrooms, a gym, and a sprawling chef's kitchen, not to mention a stunning yard with a pool on a huge swath of oceanfront. His apartment was the New York equivalent.

Located in the penthouse of a classic six with views of the Hudson River and the southern tip of Manhattan, it had sweeping views, two terraces, and a keypad elevator that took us from the building's lobby straight into the foyer. He told me he'd bought the place nine years earlier, which meant he had been all of twenty-seven when he'd spent gazillions on the piece of prime real estate.

He hadn't furnished it himself—not that he couldn't. Chris had really good taste. But I knew he had zero hours in the day for anything that didn't involve some aspect of work.

Even if he hadn't told me as much, I would have guessed by the fact that every design detail had been thoughtfully executed, including tall draperies framing the windows, which soared to a twelve-foot ceiling, and matching pillows on perfectly overstuffed couches that looked like no one had ever sat on them. It wasn't that I didn't think he had an interest in the aesthetics of his home, but I knew he just didn't have the time to browse in fabric stores or sit on various cushions to decide on the amount of fill he liked. His needs had been well anticipated by the same sort of team of invisible elves that maintained his home in France and ran the parts of his life he didn't have time for when he was working, which was pretty much all the time.

His dining room had a twelve-foot reclaimed-barnwood table and chairs that looked like he could have bought them in France, if he was the kind of person who had idle time to look at furniture in France. I knew he wasn't, and he rarely had idle time at all, so I correctly surmised he'd given an interior decorator his credit card and a deadline, and everything had happened from there.

Nevertheless, the end product he'd obviously agreed upon was stunning, especially with the early-morning sun streaming in through the east-facing windows. That was already my favorite time in the apartment, and it had little to do with the Nespresso coffee maker in the kitchen—it took the large pods, so I could make myself a generous cup of coffee on my first day there as I battled exhaustion after my redeye flight.

The one thing that struck me as odd was the lack of anything personal. He had a couple of lithographs on the wall from brand-name artists who regularly showed their work at the Gagosian Gallery. It wouldn't take much art knowledge to spend a fortune on a few well-regarded pieces that would look perfect on the soaring walls of his apartment, and I felt fairly certain Chris had said yes without looking then nodded appreciatively when the art arrived.

Aside from the lithos, his apartment was devoid of knick-knacks or even daily clutter. I saw no magazines, collectibles from his travels, or framed photos of family or vacations. Actually, there was one. It was a painting of me in a cerulean blue dress that I wore when we went to his movie premiere in Cannes. He'd asked his friend Marguerite to paint it, and there was no mistaking the expression on my face—I was staring out the window at Chris, and I was completely smitten.

He'd brought it to me when he met me on my flight back to LA, and I'd insisted he keep it. The idea of a painting of myself on my wall made me uncomfortable. But he'd never mentioned that he had it up in his apartment. Seeing the personal memento of our time in France made me happy.

I didn't mean to say his apartment lacked warmth. It lacked Chris. I knew he lived there, yet there was no real evidence of who he was. In some ways, I chalked that up to him being a guy with no interest in trivial things. He wouldn't think to hang baseball hats on nails on his bedroom wall as decoration. He would have put them on a shelf or in a box made especially for storing baseball hats.

The apartment couldn't have been more beautiful, but it also made me a little sad.

I'd spent time in New York before, so I didn't feel as if I needed to run all over to see touristy spots. If we spent every free moment on those overstuffed couches, I would be perfectly happy. The point was to connect. And talk. And whatever that led to. But then talk. Because the point was to get to know each other.

Chris was already back when the elevator deposited me in his entryway. "I don't think I'll ever not think this is cool," I said as the elevator doors closed behind me. "You have a direct elevator to your living room."

"That's why the keypad entry. I don't necessarily want my

neighbors showing up in my entryway when I'm walking around in a towel."

"I get that. But can you walk around in a towel now, please?"

He laughed. "I will do whatever you ask me to do this week." He had his shirtsleeves rolled up, and he was squeezing limes into two glasses for some sort of craft cocktail. Joni Mitchell was playing out of the surround-sound speakers.

"You like Joni Mitchell?"

"I love Joni Mitchell. And Janis Joplin. And Janet Jackson. Pretty much any female artist whose name begins with J."

"I don't know if you're kidding."

He raised an eyebrow. "But maybe by the end of the week, you will."

I loved his acquiescence in indulging my getting-to-know-each-other week together. I was also aware of the limitations—we had one week. By my own design, it was supposed to give us more solid ground on which to base a relationship, especially if it would continue to be mostly long distance. I still wasn't sure how I felt about the distance part.

What I did know was that the towel issue needed urgent attention.

"Okay. I'm asking you to be in a towel."

"Pre- or post-shower?"

"Hmmm... such good choices." I walked to where he stood in the kitchen and saw that he'd put together a crudité plate with a small dish of hummus and a bowl of olives. "I have just the decadent cheese to compliment this gorgeousness. But I'm gonna withhold it until I see the towel."

"Follow me," he said, beckoning me to a cupboard in the hallway. He opened it, revealing a stack of thick Turkish cotton towels. "Any one in particular strike your fancy?" They were all fluffy and soft, and they were all off-white and looked brand new.

I pulled two towels from the stack and pushed him toward the giant bathroom attached to his even more giant bedroom.

"Not so fast," he said, taking the towels from my hands and

tossing them onto a barnwood console table against the wall. Then he grabbed both of my hands, pinned them to my sides, and walked me slowly backward toward the bed.

"Not interested in the towels?" I asked.

His dark eyes locked on mine, and he shook his head. When we got closer to the bed, Chris scooped me up in his arms and laid me down on the downy duvet. He crawled on top of me and straddled my legs, effectively pinning them. "No towels."

"What, then?" My head was resting on a nice medium-loft feather pillow, and I was looking up at the exceedingly gorgeous face of Chris Conley. Aesthetically, my life felt complete.

"Oh, so many ways I want to have you," he said, looking smug. His eyes roamed my body as if he was deciding where to begin. I started to push myself up to meet him, but he gently held me down, shaking his head. "No." He leaned forward, lifted my hands over my head, and held them there with one hand.

I obeyed because I trusted him. He'd given me reason to put all of my faith in him and surrender, so I did.

And because it was hot to have him tell me what to do.

His gaze was hazy as his eyes took a long, slow journey from my eyes to my lips and over my body beneath him. He blinked lazily and met my eyes again. "You are so goddamn beautiful. Every part of you. I want you to know that I spend every waking hour thinking about you."

"Are you for real?" I asked, dazed by his words and my intense longing for contact.

He nodded but didn't give me what I needed, instead keeping his grip on my hands so I couldn't touch him. I was effectively immobilized, and lying there, fixed on the depth of his dark eyes, I felt the want growing the longer I went without satisfying the need to touch him.

With his free hand, he began tracing the contours of my body, over my hip and along my waist, under the swell of my breast. Every nerve ending fired at his touch. The heat of his hand made my skin blaze.

"So, so beautiful. I missed your sexy body. And your gorgeous face." He edged the bottom of my shirt higher and ran his fingers over the skin of my abdomen. I arched my back in response to the feel of his hand on me, incapable of lying still.

Using the one hand, he dragged the shirt up my torso and over my head, still holding fast to my wrists. Then he wrapped the shirt around my wrists to secure them and brought both hands through my hair at my temples. He fanned my hair out on the pillow, drew it up and away from my neck, and bent to leave a row of wet kisses from my ear to my throat.

"You taste like a summer peach," he said with a growl near my ear, sending a shiver over my skin. "Every delicious bite." His lips and glorious tongue marked a trail down my throat and between my breasts, which he began massaging with his hands. He yanked down one cup of my bra and bent his head to lick and suckle my nipple, thrilling every nerve in my body. With my hands lassoed above my head, taking off my bra would have required wizardry, so he briefly unwrapped the shirt, removed my bra, and rewrapped my wrists.

"Chris, I need my hands back. I want to touch you."

He shook his head again. "Not yet. I intend to take a slow, detailed tour of your body with my tongue. And then—only then—will I let you touch me."

He wasn't normally so bossy. Actually, he was never bossy. But I loved it.

And he wasn't kidding about using his tongue. He circled my nipple, coaxing it to harden and throb against his mouth while he sucked and massaged. My eyes closed at the sensation, and my hips bucked up against him. He gripped my hips with his knees and stilled them, which only caused my need to build even more.

"Chris," I hissed through gritted teeth. "You have to let me touch you."

"Not yet." I could tell he was getting off on the control, but mostly, he was enjoying how he'd turned me into a writhing, pleading recipient of his whims. "Not until you surrender completely. I want you to trust me, trust me to see you come undone."

"I do. I trust you," I panted. I could barely form words. His hand dipped into my panties and found its way to my soft, wet center, and he teased me with a finger.

"Tell me you know I'll never hurt you."

"I know you won't."

"I'm not gonna make you tell me you love me, because it would be under duress. But I'm going to make you love me. And I'm gonna fuck you with my tongue."

Well, now.

I'd never been with guys who did much dirty talking, and it hadn't really appealed to me before, but hearing those words from a sweet, hot guy like Chris almost made me orgasm on the spot. "Please. Yes please."

He smiled and placed a row of kisses down my stomach to the waistband of my panties, which he grabbed in his teeth and pulled down. He worked them down over my legs until I was naked and bound by my cotton T-shirt. He surveyed my body as if he'd unearthed a masterpiece, and he was appreciating every nuance. He made me feel that beautiful, and I rarely felt anything even close to that.

"It's all I've been able to think about for weeks—seeing you, all of you." He'd backed away so he wasn't touching me at all, and the ache of wanting was doing me in. "Tell me what you want."

"I want you to touch me."

"Good. Because I need to touch you." He put both hands on my shoulders, and I felt my skin ignite under each hand. He ran them lightly over my body, pausing to fondle and tease my breasts before moving lower.

The ache between my legs was driving me to distraction. I needed him to touch me, but I knew that the more I wanted it, the more he would tease and torture me.

Chris moved toward my feet and pressed my knees up so my

feet were on the bed. Then, carefully and slowly, he touched and kissed the inner side of each thigh, starting at my knee and pressing soft kisses to my skin. My body was on fire. My legs were shaking, and I was pretty sure the quiet moaning I heard was coming from me.

Running his fingers over the sensitive skin he'd just kissed, Chris leaned between my legs and exhaled a hot, sexy breath at my center, and I felt my skin melt and my insides clench.

Then he paused. I almost screamed out to him, begging him to touch me. But I knew that would fuel his torture, and I was committed to moving things along. I felt his hands gently part me. Then his tongue found my center and licked slowly, softly, making my hips rise against him and my legs return to their ceaseless shaking.

"Oh my God, Chris. You're killing me."

He looked up, his eyes blazing, and smiled—or rather, smirked.

Then he waited again. I leaned my head back and started counting silently to myself. It was the only way I could think of to keep my brain from exploding and my body from writhing with pent-up desire.

He took mercy on me with his tongue. He licked and sucked and devoured me until I couldn't hold on any longer. My hips rolled against his mouth, and I broke free of the T-shirt binding and grabbed his hair in my fists as my orgasm built and soared until it shattered me.

Oh. My. God.

I was pretty certain I would never utter a coherent word again, and it didn't matter. There were no words for what he'd just done to me, anyway.

When I opened my eyes, he was watching me with a combination of lust and devotion that made me grab for his shirt, which needed to come off. Then his belt and the buttons on his pants. I worked quickly and efficiently, because getting him naked was my urgent goal.

Chris looked wary, maybe unsure what I might do to return the favor of his delightful torturous game. I beckoned for him to come closer. When he leaned in, I wrapped my hand around his erection and whispered. "You are so fucking hot. I want you inside me."

Then I moved my hand away.

"Fuck, Nikki." He picked up my hand and put it back where it was. Damn it, I hadn't tied up his hands.

I'd thought I could return the favor of his merciless control, but I hadn't thought through our size difference. In moments, he rolled on a condom, wrapped my legs around him, and crushed my mouth with his.

It was hands and mouths and tongues and heat until he slowed his movements and paused before lining himself up at my entrance then filling me completely. I gasped at the glorious feel of him and rocked against him in steady rhythm.

He moved slowly at first, making sure to hit all the right spots. When he rolled his hips, I felt myself building to another orgasm, but I wanted to make sure he was working toward his own.

And then we were both crashing and falling into each other and reeling off into intense, fiery bliss.

CHRIS GOT up to dispose of the condom, and when he came back, he was wearing the towel. He slipped next to me on the bed and rolled me on top of him so I was resting on the soft plush of the towel and my chest was flush against his. "I'm afraid we're not going to do much sightseeing this week," he said.

"You're the only sight I came here to see."

He smiled and tucked a few loose strands of hair behind my ear. Then he kissed me.

We kissed for a long time. We were a tangle of limbs with my leg draped over his and one of his arms wound around my back and the other tangled in my hair, which he combed with his fingers. He was quiet, but I knew he wasn't asleep. I also knew he wasn't thinking about work. I'd learned to tell when he drifted to the work place, and he was one hundred percent in the moment. It was like watching a hummingbird land for a split second. In that time, it was possible to see the sleek body and nimble wings that allowed it to fly, but in its stillness, it almost seemed beautifully ordinary.

I loved the moments when Chris was still. I hadn't felt it when he'd been in LA for twenty-four hours—or even less—when he'd visited and tried to keep our French fling alive, almost in a desperate attempt to stop an inevitable abyss from opening between us. That desperation, coupled with the stresses of his work that he simultaneously juggled, made those times together feel forced, if still enjoyable.

But as we lay together, I felt him fully give over to the present. It was a lovely thing, the detachment from anything that came before—no memories or guilt or apologies or stress, and no concern for what would come next.

And I had an epiphany. I knew it sounded grandiose, as if some sort of lightning bolt severed the clouds and sudden clarity rained down. But it was sort of like that.

"Chris," I whispered.

He moved his arm from my back to my hip so he could roll to the side and meet my eyes. "Yeah?"

"I think I just figured something out."

"What's that?"

I had to untangle myself a little more so I could see him better, but I didn't want to let go of him, so I carefully moved only as far away as I needed to focus on him without going cross-eyed. Then I sighed. He was so beautiful.

I couldn't help smiling at him, just because he was him and I was a hundred percent in. I knew I loved him. There was no other way to describe how I felt. "I understand what it means to be fully present. Right now, the way we are together, it's like it's frozen in time. My heart is full. It's a perfect moment."

"I agree. Only I don't think it's just a frozen moment. Because I feel this way about you all the time."

"You do?"

"Yes."

He kissed my temple and kept his lips there.

"Chris." My voice was barely a croak, because I felt overcome with emotion and my eyes welled with tears. I struggled to swallow and normalize my voice because I needed it urgently. He heart the struggle in my voice and stroked my cheek in response.

"Chris, I love you."

He backed away slightly so he could study my face. He looked more surprised than pleased. "Is this the duress speaking? Are you still under the fog of orgasm, or do you really mean that?"

"I think I've been in love with you since you kissed me on the bridge in Paris. I tried to stop my heart from going there because it hurt too much when I couldn't be with you. But you deserve to know how I feel. And I am so in love with you."

He ran his hand over the hair at my temple and cupped my face. His thumb traced a circle on my chin, and he stared into my eyes. I was consumed in the depths of his and couldn't look away. Chris covered my lips with his, kissing me deeply and lovingly, telling me everything I needed to know about how he felt.

CHAPTER TWENTY-THREE

Chris

TWO THINGS BECAME ABUNDANTLY clear within two days of Nikki arriving in New York: first, I was happier than I'd been in three months, and second, I never wanted her to leave.

I knew that wasn't realistic, given our jobs.

Or maybe you've been using the work excuse long enough.

I wasn't ready to see a therapist or think too hard about why I worked so much. I just wasn't. Even thinking about thinking about it felt like moving a mountain.

So I chose to focus instead on her and the possibility that she liked being with me in New York more than she liked being in LA with her job.

From everything she'd said about her work, she liked it, but she didn't love it. I began to wonder if she would consider a different job that she could like just as much at a firm in New York. Part of the reason I felt justified in asking her to make such a life change was that I'd seen her art. A person couldn't be so talented and passionate about something and not want to do more of it.

As I walked across Canal Street toward the Westside Highway, I enjoyed the feeling of chilly fall air and the warm sun hitting my face. Passing a stand of cheap sunglasses, trucker hats, and souvenirs, I stopped and bought a tiny replica Statue of Liberty for Nikki because she'd remarked on the view of it from my apartment and said she'd never been to Ellis Island. We would have plenty of time over the course of a week to take a boat out there, but she insisted she didn't want to do any sightseeing.

I was lucky that the production offices of the company behind my next film were in Tribeca, which meant I could walk the few blocks to my meetings. That rarely happened, and I felt fortunate. When I got to West Broadway, I hung a right and walked a couple blocks to Cipriani, where Nikki and I planned to meet for lunch. She was already there, sitting at one of the round outdoor tables under the yellow awning and munching on a breadstick from a glass jar on the table.

She smiled, and her eyes lit up when she saw me and when I bent to kiss her. I lingered longer than was probably appropriate for a public venue, but I didn't care. The paparazzi could kiss my ass if they wanted to try to take photos of us, because I kept my back to the street and both hands on Nikki's face. They would have been hard-pressed to get a good shot.

Nikki had taken the seat facing the street because she knew I usually liked to face inward. That day, I didn't care. I pulled my chair around so I could sit next to her, facing the sidewalk. She looked surprised. "Aren't you photo averse?"

"Not when I'm with you. They can take all the pictures they want and write all day long about how I'm 'smitten with my girl' or whatever the hell. They're right."

She smiled, leaning in to brush my lips with hers. "You're sweet," she said. "I ordered us some iced tea. And calamari."

"See, you already know so much about me," I said, teasing because she still kept insisting that we didn't know each other. I wasn't sure what it was going to take to convince her that we didn't need to go through the charade of getting acquainted.

She stared at the menu. I'd been there before, so I stared at her. A few seconds later, her eyes shifted over the top of the menu to connect with mine. "What?" she asked. "You're in a daze."

"Yes. I'm in a daze of you. I could daze at you until the end of days."

"How are you a real person? I feel like you're someone I'd dream up, but then I'd wake up and realize I have to live in a depressing world where you don't exist. Which would make me very sad."

"I exist."

"I'm grateful you exist," she said, her lashes shading her eyes as she looked down at the menu again. I could see the hint of a smile on her lips.

When I placed the tiny Statue of Liberty on the table in front of her, she yelped and studied its tiny details. "This is adorable. Thank you. And someday, I hope to visit her in person with you." She leaned in and kissed me.

"We can go while you're here," I offered again.

"Nope. No touristy stuff. Just you and whatever tour of your hot body you'd like to give me."

"This tour guide is at your mercy—I mean, at your disposal." I couldn't help but smile at her like a smitten schoolboy.

Our waiter came by, and we ordered—she picked a salad, and I chose an antipasto platter. I assumed we'd share both, because that was what we typically did without discussing it first or debating about it later. It was yet another sign we were compatible.

It was the kind of late-fall day when most of the leaves had dropped from the trees, which gave the sun extra places to shine. The sidewalks were their usual busy—people walked to lunch, rushed between meetings, took kids to the park—and sitting outside, even under heat lamps, wasn't always a given. That was one reason I liked the place. The other was the food, most of which I would not be eating, since it was only lunch and I didn't want to put myself into a food coma for the afternoon.

We watched as a squirrel ran down the trunk of a tree and try to make a dash across the crowded street. It barely managed to get across with its life, but somehow fate smiled, and the traffic parted for its tiny paws. "That squirrel needs to reevaluate its life choices," Nikki said, rolling her eyes. I loved that concept.

"Can I ask you something?"

Nikki looked up when I said it. We'd had a conversation recently about how she hated when people asked if they could ask something because then they were actually asking two things. I didn't have a problem with the double question, and I hoped she wouldn't take the opportunity to bring it up for discussion again. "Sure."

"Have you ever thought about turning your artistic talent into a career?" I don't know what I thought. Maybe that she'd be flattered I thought so highly of her art or that she'd have her eyes opened to something she'd never considered.

I didn't expect her reply. "Yeah, no."

"Why not?"

"I mean, thank you for the thought. I appreciate that you think I could make some kind of job out of it, but no."

"You're really talented. I don't know how you can't see it."

She took a bite of her breadstick and a sip of her iced tea, being very deliberate in her movements. Was she stalling? "I do see it. I know it's something I have a knack for," she said.

I held up a finger to correct her. "No. You have a gift."

"Thank you. Whatever you choose to call it, it's a passion hobby, but it'll never be a job."

"Why not? I thought you said you didn't love PR."

"I don't. But I'm good at it, and I like being good at it."

"And that's enough for you? Being good at it but not loving it?"

"I don't need to love it. I love making art. That's my passion. And my friends are my passion. And watching the ocean. My passion is having balance in my life, not doing one thing to the exclusion of everything else." Her eyes got wide. "I mean, I'm not criticizing your devotion to your career."

"No, it's okay. You're not wrong. I do devote myself to it, maybe too much."

She didn't disagree with me. Maybe I wanted her to, at least a little bit. And maybe she would if she gave into her love for art and made it a bigger part of her life. "I guess I don't understand. If you have a passion, and you're phenomenal at it, why wouldn't you want to do it as your career?"

"Because it wouldn't be fun anymore. If I was trying to make a living at it and turning it into a source of stress, all the joy would go. I'd rather have a job I know I'm good at and a hobby I'm great at that I love. That's how I've prioritized it."

"Hmph." Her perspective was interesting. I grabbed a breadstick and broke it in half. Then, unsure which half I wanted to eat, I put both pieces down on the bread plate. She'd scrambled my logic, and I had a feeling hers was superior.

I decided that as long as we were at it, I would gently broach the subject of her job and the possibility of doing a similar job in New York. Her own firm had an office there, for crying out loud—it wouldn't be that hard. But she had to be willing.

"How was work?" I asked.

"Eh, fine. Nothing too earth-shattering. I wrote some press releases and had a conference call."

"So it's not disrupting your workflow to be here, out of your regular office?"

She slid the jar of breadsticks toward me, and I took another one, but I didn't eat it. I was still too focused on the conversation. "Not really, but I'm only doing like a third of the stuff I normally do. My boss doesn't realize it, but I'm neglecting half my clients. But it's fine. I'll make up for it when I get back. All good."

"But you like that particular firm?"

She leveled me with a look that said she was on to me. "Why do you ask? Do you have a different job in mind for me, perhaps something that requires me to wear a revealing costume of some sort?"

"Well, yes. There's always that. And let's definitely put a pin in that to discuss later. But no, I was just wondering how rooted you are to your job. In LA. How rooted you are to living in LA?"

Now she looked wary, clearly unsure what I was suggesting. "Meaning what?"

"There are a lot of PR firms here."

"You're suggesting I move?

"You could."

"I could." She nodded her head like she was considering the concept. "I would consider it."

"You would?" I was overjoyed. That had been so easy.

She nodded, but then her gaze pierced mine. "But I have a question for you. Would you consider working less than you do? Taking weeks or months between projects instead of days?"

I felt my face fall into a frown. I didn't mean for it to happen, but she'd caught me off guard, and I'd never—ever—considered working less. If I slowed down, I might quickly coast to a stop. That was what my agent always said. I'd always believed him.

"I know. It's asking a lot," she said. "But hear me out. I look at you, and I see how much you enjoy the time when you're not working. And I know you love your career, but you don't have much of a work–life balance. I'll bet you could give yourself the gift of more free time and not sacrifice your career."

I had no answer to that. And the idea made me nervous. "I… I mean, maybe…"

She immediately grabbed my hand. "Hey. It's okay. I'm not saying you need to make a big change all at once. I'm just saying think about it. Get a little more comfortable with the idea."

Why is she talking to me like I'm a scared child?

Because you are terrified of changing your life, and no one's fooled.

"Right. Sure. I can think about it. I suppose it's possible." I hemmed and hawed, not knowing what the right answer was. What she was proposing wasn't crazy. I knew most people had a much better work–life balance than I did, but my situation had never bothered me. In fact, the constant busyness fueled me.

The idea of doing things differently did not fill me with excitement.

It scared the hell out of me.

CHAPTER TWENTY-FOUR

Nikki

MY WEEK in New York was amazing. We walked all over the city. We laughed. We spent hours and hours in bed—and on the couch, in the kitchen, and on the bathroom floor. I fell in love with Chris over and over again. We ate dim sum for Sunday breakfast, and we watched the sun setting over the Hudson from his balcony every chance we got.

The best thing about us was how easy we were with each other. I felt like Chris was the missing half of myself I never knew I needed. I knew I loved him. And I knew loving him was about to get a lot harder, because he'd soon be on location for a new project, and we wouldn't see each other for months.

I wasn't really okay with that.

Before I realized it, we were walking in Central Park on my last day. It felt oddly familiar, the foreboding of an imminent and unwanted goodbye.

"Would you consider staying? A few more days? A few more years?" Chris asked as we wandered past the boathouse and took a moment to gaze out at the water.

"I would love to stay. But I have work."

"You know that's not what I meant."

"I do know."

He pulled me in with one arm around my waist and tilted my face up to meet his. His lips were soft and inviting, communicating his sincere desire that I never leave. I never wanted to leave. And that was the problem.

When we broke the kiss, I felt like I needed to explain it differently than I had before. He needed to understand what I wanted. I needed to tell him what I wanted. Thus far, I'd been afraid to do that. "The thing is, I do want to stay. I want to be all in."

"Really?" He looked childishly optimistic and pressed his forehead to mine. "You would move to New York? Please say yes. Please say yes."

"I would. But it would be for the wrong reasons."

"How could there be wrong reasons when it means we can be together?"

He really didn't get it. Maybe he never would. "Chris, me moving to New York would mean that instead of being in LA and missing you because you're always working, I'd be here, missing you because you'd be working."

"Not all the time. I get breaks."

"Not that I've seen so far. And Chris, you've been great. I know how exhausting it was to fly to LA for twenty-four hours. That was insane. I know you care about us. But you're constantly working. I don't want to move my life here so I can sit in an empty apartment most of the time, waiting for a FaceTime call. It's not about my job or whether I'm passionate about my job or whether I'm in the right job—it's about wanting more. I'm saying it. I want more. I'm asking for more. And if you can't give it to me, I understand, but I have to ask. Because that's what I want."

I'd finally laid it all out, and I felt great. Whatever happened from that point forward, I would know I advocated for myself and asked for what I wanted.

He nodded. "I hear what you're saying. But does it have to be all or nothing? If we live in the same city, we'll see each other more than we do now."

"More. But not enough. I want it all. You told me I should ask for what I want, and that's what it is. I want a partner who's with me. Not all the time, but at least most of the time. Because I want to share the everyday stuff. The newspaper headlines over coffee and spontaneous late-night sex."

"And you can't do that with me. Because of my job." He looked dejected. No, he looked lost. And for a moment, I had a glimmering thought that maybe he was reaching the limits of how satisfying his workaholic existence was. Maybe I could help him adjust, even a little bit at a time, to finding more of a life balance. But then he said, "I get that."

"Chris, I so respect your career and how hard you work at it. And I know you're really trying with me, but your commitment to your job—the amount of time you work—doesn't leave enough of you left over. I can't ask you to give up projects you have your heart set on. I can't ask you to work less."

"You could."

"You'd resent me for it."

"I don't think I would."

"I can't do this for you. You have to *want* to want it."

There was a bench a few paces away, and he led me there. We sat. "So are you ending things with me? Because, just to be clear, that's not what I want. Not at all."

"It's not what I want, either. And I'm not saying we end things. I really love you. I don't want to end things. I just don't know where we go from here. I don't know how we can move forward."

"Maybe right now, we can't. Are you happy enough doing what we're doing? Maybe we can see… if something changes?"

His desperation to believe made me sad. "Chris… do you honestly see that happening? You have to want it to change."

A balloon floated past us, and a boy ran over to retrieve it. His navy coat was buttoned up to his chin, the down so thick that he could barely move his neck to see where the balloon had gone. Chris picked it up and handed it to him. "Here you go, bud." He bopped the balloon up into the air, and the boy chased it gleefully.

"So like that... kids... having a family..." I felt for him. He'd been on autopilot for so long, he'd never taken the time to think about what he was missing. Like kids. Or having a family.

"You can have all of that. But not if you're working yourself to the bone every day of the year. It just doesn't compute. What would be the point of having kids if you never saw them? You'd have to find a reason within yourself to change. It's a big deal. It's not a one-conversation-in-the-park sort of thing. It's a lot of conversations and a lot of thinking."

I watched the boy, who was completely bewitched by his balloon, and I desperately wanted Chris to have more than what he was allowing himself. He was a good person. He deserved to let himself out of his career jail, but he could only do it if and when he was ready.

Chris was silent for a while, so I couldn't be sure whether he was still thinking about our conversation. Then he shook his head. "Maybe this is why I'm meant to be an actor and nothing more. Fictional characters are superior and I can play them really well. They have all the right words, the scripts tell me what to think and feel. The directors make me look better than who I really am."

"I call bullshit on that. I'm not even going to let you believe that for a second. You're better than any story any movie ever told. So just stop it."

"But what if I can't give you what you want? Me, the real guy. What if I'm not good enough because I'm scared to make sacrifices in my career?"

Hearing him say the words broke my heart. My only hope was that he said them out of fear and didn't entirely believe them. "Chris, you are better than good enough. Please know that. And listen, I'm not asking you to sacrifice everything. I'm not planning to sacrifice everything for you either. But I have to give up some things, and I'm okay with that. The sacrifice gives how I feel about you more meaning."

He looked at me. "I like that. It reminds me a little of…" He looked unsure about continuing.

"What?"

"In the movie I did—with Triss—that was an issue her character struggled with. I told her that loving someone completely and leaving that person to go to war made the sacrifice that much greater."

"And that much more tragic."

"I overlooked that aspect. But I see it now."

I couldn't help smiling at him. He was so sweet and so like the baby birds on my balcony, singing at night because they didn't know any better and just learning how to fly. I took his hand and kissed the center of his palm.

He inhaled deeply and held it. When he finally let it out, his resolve seemed firm. "I guess I need to reevaluate my life choices."

It was so sincere and sweet, I felt my face crack into a wide grin. "Yes, you do. You need to reevaluate your life choices."

CHAPTER TWENTY-FIVE

Nikki

DURING DINNER on our last night together, Chris told me about his parents.

We'd walked to St. Tropez on West Fourth Street because Chris liked the idea of recapturing our time in the South of France, at least through the food and vibe of the restaurant, which had square wooden tables decorated with a small succulent in the center of each and twin bottles of oil and vinegar.

We sat side by side at the bar, facing a wall of wine bottles and a single bartender who poured wine flights and served the handful of us sitting there. The benefit of the bar was that we could sit next to each other, which meant Chris either had his arm over the back of my chair or he leaned in toward me, crowding my space and pressing kisses to my temple, cheek, and neck like I was a most cherished possession he needed to keep close.

Chris chose a bottle of red wine for us to share, and while the waiter uncorked the bottle, he rattled off half a dozen appetizers he wanted us to share. We had similar taste in food, and he knew that as long as there was salad involved in a meal, I wasn't picky.

"How about the mussels, the zucchini tart, the flatbread, and the grilled octopus. Oh, and a salad," he said, smiling at me and raising an eyebrow at my creature-of-habit ways.

The waiter zipped off to put our order in, and I pounced on the chance to learn more about his family. I was surprised by how insistent he seemed about talking about his parents. It seemed important to him. Then I learned why.

He was careful to explain that the reason he'd told me the sanitized, fictional story about them was partly out of habit, partly out of protectiveness. He grabbed my hand and didn't let go of it, even when it came time to taste the wine and sample the oysters.

His foot tangled with mine under the bar top, and I spent most of the dinner staring into the dark pools of his eyes. I wanted to memorize everything about his face and take it home with me.

I could tell that talking about his parents was hard for him. He liked to be picture perfect, or at least he didn't like drawing attention to what he saw as shortcomings.

"They're completely co-dependent, bound together by guilt. It's not love, it's guilt," he said. "My dad should leave, but he loves her too much. And she should let him go, but he puts up with her affairs, and she likes the comfort of having known him most of her life. It's totally twisted."

"Or..." I said, treading lightly, because I knew he was raw and vulnerable, opening up about something he'd stuffed away for years. "Maybe it works for them."

He shook his head. "My dad loves her too much."

"What's too much? How do you define too much? Is he happy?"

"I never thought about the possibility he could be."

"Think about it now."

Chris was silent and stony faced. I wasn't sure if he was thinking or placating me for suggesting it. "I guess, maybe. It's very different from how I'd be happy."

"Yeah, I know."

He was quiet for a while, and I could tell he really was

thinking about them and trying to come to terms with who they were. I was surprised when he asked, "Would you like to meet them?"

"I'd love to meet them. Of course."

"They'll love you. I know we have at least that much in common."

I had no idea when I would next be in New York, which was all wrapped up in the uncomfortable subject neither of us wanted to discuss. I'd told Chris what I wanted, and he still hadn't figured out a way to meet me halfway. I had to get my brain around the idea that maybe he never would.

"Parents should be given user manuals before they're allowed to have kids. It might help," I said as I considered what he'd told me about his family.

"It's not a bad idea. You think your parents could have benefitted from that too?"

I shrugged. I loved my parents, but they had as many flaws as the next person. We all did. "You know how I told you that I tend to beat myself up for being too serious? How I always felt like I lacked spontaneity?" I asked.

"Yes, and I disagree. I don't see your seriousness as a problem."

"Exactly. I think I was confusing being crazy and spontaneous with living my life and being present."

"So you're saying you don't want to be crazy or spontaneous? Because I may have to argue against that. I like it when you're spontaneous. Like agreeing to come to New York." He kissed my forehead. "And I especially like it when you're a little crazy, like… oh, so many examples… hard to pick just one." He reached for the hair at my temple and followed the strands down to the ends. He did it slowly several times. The effect was hypnotic, and I almost lost my train of thought.

"What I'm saying is that just like your parents, my parents did a number on me. I still love them, and I know they didn't do it on purpose, but I'm starting to believe that where we end up in life has a direct correlation to the ways in which our parents gave us the wrong message."

He looked interested in that topic of conversation. "Explain, please."

"Well, you know my parents live by the beach in SoCal."

"I do know that, but that's all I know, because you've been purposefully vague."

"They live in an Airstream trailer. They move around and travel when they feel like it, but when they're home, they're parked at Dockweiler Beach, making use of the county barbecue grills and public bathrooms."

He nodded, but his eyes left mine, like he was picturing them grilling. "Doesn't sound too bad, actually."

"It's not. It works for them. They're total leftover-from-the sixties hippies. They used to follow the Grateful Dead, and now they follow Dead cover bands. My dad sells T-shirts, and my mom has a store on Etsy. They make a shit ton of money. Living in a trailer is a choice, not a hardship."

A genuine smile spread across Chris's face. "I would so love to meet your parents. They sound awesome."

"They are awesome. They love me, and they're supportive of me… to an extent."

"What does that mean?"

"They have this life rule that's very Deadhead. It's all about living in the present and not stressing. Well, I'm a stresser. It's part of my DNA. And I always felt like I had to apologize for it. But now… I get that I can be both."

"I'd say you've hit a good balance."

"Yeah? It wasn't always the case. But I do think I've made remarkable progress."

Chris raised his glass. "Cheers to that," he said.

I clinked and drank and loved how we were together. I tried not to question how we could be so compatible and so in love and potentially not work out as a couple. I couldn't even lay odds on our chances for success, because I didn't know if Chris could change his workaholic tendencies. Neither did he.

What he did know, however, was that he'd be in LA the following week for a movie premiere, and he wanted me to go with him.

"Of course, I will come if you're sure that's what you want. You know me and premieres." The one in Cannes hadn't gone especially well.

"Very funny."

"I'm serious. Are you sure you want me tripping down the red carpet with you? Getting the paparazzi all excited about your klutzy arm candy?"

"You really think you're hilarious, don't you?" He signaled the waiter so we could order more food. We tucked the menus to the side and sat back to enjoy the view. It was nice not to feel hurried. I didn't want to think about tomorrow, when I'd be home and we'd have to revert to texts and FaceTime.

Chris looked at me as if he had something on his mind.

"Yes?" I asked.

"What? I didn't say anything."

"I see the gears moving in your brain. You're worried I don't have the right dress for the premiere. And knowing you, there's probably some atelier a few doors down from here, where a bunch of elves are waiting to sew me into some princess clothes."

"Is this what happens when I don't see you for three weeks? You lose your sanity?"

"Tell me you weren't thinking about a dress."

"I wasn't thinking about a dress," he said.

I just waited. I knew I could sweat him out if I didn't say a thing.

Finally, he couldn't stand it any longer. "Do you have a dress?"

I grinned. "I have a dress."

"See? I wasn't worried."

I eyed him suspiciously. I hadn't been needed at work that day, so I'd spent a little time shopping. I'd found Chris a pair of socks with clouds and a matching Joni Mitchell quote. It was crazy to me that such socks existed, but after a quick dash through MOMA —I couldn't leave New York without seeing more art—I went to the museum gift shop, and there they were.

He was wearing them, and I was wearing my purchase, which was a tight tank dress in cerulean blue, the color of the dress I'd worn to the premiere in Cannes. When I'd walked out of Chris's spare bedroom in it, his eyes had slowly roamed the length of my body, which was hugged at every curve by the dress, leaving little to the imagination. "You look gorgeous," he'd said quietly. I sensed that he had more to say, but he was still gathering the words. His gaze looked hungry, a fire ignited in his eyes that hadn't been extinguished over the course of dinner.

"On the subject of dresses," he said, melting my eyes with his intense stare.

"Yes?"

"I love you in this one."

"Thank you."

"I love you no matter what you're wearing. And even," he said, running his hand down the length of my arm, eliciting a chill, "when you're not wearing anything." He leaned in close to my ear, and his breath feathered against my skin when he spoke. "Especially then."

I lost all interest in the remaining courses of our dinner, which Chris had boxed up and paid for within three minutes. He took my hand and helped me off the barstool, his eyes never wavering from mine. As he led me out of the restaurant, walking close to my side, he leaned in again. "Apologies in advance if I end up ripping this dress in two."

I looked at him, and the heat rose in my cheeks at the suggestion of his carnal want. I swallowed so as not to drool. Then I nodded.

It wasn't a long walk. But it was long enough for Chris to keep making suggestions about how quickly and how aggressively he needed to get the dress off my body. "I might not make it all the way home," he whispered, gesturing to a park, where the grass looked comfortable but very, very public.

"How do you feel about making love in an elevator?" he growled, pulling me in closer, wrapping his hand around my waist, and squeezing my ass hard.

I wanted to answer, but every time he spoke to me, it shot a white-hot, delicious flame to my center, and I fell speechless again.

"Or do you prefer the bed? The soft sheets against your naked skin and me against you?" he asked when we'd stopped at a traffic light, brushing my hair back from my neck and attacking it with a row of hot, wet kisses from my ear to my throat.

My knees felt weak, and I looked desperately up the block to count how many more buildings we had to pass before we made it back to his apartment.

Maybe he sensed the weakness in my knees, or maybe he couldn't wait any longer to meld our bodies closer together, because he lifted me up, cradling me in his arms for the last few yards to his building.

The park was out, and we never made it to the bed.

But the private elevator was in use for a very long time.

CHAPTER TWENTY-SIX

LOS ANGELES
Nikki

THE TRUTH WAS, I didn't have a dress for the premiere. Before I met Chris, the only times I'd ever needed to wear anything remotely dressy was when I was a bridesmaid in a couple of my friends' weddings, and I didn't think a long baby-blue halter dress with a matching bolero jacket was the move for a Hollywood premiere. To say nothing of the iridescent-green maxi dress with an organza shawl.

"You don't have a perfect go-to cocktail party dress?" Jemma asked.

I wanted to tell her that I didn't go to perfect cocktail parties, but I worried that might make her not want to help me. Instead, I asked if there was any chance she knew of a store that sold really cool, glamorous, inexpensive evening or cocktail dresses. She did a spit take of Caesar salad and shook her head at me.

"Yeah, those are oxymorons. You're gonna drop at least a grand on a dress."

I didn't want to drop that kind of money on a dress.

We were at the barely edible Italian place near work, and I'd decided to forgo pizza for the time being for the sake of fitting into the mythical fabulous-but-cheap dress.

"Do *you* have a perfect little black dress?" I asked, unexcited about the fancy lettuce salad that cost me thirteen dollars. "And can we head back to the office? I have a conference call in fifteen minutes."

"Sure." Jemma pushed her chair back and went to the counter to ask for a to-go box for the rest of her salad. I snuck a look at her from behind. We were roughly the same size. Even though Jemma favored blousy caftans and leggings with slouchy boots at work, she could have had a perfect premiere dress hanging amid her work attire.

"And in answer to your question, I have a black velvet cocktail dress from Banana Republic."

"Could I borrow that? Do you think it would fit me?"

Her laugh was sarcastic. "I was kidding. Do you think I shop retail? I'm all about secondhand clothing stores and Goodwill," she said. Suddenly the grandma-like caftans made sense. But I doubted Goodwill was the direction I should go when there was a good chance I would end up standing next to Chris, who would look amazing, in photos.

"Don't you and Chris have any fancy friends? People who go to the Oscars and have loads of dresses? This is LA. Someone must have a dress they've worn to an awards show or a museum gala."

"I'm sure lots of people do. I just don't happen to know those people."

"Hey!" she said, clapping her hands for her new idea. "I'm sure there are lots of designers who'd love to put a dress on Chris Conley's girlfriend. I still can't believe you're dating him, can I just say?"

We were standing close to the line of people waiting to order, and as soon as the words were out of her mouth, Jemma obviously realized what she'd done. At least ten people were staring at me. We turned and practically ran out of the restaurant.

"Wow, sorry about that. I didn't realize that just saying his name was like human clickbait."

"Welcome to my world."

"So yeah. What's that like?" she asked as we walked.

"Um, it's been fine for the most part. He's really good at navigating so he can sit facing away from crowds, and most of the time, people don't notice him. Or if they do, most of them are discreet with their pointing."

"That's good."

"Yeah."

"But how is it for you? Is it weird being with someone who's, like, rock-star huge?"

"That's what I mean. It never feels that way. I don't watch those kind of movies, so I don't think of him as huge. He just seems like a normal guy."

"Wow. That's...interesting."

Annie's mom was a therapist, and she used to complain that her mom used the word "interesting" to avoid saying what she really thought about anything. "His new haircut—that was interesting," she would say. Or "Her parents left her at home without a babysitter. That's interesting."

Lots of people used the word as a substitute for something more descriptive. I had no intention of letting Jemma off without telling me what she really meant. "It's not interesting. Say what you're really thinking."

"Sorry," she said. "I guess I was thinking you're living in kind of a bubble, aren't you? Like, you don't see superhero movies, so he's just a regular guy. You do realize those movies make a billion dollars. Each."

"So?"

"So he's a really big deal to a lot of people. You should be aware of that is all I'm saying. When do I get to meet him?"

"Ah, that's where this was all really leading, right?"

She shrugged. "I'm your very close, capable work friend. I should merit a meeting. And maybe a date with one of his hot actor friends."

I laughed at her generous description of our work friendship.

"You know there's not a hot actor club. They don't all know each other and hang out together."

She shrugged and pulled open the heavy glass door to our building. "Hey, here's a thought about your outfit dilemma. What about Rent the Runway?"

"You mean, rent a dress?" I asked. I'd never looked into doing anything like that. I'd never had a reason to. But it kind of seemed like the perfect solution to my wardrobe issues.

Jemma was already googling the site. "This is perfect. For fifty bucks, you can get something swoon-worthy for the premiere. You might need to pay a little more for expedited shipping, but this seems made for you."

Both of us were so firmly glued to Jemma's phone, swiping from dress to dress, that we missed our floor in the building and had to ride down to the basement before going up again. But the dresses on her phone were worth it. One of them would be perfect.

When we returned to our respective offices, I thanked Jemma for her help, and she grinned at me like the fairy godmother who was sending her Cinderella off to the ball. A part of me wanted to tell Jemma the truth—after the premiere, there might not be a Chris and Nikki. But I couldn't bring myself to say it.

Ever hopeful that something would change, I clung to the idea of our rom-com movie ending, even though I was fairly certain Chris hadn't reevaluated his life choices. He would have told me if he had.

When I really thought about getting dressed up and spending one last glamorous night with Chris, I felt depressed. I didn't want to go. I didn't want to say goodbye and have my last memory of us be picture perfect—or worse, captured in a magazine for me to cry over later.

We weren't perfect. We were messy. We'd achieved that level of normalcy, and I loved it. We'd gotten close to something that could have worked, something with a future. If only…

But no.

I was done with hoping and wishing. I'd already done that with one boyfriend, and there I was, thinking about doing it again. The best thing I could do for myself was to see the situation for what it was. If Chris couldn't find a balance in his life between work and everything else, I had to move on.

CHAPTER TWENTY-SEVEN

Nikki

I HAD ALWAYS LOVED the month of December. Even though living in Southern California meant that I never had a white Christmas or even much weather to speak of, it didn't matter. Twinkle lights wound around trees and holiday music always made me happy. In fact, I might have been the one person on earth who never tired of Christmas music. It didn't matter that it started before Thanksgiving and played its final notes in the wee hours of December twenty-fifth. I would take all of it, as many renditions of "Santa Baby" as the in-store sound systems wanted to throw at me.

That meant I was in a great mood all month, and not just because Chris would be in town in a few days, although that helped a lot. I was in a great mood even though he was planning on dragging me to another premiere. I felt almost certain it was an action movie he'd shot last year, and I felt nearly positive that he'd told me the name of the movie… but alas, I would always be an arthouse movie girl. And when he spoke about action and adventure and superheroes, they all blended together in my mind into one loud, big-budget film with elaborate action scenes.

I felt a little bad about my lack of finesse when it came to those films. I really did try to keep them straight, and I had watched every single one—there were a lot of them—since we started dating. I watched all his movies carefully so we could talk about them, which I enjoyed even more than he did.

"By the time the movie comes out, I've mostly forgotten it. You realize that, don't you?" he would say when I insisted on dissecting the action sequences and talking about why there needed to be so much destruction of property to get the point across. I secretly thought maybe he, too, thought they were all the same.

"Well then, this is a good refresher for you. You'll be all prepared for your press junket, because I need you to explain why thirty-six police cars needed to collide in that last scene instead of just two. The point would have been made with two."

He'd humored me and explained how the buildup of action scenes was the whole point. "The police cars colliding is the end result. The action is the helicopter tracking the van, the explosion on the bridge, the near death of the driver and last-minute hop on top of the police car, which then drives into a dead-end road and a major showdown. It's an action film. Exciting action is the point."

Then I asked him to break down how much of the film's budget went into sets and stunt people and destruction of property. "You realize you could make ten indie films for what it costs to film one car chase."

"Yes, I know. Ten indie films that would collectively make an entire nation want to drown its sorrows in a bucket of chardonnay... if they could see through their tears well enough to reach the bucket. I'd rather be the one riding on top of a police car on a death mission than watch a destitute mother sell her oldest child in order to feed the rest of the brood."

"You heartless, heartless man."

"You safe-driving, rule-following woman."

On movies, we had to agree to disagree.

~

I PANICKED when I figured out that the couple days Chris would be in LA were also the two days Annie planned to be in town for work. I'd promised my best friend that we would get together. I knew I could spend time with both of them, but selfishly, I didn't want to do that. I valued my alone time with each of them.

Fortunately, the scheduling deities took pity on me. Chris needed to shoot a segment on *Jimmy Kimmel Live* and had to stick around for a dinner meeting with his agents afterward. We'd agreed to meet at the bar in the back corner of a hotel by the beach at around ten. That gave Annie and me a chance to eat and catch up.

Annie and I grabbed salads at Whole Foods and set up our bachelorette dinner picnic in my apartment. Annie munched her salad in silence for a few minutes, which gave me a chance to get out of my head and think about the fact that she hadn't mentioned anything about the work promotion she'd expected the last couple times I'd talked to her. She'd been so excited, so certain it would happen, and then… nothing.

"Annie," I said, watching her chew.

It was almost as if she'd read some article about how important it was to chew each mouthful fifty times before swallowing. She didn't seem to want to talk. Finally, she swallowed and couldn't ignore the fact that I was staring at her. "Yeah?" she said then scooped another forkful of feta cheese and a cherry tomato into her mouth and began a marathon of closed-mouth masticating.

"What's up with the promotion? I've been meaning to check in with you."

Her expression didn't change. She kept gently chewing. I knew it didn't take that much effort to make a tomato fit for swallowing. She was stalling. Finally, she swallowed and looked up at me, a blank expression still disguising any emotion. "Parsons got it."

I was shocked. Annie had been on the partner track at her law firm from the moment they'd hired her as a summer associate. She'd aced the bar exam and litigated her way to millions of dollars for the firm. Her words didn't make sense. "That's impossible," I said. "You deserved it."

"Not this year. At least that's what I was told."

"So what does that mean?" I still felt dumbfounded by what she was telling me.

Annie pushed her salad away, suddenly looking tired. "I don't know what it means. I guess I could look for another job. Or I could keep working my ass off there and hope they see things differently in a year."

"That sucks. I'm so sorry."

"Yeah. Thanks."

"When did you hear?"

"Three weeks ago," she said.

"Wait, seriously? Why didn't you tell me?"

She looked at me like I was daft. "Are you kidding? You were busy in Chris-land, trying to work out your schedules, and stressing about everyone at work seeing you differently. I didn't see the point."

I pushed my own salad away, feeling suddenly sickened by my friend telling me I'd been too self-involved to bother with her problems. I got up from the table, retrieved the lid to my salad, then replaced it. There was no point in opening the popcorn I'd bought. I'd lost my appetite. "I'm so sorry."

"It's not your fault."

"It is. I've been a terrible friend."

"You've been fine. This is on me. I didn't want to weigh you down you with my stupid failure."

I watched her as she poured filtered water into my orange teakettle and put it on the burner. "First of all, you're not a failure. And second, I *want* you to weigh me down. Weight on me is less of a load on you. Unless it's pretzel bloat, of course, in which case it's just bad all around."

She grinned, and I realized it was the first time I'd seen her smile that day.

I wondered how it had been lost on me that something was bothering her.

"Careful what you wish for, lady. I will be a monster botherer."

"I can't believe Jordan didn't say anything to me." Jordan, my boss when I'd worked for a startup in the Bay Area, had been dating Annie for a couple years, all through her pink-hair phase, her platinum-blond phase, and the red-hair phase that made her look like Ariel from *The Little Mermaid*. Firmly settled into a brunette phase, Annie had hinted that she and Jordan might be moving in together. I'd just called him with a venture capital question the week before, and he hadn't mentioned anything.

She looked sheepish. "He doesn't know."

"You have to tell him. He'll want to know. And he'll be supportive—you know that."

"I know. It's just that I keep thinking that if I don't tell anyone, maybe I can still turn it around."

"Is there a chance of that?"

Annie shrugged, but she was the type of person who never uttered a thought before considering all the angles. If there was a chance of still winning the promotion, she would have already doggedly pursued it. "Probably not."

"So is it a matter of waiting another year, or do you feel like it was this time or never?"

She smiled ruefully. "Honestly, I just thought it would be this time. I have no idea about never." The water had reached its boiling point, and the kettle had barely started to whistle before Annie turned off the heat. She reached into a drawer filled with boxed tea bags and rummaged around until she found what she wanted, a box of decaf chai. "You want a cup?" she asked.

I looked at the assortment and chose an Earl Grey, figuring I had a late night ahead, and the extra burst of caffeine might help me along. While we waited for the bags to steep, I thought about how I'd missed the signs that something had been bothering Annie over the past few weeks. "You need to call Jordan tonight and tell him. That's probably half of why you feel bad about it—you're carrying it around alone. You've gotta tell him."

"Yeah. You're right," she said.

"I know I'm right. Listen to me." I felt very insistent that I knew of what I spoke. Because I was great at relationships—anyone's except my own.

CHAPTER TWENTY-EIGHT

Nikki

I STARED at the dress hanging in its hermetically sealed clear pouch and almost decided to leave it on the hanger and pull my old standby black dress out of the closet. There was nothing wrong with it. It had gotten me through several weddings and one Christmas party at work.

The best thing about it was that it was plain. I could make it look a little more interesting by pairing it with a pair of dark-red silk stilettos and a cute handbag that matched, or I could let it fade into looking rather ordinary with black pumps and a blazer. I liked its versatility, I told myself. Really, I liked the idea of fading into the woodwork.

The dress Jemma and I had finally decided on was not a wallflower dress. It was a come-check-out-my-cleavage-in-my-pushup-bra kind of dress. It was a strapless pale pinkish-silver column of smooth silk that hugged my waist and accented the hourglass tendencies of my hips. It fell to just above my knees, and its sleek texture made me look like a slippery silver-pink eel.

In a good way. At least that's what Jemma had convinced me to believe.

"Trust me, you'll be so happy in this dress. You can breathe, right? Breathing's important," she'd said.

Once I'd assured her I could in fact breathe, she signed off on the fashion choice by taking about a million pictures of me in the dress. Sort of. She cut my head off, so really it was just the dress. But then she posted them on her social media accounts, because in addition to being a budding publicist, she was also working on being a fashion influencer and wanted to exploit the dress while she could. It was sort of our quid pro quo after she'd agreed to help me find said dress.

I was actually relieved she'd cut off my head.

The soothing sounds of coffeehouse music played on a satellite radio station on my computer. I usually listened to that kind of music when I worked on art, but pulling myself together for the premiere felt like a sort of performance art, so I decided the music felt appropriate.

Chris's handlers had sent a hair-and-makeup team to my apartment without asking if I wanted them. It almost felt like it would require too much of an explanation to turn them down, so I acquiesced. I wasn't great with makeup, anyway. Other than lip gloss or a little mascara, I didn't wear much, but I knew the red carpet and the potential for photographers required more work.

Unlike the premiere we went to in France, the one in LA didn't strike the fear of God in my very soul. I wasn't as worried about what other people would think of me. By then, enough photographers had snapped pictures of us together and enough gossip magazines had written their breathless stories that Chris and I were old news.

That meant I needed to look the part of his arm candy, but there would be no wagging tongues speculating on our relationship status. I focused on the arm candy part and let the hair and makeup people work their magic.

The hair stylist decided to flat iron my normally wavy hair

into a sleek, long sheet, pinned back on one side with a glittery clip. The makeup was mostly in hues of pink, which brought out the pink shimmer in the pinkish-silver dress.

By five fifteen, Chris was waiting outside my building, the town car idling in the street and the driver standing by.

He looked handsome in a way that was unfair to the rest of the male species with his hair slicked back, his face clean-shaven, and his dark suit. "Hol-yyyy," he said. "You look… there are no words for it. You look absolutely gorgeous. I am the luckiest guy alive."

A deep blush crept across my face, not so much because of his words but because of the way he was looking at me like he wanted to devour me. He actually licked his lips.

"Let's get in the car," I said, "before you chase me upstairs and tear me out of this dress."

"Oh, I can make quick work of that in the car. Don't you worry." For good measure, he showed me his Joni Mitchell socks, as if I could have loved him more.

I made a move to evade him and get to the car, but he grabbed me from behind and wrapped his arms around my waist while planting soft kisses along my neck and walking us to the car together.

"Don't worry," he whispered into my ear, sending a chill over my skin. "I can find many, many places"—he kissed my shoulder —"to kiss you." He nipped at my chin. "That won't mess up your makeup one bit." He kissed the sensitive skin behind my ear as the wet heat from his lips blazed a path through the center of me.

"I…" I started to say something. But the words died on my lips, and my brain went into free fall. To hell with my makeup. I just wanted to kiss him.

I was glad we had a long drive all the way across town.

I prayed for traffic.

THE OUTSIDE of the theater on Hollywood Boulevard had two sweeping spotlights crossing in the night sky and heralding the arrival of the movie with the kind of fanfare typical of a premiere. But since I'd survived the press gauntlet at Chris's side once, this time it felt a little less stressful.

The flashbulbs assaulted us, and Chris got pulled this way and that to pose for photos, but the carpet itself was rather short, so it didn't take very long to walk on it. I did my best to stand up straight, smile when asked, and move when someone wanted a photo of Chris alone.

Then we were done.

We walked through the glass doors of the movie theater, just as we had in Cannes. The scene was similar. People loitered in the lobby, hoping to catch one more glimpse of the film's stars before taking their seats. There were buckets of popcorn and cold drinks on offer by the doors to the auditorium, where most seats were filled by the time we entered the lobby.

I knew there would be reserved seats in front for us and any other guests of the film's director and actors.

At the premiere in Cannes, Chris had opted to do an interview instead of sitting in the theater, so I wasn't sure if he'd be accompanying me inside, but he didn't let go of my hand as we made our way through the lobby. There were two sets of double doors leading into the auditorium, and I didn't think much about it when we passed the first set. I figured maybe Chris liked to walk down on the left side, where there were fewer people.

But we passed the second set of doors too. He kept a tight grip on my hand, almost as if he was afraid I might escape. "We're not going in there. We're going this way," he said, leading me down a hallway to a different set of double doors and what looked like a second theater.

I didn't hear the same level of commotion emanating from that one, and I wondered if it was some odd overflow area for people who couldn't get seats in the main theater. Honestly, that was fine by me, since Chris had obviously seen the movie and didn't care where I sat. "Is it a smaller theater? Does that mean we can make out in the back row?"

"Something like that," he said. His expression was tight, and I saw a muscle flinching in his jaw.

"Chris," I said, stopping in my tracks, which forced him to stop. He looked at me, and I could tell something had changed from the time we'd stood outside in front of the cameras. He no longer looked confident. "Is everything okay?"

He didn't answer but started walking again toward the other set of doors. I was confused by his change in demeanor. But maybe that was what seeing his own films did to him. Maybe he was just nervous. I'd only seen his movies in the privacy of his apartment, where he didn't have to worry about the reaction of anyone but me. And he already knew how I'd react. "Everything's fine," he finally said.

"It doesn't really seem fine. Are you sure—?"

"Yes, I'm sure."

I decided to let it go. I didn't want to add to his stress. I would just sit with him and be supportive in whatever way he needed.

Chris pulled on the handle of one of the doors and ushered me inside. It was a smaller screening room, but it was completely empty except for us. I'd seen movies in that very theater and had never known this other screening room existed. It felt like our own private theater, at least for the time being. Of course, the rest of the seats would get filled quickly enough.

"I like this," I said. "Where should we sit?"

"The best seats are in the middle and slightly to the left," he said quietly.

I walked to the seats he was gesturing to and sat down. He sat next to me. "Did you get them to open this other room so you wouldn't have to sit with the riffraff?" I tried to joke because I still didn't know why he was suddenly so serious.

"It's just us."

"What?" I wasn't sure if what he meant by that or why he'd led us in there, for that matter. Unless… "Does this mean we can make out?" The thought of that excited me more than the movie, but Chris still didn't look relaxed. It was strange. If it was just the two of us, he should be more calm, not less.

I really didn't know what to make of him, his nerves, or our private room, so I told myself the same thing I'd been saying all day: just go with it. I grabbed a handful of popcorn out of the bucket between us and used the other hand to eat it, one kernel at a time.

Chris looked over at what I was doing and started to laugh. "You look like a bird."

"Maybe I am a bird." I offered him what was left in my hand, but he waved it away.

"Listen," he said. "I wanted to talk to you today, and I know earlier wasn't a good time, and I'm not sure what you're doing later…"

My face fell, and I sensed the heat rising in my cheeks, because he was making it clear that whatever I was doing, it wouldn't be with him. "I have no plans," I said, trying to keep my voice steady and hoping he didn't notice the crack.

"It doesn't matter. We can talk now."

I realized what it was—the goodbye conversation. He probably had plans right after the movie with his people. There had been a party after the Cannes premiere, too, and he probably had a big night ahead of him. He hadn't mentioned anything about it to me, which clearly meant I wasn't invited. It was fine. He could say goodbye, we would watch the movie, and if I was lucky, I would escape the theater before I cried or did some other embarrassing thing.

So I steeled myself for whatever he had to say. I was a big girl. I could handle it. I could say goodbye right back to him and hide my emotions in the darkness of a two-hour movie after that. "Sure, okay," I said.

He looked straight ahead, and I wondered if he planned to say goodbye without looking me in the eye, which seemed cowardly. Then again, I didn't need the visual of his actor-perfect emoting. I heard him exhale a deep breath, and he turned toward me. His hand reached for mine, and he interlaced our fingers. I immediately felt the heat of his skin, and an unwelcome twinge ran straight through my stomach and ended between my thighs.

Damn it. He was going to torture me.

Before he could spit out what he wanted to say, the lights dimmed all the way so the movie could begin. "It's fine. We can talk afterward," he said. Then he pulled away and tucked back into his own seat, still holding onto my hand. "Just… let's watch the movie."

I could hear the projector start above and behind us. "Wow, since when are you so uptight about watching your movies with me?" I turned halfway around in my seat to look him in the face.

He wouldn't look at me. Instead, he kept his gaze focused on the screen.

I had no choice but to join my stick in the mud for his movie, so I turned back around. But the opening scene didn't look anything like his usual movies. It had subtitles, for one thing. And it was in French. And it was… an arthouse film I'd been telling him I couldn't wait to see. It wasn't out in theaters yet. I knew because I'd checked as recently as that morning.

Oh my God. I couldn't believe it. "You had this movie screened just for us?" I asked in sheer disbelief that he would do something so utterly kind. And the arthouse-film hater was watching it with me. "But what about your movie?"

"I've seen it a dozen times. This is for you." He looked forward at the screen when he spoke.

"I'm so… touched. You're amazing," I said. I knew I was ruining the opening scene by talking, but I also knew that I probably wouldn't miss much by looking away from the screen and staring—still dumbfounded—at Chris. "You hate subtitles."

He turned to meet my eyes. He didn't look as stern, but something about his expression still seemed nervous. "I love you more," he whispered. He interlaced his fingers with mine and brought the back of my hand to his lips, where he kissed it. I sighed like a Southern belle, and he chuckled quietly. "And I speak French."

He did speak French. I'd forgotten.

The movie was gorgeous and touching and thoughtful. I loved it because I noticed the tiny details and the subtle themes. The cinematography was stunningly beautiful, with long tracking shots over lush fields and gossamer flower petals. A pair of childhood friends realized they loved each other too late to be together. She was married. He was devastated. She was devastated. Their star-crossed love went unrequited.

Big, sorrowful tears rolled down my face because I wanted her to cheat. I wanted them to be together. I needed her to say she'd made a mistake. But she didn't.

I stole a look at Chris, wondering if he'd think I was an incredible sap for getting so wrapped up in the on-screen relationship that I was brought to tears, and I saw that his own eyes were wet with the same emotion.

"Chris," I whispered so he'd look at me. When he turned, I put my hand up to his face, cupping his cheek so he would tilt down toward me. I needed to kiss him. I needed to feel his lips on mine. I needed to tell him I couldn't let him go. "I'm so in love with you. And I do want more, but I don't have to have it now." I felt desperate, needing to assure him that I wasn't going to change my mind, that it wasn't one more of my equivocating pronouncements. "I know I've been bossy and demanding, but I just wanted you to consider what I was saying."

"No," he said, looking away then picking up his jacket off the chair and unfolding it. "That's not good enough."

"Wait," I said. I couldn't let him finish his sentence and put on his jacket and walk away. "I have more to say. Don't go. Please don't."

Maybe it was the look of abject panic on my face, but Chris took both of my hands in his and pulled me to him. "Nikki, relax. I'm not going anywhere."

"You're not?"

He shook his head. "I was starting to say, however, that you can't ever stop asking for what you want. You have to fight for it. Especially because you and I want the same thing."

"We do?"

"We do."

"You don't ever want to be apart? You want us to live together all the time? You really want some water because… salty popcorn?"

He nodded and reached down to grab a fresh bottle of water for me. "All three. Plus… there are a couple things," he said, vulnerability in his dark eyes. "First, I spent most of the day lifting contingencies and signing escrow papers on a house."

"I'm sorry. What?" The words made no sense.

"I bought a house."

"You bought a house." I realized I was repeating what he'd said, but I couldn't help it. He was saying words. I was saying them too.

"In Santa Monica Canyon. It's been on the market a long time, and the owners were thrilled to hear from a buyer who appreciated the handmade tile and the treehouse views."

My eyes went wide. I was likely in shock. "You bought the place I want to sit in when it rains?"

He nodded. "All nine days of annual LA rain. I also cleared my schedule for the next six months. I don't start a new film until next summer."

I blinked at him, trying to process what he was saying, because it sounded like he was saying the things I'd fantasized about him saying, but that was impossible. He didn't want them.

If he didn't remember that he didn't want those things, I needed to tell him. "Chris, you can't do that. You live in New York. You have a career, and you can't just *not* work for six months."

"I can."

"It's too big a sacrifice. I can't let you do it." I grabbed his hands and tried to shake some sense into him.

"It's funny, that whole thing about sacrificing. When I decided not to do the movie, it didn't feel like I was giving up anything. It felt like a net gain. I'd get to have balance in my life, and I'd get to have you. That makes me the big winner in that scenario."

"No. It's crazy. You'd be doing it for me. You can't do this for me. You'll hate it, and you'll end up hating me."

"Nikki, you gave me something I care about more than work. You gave me the chance to have balance in my life. And you gave me love."

My brain charged off in ten directions at once—elation, fear, confusion, and elation again. "That's a big change for you. Are you sure? You might try it for a few weeks and freak out, even though you never freak out about anything—that's my department—but still. This is a big deal, Chris. Have you thought this through?"

He nodded and brought a finger to my lips to stop my protestations. "I've thought it through. I reevaluated my life choices, and what I want is to have a life with you. I'm doing this for us. And selfishly, I'm doing it for me. I'm only happy when I'm with you, so I need to be with you all the time. It's just the way it has to be."

I didn't know what to say. "Chris…"

He held up a hand to stop me. Then he leaned over to deliver the king of kisses. It was a warm, commanding, hot kiss with a sweep of tongue and a dizzying bite of my lower lip. He soothed that with his tongue and left me wanting more.

"And," he said, bending down for what I assumed was a bottle of water for himself. "I want one more thing."

"I don't care what it is. If I can give it to you, I will."

He reached his hand for mine. "I want you."

"You have me."

"I want forever."

"I want that too. Like, really forever."

He laughed. "Only you have more than one version of forever. I'm going with the one that means I want you for life. Until the end of days. I want to be married to you. If… you approve," he said, holding out a dark-blue velvet box that he'd procured as if from nowhere.

I would have thought I was all cried out after the movie, but my eyes went for bonus points with a new round of stinging tears that rolled down my cheeks. "Yes, please. I want to be with you forever. And I want to kiss you right now. A lot."

He bent toward me and swept his lips gently across mine. It was sweet, searching, loving. "Nikki."

"Yes?" I wanted less talk and more kissing.

"Do you want to see the ring?"

Oh my God. The ring. It hadn't even seemed necessary to see it, because I knew I wanted him. I would have been ecstatic with a twisted, knotted cherry stem around my finger for life. "Yes, please. I'd like to see the ring," I said calmly.

He opened the box, and I nearly went blind at the sight of the sparkling solitaire diamond in an antique setting with two small sapphires on either side. "The setting is my mom's. She wanted you to have it. I added the diamond."

And it was some diamond. But I focused on the other part. "You spent time with your mom?"

He nodded. "Last week. I spent the day with both of them. It was strange… but also nice."

"Think you'll do it again?"

He shook his head but then smiled and nodded. "I think so. She'd really like to meet you."

"I would love to come with you. Because I love you. But if you don't kiss me now, I'm gonna lose my mind."

He pulled me hard against him and crushed my mouth with his, but only for a moment. Then he seemed to reconsider. "One more thing, because I don't think I remembered to say it: I love you."

Then he kissed me again in the dimly lit theater, with the sounds of sixty crashing police cars echoing in a beautiful serenade from the room next door.

EPILOGUE

SANTA MONICA - Two months later
Chris

"YOU OWE ME TEN DOLLARS," Nikki said, racing down the wooden staircase in Ugg boots and a long T-shirt. I didn't ask what had happened to her pants, because I preferred her the way she was.

She pointed out through the tall windows, where I could see drops of water on the leaves. It was raining. Not so unusual for February, but it was the first time it had rained since we'd been there..

The house really did feel like a treehouse. There was a metal awning over the kitchen window, and when the rain hit it, the sound was amplified. Looking out through the windows, it felt like we were in a warm, safe oasis in the forest, even though I knew that if we walked along the street and down a hill, we'd be at the beach. It was the perfect place to live, hidden away enough that we felt normal.

Nikki made me feel incredibly lucky every day that I'd been with her—sixty-four since the night of the premiere. Yes, I liked to keep track of those kinds of things. Eventually, that number would get pretty big. I'd use a calculator if necessary.

"I'm pretty sure the bet wasn't ten dollars."

When we'd moved into the house, it only made sense to put a small wager on the likelihood of Nikki getting her rain days in the treehouse. It had been a bit of a drought year, so I felt like I had an unfair advantage, but I took the bet anyway.

"It wasn't ten dollars?" she asked innocently. "I thought if you won the bet, you got to boss me around in the bedroom, but if I won, you'd give me lunch money for the crappy pizza near work."

I walked to where she stood, looking out the windows at the glistening leaves. "Is that my shirt?" I asked, standing behind her.

"Um, maybe. It was in the laundry pile, and it looked comfy."

She was adorable. And also incredibly sexy. I ran my hand under the hem of the shirt and put my palm on her warm stomach. When I leaned in and whispered against her neck, I felt her clench and shiver at the touch. "I'm prepared to give you whatever you want. You won the bet, fair and square. But if all you want's ten dollars..."

She turned around to face me. Her eyes sparkled, and I caught the faint smell of plumeria from her shampoo. She put her hands against my chest and lifted her head to kiss me. "I want you to boss me around in the bedroom *and* I want the ten dollars." She grinned like she'd won the lottery, which was sweet. And wrong, because I'd been winning every day since I'd met her.

"You can have anything you want. Always."

"Well, I guess I made a sucker's bet, then. Because I already have everything I want."

I kissed her again, because I could never get enough, and after a few minutes with her plastered against the plate glass window, I was pretty sure we'd never make it to the bedroom.

We were pretty damn happy. We both had careers and we'd figured out a pretty good life balance.

But I still felt like I was getting the better end of the deal. Because I got her.

THE END

SUBSCRIBE TO STACY'S Super Fun Newsletter for exclusive bonus chapters, sneak peeks, and Stacy's favorite drink recipes https://bit.ly/3cUT55Bnewsletter

PREORDER STACY'S NEXT RELEASE, In Trouble with Him (Book Three in the Summer Heat series)

Read on for a Sneak Peek…

ABOUT THE AUTHOR

Stacy Travis writes contemporary romance novels with strong female characters and the men who love them for their badassery. When not writing, she is probably dashing about in running shoes and complaining that all roads seem to go uphill. Or she's on the couch with a margarita. Or fangirling at a soccer game. Stacy lives in Los Angeles with her husband, two sons and a poorly-trained rescue dog who hoards socks.

I love to hear from readers, so please connect with me!

Super fun newsletter: https://bit.ly/3cUT55Bnewsletter

Awesomest Facebook reader group: https://bit.ly/2B1psS4fbgroup

Goodreads: https://www.goodreads.com/stacytravis

Email: stacytraviswrites@gmail.com - tell me everything!

Want more Stacy Travis wordsmithing? Read on for:
1. Sneak Peak of The Trouble with Him, a standalone romance in the Summer Heat series
2. Sneak Peak of French Kiss, a standalone friends to lovers romance

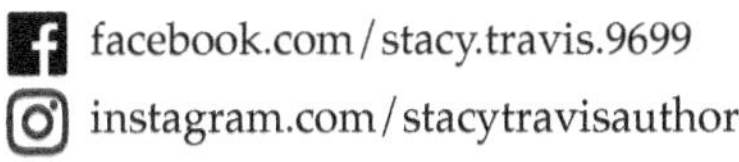

ACKNOWLEDGMENTS

In the immortal words of Hillary Clinton, "It takes a village." I may work ridiculous hours—many of them during the traditional sleeping hours—to get these books out, but I couldn't even find my morning coffee without the village.

First, Jay, Jesse and Oliver: I've missed some dinners, I've crawled into bed when the sun was coming up and I've thrown a few hotdogs at you rather than cooking something decent. Thank you for forgiving all of it and supporting me always. Love you three giant men.

To my beta readers, editors, proofers, givers of feedback, and supporters—Amy V., Christine, Kate, Kim, and Melanie. Amy L. and Jen T., I wish I had 50 cheerleaders of your caliber.

Alyssa, your design genius amazes me and I'm grateful for your skill and patience.

Thank you Jenn and the Social Butterfly team for expert advice, brilliant execution, and other superpowers.

Bloggers, bookstagrammers—thank you for embracing my books and exposing my writing to readers. Glad to have you in my village.

Readers: I could not do this without you. I'm grateful for every word you read, every kind review, every thoughtful click and like and comment. Love you all.

And to my fellow authors: as always, I am honored to type among you.

~

IN TROUBLE WITH HIM

SNEAK PEEK! RELEASING IN OCTOBER

Chapter 1
The Wedding
Annie

I caught a glimpse of myself in the mirror to my right as I sat on a giant, round pouf of a chair. What I saw was a twenty-nine-year-old woman with a pile of peach silk and organza gathered from the floor and draped over one shoulder so as not to tempt fate and whatever unidentifiable germs lurked on the restroom floor. I also saw a tiara. Yup, a freaking tiara.

Nikki was to blame for that. She'd gifted them to her bridesmaids with the misguided belief that, "who doesn't look good in a tiara?" I thought it made me look like a Disney princess who'd lost her way after escaping from the wicked queen. So I took it off. The ceremony was over, photos had been taken, and I was free to pull my tumble of dark wavy hair into a knot that would keep it out of my face.

The dress, with its layer of organza over the silk and its spaghetti straps and square neckline, that was all my doing. I'd seen the dress and loved it on the hanger, convincing myself that it would look equally good on me. For the record, I don't have the body of a hanger, but the dress, as it turns out, looks even better with hips and other curves filling it out.

"Wear whatever you want," Nikki had said when she asked me to be her maid of honor. At the time, we were sitting on the rooftop of the Waldorf Astoria Hotel, which was my favorite place to stay when I came to LA for work. They had a cocktail with a flower floating on top that I dreamed about sometimes when I was home, drinking cheap wine in the eternal fog bank that was San Francisco.

"Seriously? That's very un-bridey. Isn't your moral obligation as bridezilla to force me into some hideous polyester monstrosity that will all but ensure I won't get laid after the wedding?"

"Annie, do you want me to pick your dress?"

"No, I absolutely do not."

"So you're just arguing for the sake of arguing." I hated that she was so rational. I was generally the most rational person in the room and her levelheadedness threw me off. We needed some bit of crazy, and if she was determined to breathe slowly and evenly, I felt forced to amp up the hysteria just a little bit.

"I'm just making sure you understand that according to the bridesmaid manual, I'm obligated to wear whatever horrible bushel of taffeta you send my way and smile in all the pictures with an expression that makes me look ecstatic for you, but not pretty enough to outshine you. I know this. I understand my role."

"Where are you getting your information?" she asked, her rational brain again not understanding that there were rules about these things. Friend-torturing rules. It was the final act a maid of honor could perform to show undying devotion to her best friend.

"I've been in a lot of weddings," I said. I had supplied my local thrift shop with a trove of future costumes as a result.

"Who are these women who make you wear awful dresses? Do I know them?" she asked. Nikki tossed her blonde-streaked mane of wavy brown hair over her shoulder and sipped her drink.

"They're mostly high school friends. And when I say *friends,* I mean that we were friends in high school and our friendship now rests mostly on the memory of homecoming dances and pajama parties."

"I have enough to do finding my own dress. Wear whatever you want. If you like it and feel good in it, I'll be happy," Nikki had said. Then she snickered at me and I knew there was a fifty-fifty chance she'd bring up the fact that I was a cheerleader in high school. Nikki held her tongue, but it didn't matter. I knew she was picturing me skipping through the bleachers wearing fuchsia lipstick and holding pompoms.

Yes, the woman who now cringed at the patriarchal idea of young women cheering for male athletes was once a cheerleader. I grew up in a small Central California town and never questioned the idea that being a cheerleader was an important goal. I didn't question anything back then. I rolled with whatever the people around me were doing.

I wasn't particularly graceful but the cheerleading coach thought I was cute and would look good a short twirly skirt, standing at the top of a human pyramid. I did this for three years and went on to wear my first tiara as homecoming queen. My studies were an afterthought, but school was easy, so I got As without taking time away from my social life and some wild nights spent with homemade hooch and whatever could be done within the confines of an empty barn.

Somehow, I'd survived all that with enough leftover brains to get into Berkeley, where I embraced everything that allowed me to think for myself—philosophy, feminism, Keynesian economics, intellectualism, political determinism. I pushed right through to law school with my eye on doing important work and left my small town upbringing firmly in the past.

This was how it came to be that at the tender age of eighteen, when Nikki and I met in the dorms at Berkeley, blessed by the universe which somehow knew how much we'd need each other to be the yin to each other's yang, we never questioned that we were going to be friends for life.

This was also how I'd come to be sitting in the well-appointed restroom at the Bel Air Hotel. The design rivaled the nicest rooms I'd ever seen, rooms whose primary use was not primping or pooping. There were metal flowers blooming from the walls and tall arched mirrors behind a series of pedestal sinks arrayed against the oval shape of the wall.

The pouf on which I sat was pulled up to a small white table equipped with perfect orchids, magnifying mirrors, tissues, and other goodies that lent themselves to self-maintenance. What I really needed wasn't in this bathroom. It was at the bar.

But before I could go there I needed to collect my thoughts—not thoughts about my lack of romantic prospects or my lack of desire for the complications of romantic prospects, or even other stray emotional strings that generally come loose after watching a beautiful wedding. That wasn't where my mind was.

I was trying to get my brain around moving my life to Los Angeles after ten years in the Bay Area. I knew I'd been using Nikki's wedding as a distraction for the past month since I'd moved, and I'd allowed the bustle of physically moving and starting a job at a new law firm to occupy the rest of my brain space. And yet, it was starting to hit me that I'd completely uprooted my life and was possibly in a state of shock about the whole thing. I wasn't even practicing in the same area of law. Now that the wedding was over, I'd need to face whatever my new life in LA had in store. I feared that instead of a mom and pop store, I'd face a monolithic, multilevel department store filled with crap.

But I loved the dress.

I'd known it from the moment I saw it on the sale rack at a cool boutique near my office in the Embarcadero. I loved that it draped and flowed. It was comfortable but it had a glamour factor.

"I love it," Nikki said when she saw me slip into it earlier in the bridal suite.

"I'm so glad. I love it too."

"It wasn't what I imagined when you described it."

"What can I say? I'm not a visual person. How would you describe this dress?"

"I'd say it had layers of silk and it shimmers when you walk and it's a deep blush color."

"Isn't that what I said?"

"Annie, you said it was like a salmon colored nightgown," she said, grimacing like that wouldn't have been acceptable. I was actually impressed that I'd come up with such descriptive terms.

"Whatever. Deep blush? Is that even a color?"

Nikki shrugged, not in the mood to let anything bother her. In all the weddings I'd been to, I'd never seen such a happy bride, and I'd never seen her so happy as she was at the idea of marrying Chris. Those two were meant for each other, which sounds like a cliche, but in their case it was true.

Nikki was sipping champagne to calm her jitters and laughing about some crazy idea her wedding planner had tried to include for the reception. "She told me we had to have a vodka tasting room made of ice," Nikki said, shaking her head. Chris, who had gazillions of dollars thanks to the many, many superhero action films he'd starred in, insisted on hiring the planner because he thought it would take some of the pressure off of Nikki, but the plan had backfired. "So she had this idea that we'd have a rack of fur coats and before each person went into the tasting room, which was going to be like twenty below zero, they'd put on the coat and pose with a live seal."

"Is Chris a big vodka drinker?"

"No. Not even. It was just a thing. She was seeing his wide open checkbook and pulling out every trick she could. She figured the whole reception would end up in a magazine spread of something with her name all over it."

"She sounds like a nightmare. You told her no to the ice room?"

"I told her she was fired. I planned the whole thing myself."

That sounded more like Nikki. She was never one to suffer fools, especially the sort that came along with the trappings of Chris's celebrity life. They were about as un-celebrity a couple as you could get.

The wedding had been beautiful. The way she and Chris looked at each other made it clear they didn't see anyone else in the room. That was how it had always been with them.

I thought about this, sitting with my dress wrapped over my shoulder and an expression staring back at me that I knew well. It was resignation. I could live in LA and do my job like no one else was in the room.

And with that thought, the fog of uncertainty lifted. Like I'd flipped a switch.

Now I saw the look of a person ready to celebrate her best friend's wedding, a person who needed to have some tequila, some stupid fun on the dance floor, and maybe an even more stupid hookup. Preferably in the form of one of Chris's hot fellow actors who had to be roaming around the reception someplace and would leave on the next plane to film a movie overseas.

I hadn't gotten a chance to check out my fellow guests earlier because I'd been held captive in the bridal suite with Nikki's other two bridesmaids and her mom, but there was at least one groomsman who I was pretty sure I'd seen without his shirt, playing an air force captain in a movie. I wasn't picky. Any actor/model/whatever would do. I just wanted to forget about work and this strange city for a while. That was tomorrow's problem.

Tonight's problem was easily solved at the bar and the singles table.

***

Nikki had described the game of Tetris that went into fitting everyone into a seating chart and she assured me that my table was "the most fun." But I never actually made it to Table Ten.

The line to get drinks in the outdoor reception area near the Swan Lake garden had morphed into a medusa of four or five sprawling lines that converged on a single immovable point.

"You know, there's another bar," said someone with a deep, quiet voice behind me. He spoke so quietly, I felt fairly certain he had to be talking to someone else, but he'd spoken so near to my ear, it felt intimate. I turned around, expecting to see a man whispering to a woman close to me.

I didn't care about the intrusion on my space, but I wanted to see if I could follow his journey to this other bar because the one where I stood was going nowhere fast. When I turned, I met a pair of deep green eyes that immediately felt familiar. In a strange firing of synapses, my mind went straight to my favorite marble in the set I used to play with as a kid. I hadn't seen the marble set in two decades but I was certain his eyes were the exact same color. I was struck by the idea that a memory could be so instantly triggered by a color.

I stared longer than I should have at his eyes and immediately realized my mistake when his lips started moving and I didn't hear anything he said.

"I'm sorry, what?" I asked, finally pulling my focus away from his eyes and noticing that the rest of his face was equally arresting, but not because he was trying to smolder in some model perfect way. He just had a really gorgeous, angular face, dark hair that was combed and gelled nicely, and crinkle lines around his eyes which indicated he either smiled a lot or had spent many hours in the sun. He wasn't smiling at the moment but it didn't dim the wattage of his bulb.

"I said there's another bar. No one seems to have noticed." He pointed to the opposite corner of the lawn where we stood. Sure enough, there was a second bar with no more than four people standing around it.

"Works for me." I tilted my head to indicate we should go

and wove my way out of the crowd and walked through the verdant space toward the other bar. The man walked behind me, saying nothing. After a few moments, I turned to see I he was still with me and saw he was a few paces back, looking at his phone. He'd put on a pair of nerdy-looking reading glasses which made him look a little like Clark Kent. When he saw me stop, he stowed the glasses and walked faster to catch up.

"Sorry. I'm on a short leash," he said, his voice still low. He seemed serious about whatever was going on in his world.

"Hopefully your leash is long enough for one drink," I said, wondering a little about who had him tied down. My initial thoughts ranged from girlfriend to serious corporate job. Or, if he was an actor, manager or agent were a possibility. But I didn't know him well enough to ask.

We sidled up to the bar, where the bartender was looking across the lawn in sympathy. "People just follow people," my new companion said, indicating the other bar. I put his height at over six feet tall, which meant I had to stand back a bit so I wasn't looking straight up at him. It just over five six *with* my tall stiletto heels, I was used to looking up, but I didn't want to kink my neck in the process.

The bartender nodded. "Yeah, it happens all the time. Most people don't look around. They look for the crowd."

"Lucky us. What are you drinking?" he asked me.

"Nothing yet, but I'd love a tequila and soda with a lime."

"Sure thing," the bartender said. "How about you, sir?"

"Dry martini, please. One olive."

I raised an eyebrow. "Only one olive?"

He returned my skeptical gaze. "You think I'm making an olive faux pas?"

"I mean, it's your call, but I thought the whole point of drinking a martini was as a vehicle for eating olives."

He turned back to the bartender. "Make it two olives."

The bartender nodded went about making our drinks and the

man extended his hand. "I'm Finn. And I'm quite interested in your olive theory."

I shook it and took the opportunity to look again at his eyes. Yup, exact color of my marble. He was definitely handsome. I laid odds he was probably an actor, though I couldn't place him in anything I'd seen. "Annie. What would you like to know?"

"Well, by your logic, your drink should contain as many limes as possible but you only asked for a single lime."

I held up a finger. I liked that he was parsing condiments, but he was wrong. "The lime in my drink is for seasoning. The olive in yours is actually a snack."

"Ah, now I see. So really, to you, a martini is just a soaking bowl for olives."

"Yes, but I don't actually drink martinis so it's really just academic."

He nodded and it seemed like he was assessing me, but he didn't say anything else.

"So… are you a friend of Chris's?" It was just a guess because I was new to LA and didn't know all of Nikki's friends.

"Nikki's. We knew each other at USC and stayed friends." Nikki had gotten a Master's degree in communications. He certainly could have studied at the film school there and gone on to an acting career. I realized I was willing him to be an actor, mainly with the idea that actors were sluttier than regular people. I had no evidence to prove that assumption; just hope.

"Ah, so do you work in a similar field as Nikki?" I asked. I hated small talk, but I liked finding out the interesting bits about people. And asking mundane questions was the only quick way to get to know a person.

"Eh, it's a party. I don't really want to talk about work," he said, scooping our drinks off the bar and handing me mine. He held his glass up for a toast. "To new friends."

I couldn't help smiling because he was speaking my language. The last thing I wanted to talk about was work. "To new friends."

I sipped my drink. It was strong. I was thirsty. In under a

minute, I'd already downed most of it, and I already felt a little tipsy. I smiled at Finn. He smiled back.

"Maybe we shouldn't wander too far from the bar," he said, leaning his elbow on a tall cocktail table and looking slowly over my face. He didn't seem inclined to wander anywhere, which was just fine with me.

***

Finn and I stood next to each other when Nikki and Chris had their first dance, and he obliged as my dance partner when the wedding party was invited to join them on the floor. He was a good dancer. He moved with ease and knew how to lead. Holy crap, he was a really good dancer.

"I like your dress," he said, his and moving down my arm to where he rested it on my hip. "Doesn't look like the usual bridesmaid fare."

"Spoken like a man who's danced with a lot of bridesmaids." I draped both hands around his neck. It seemed appropriate and not overly familiar, though the feel of his hand on my hip elicited all kinds of other desires that I needed to keep at bay.

"I've danced with a few." He didn't elaborate. I wasn't used to men of few words. Most of the people I worked with at my now-former law firm couldn't get enough of hearing themselves talk. Finn was a relief.

The song was slow and romantic and he wrapped one hand around my waist and held my hand in the other. I had to look up to see his face. What I saw was a mask of stoic good looks which he seemed to wear when he looked around the room, but his gaze immediately softened when he looked at me. I liked the way it felt.

The way his expression shifted reminded me of the way I sometimes felt when I was in court arguing a case. I knew I was good at that part of my job because I became a different person. I felt myself putting on a mask to keep my inner self safe from the hard-edged litigator who made enemies if necessary to argue a case. Starting over at a new firm added even more reasons to wear that mask until I found my comfort zone.

"What're you thinking about?" Finn asked, rubbing his hand lightly up my back and combing his fingers down through my hair. Then he did it again and I felt the heat rise in my cheeks and a clenching in my stomach. His touch was intimate for a dance floor full of people when we'd just met a half hour earlier, but I didn't want him to stop. I edged my body a little closer to his and ran a fingernail through the hair at the nape of his neck.

"Oh, just the real world creeping in for a moment. I had an unwelcome thought about the work I have to do tomorrow."

"What do you do?" he asked.

"No, you were right. Let's not talk about work. I'd just as soon avoid thinking about it as long as possible."

"Fine by me."

We danced until the song ended and the band kicked into a set of pop cover songs. I pulled my hand back from around his neck and we each took a step back, but he didn't let go of my hand. We looked at each other, assessing whether the other wanted to stick around. I shook my head and he led me off the dance floor and back out to the garden where we'd been before. It felt like we didn't have to talk to know that we both wanted to leave the crush of people and the loud music.

The sudden quiet on the lawn immediately calmed me. I was no longer thinking about work or trials or whether my drink needed refilling because I'd already finished three and I knew my limits.

Finn wordlessly dropped my hand and took off his suit jacket, which he draped around my shoulders. "You'll freeze out here," he said, explaining the gesture.

"I was okay, but thanks." I wasn't used to kind gestures from men. I was good at taking care of myself, so I didn't look hard for people to lighten my load. But it was sweet and I liked that he did it without asking.

"Come." He led me through the garden and down some

winding pathways between bungalows, some of which were larger than my San Francisco apartment. Finally, we arrived at what seemed to be our destination—the pool.

No one was sitting on the lounge chairs at that hour, but the tiny twinkling lights made the setting look like it had been designed for a midnight tryst nonetheless. Finn grabbed a stack of plush towels and spread them out on the plush cushion of a lounge chair and tilted it to full recline.

"Wow, you get right to it," I said, sort of impressed that he was moving right to writhe around on a lounge chair and make out mode. He looked at me quizzically and proceeded to put towels on the lounge next to it and tilt that one back as well. He gestured for me to sit on one of the chaises and he took the other one. Then he picked up my hand again.

He lay all the way back and after some momentary hesitation, I did the same, still confused because I'd thought we were on the same page. Didn't most normal single people hook up at weddings? Wasn't that where he was leading with his sultry stroking of my back and all the hand holding? And now we appeared to be gearing up to take naps at a great distance.

The thick cushions were comfortable, and I supposed I could think of worse ideas.

"So, I take it from your comment, you were expecting me to have my hand up your skirt by now?" he said.

"Oh. I mean, not really, but I guess… well, yeah."

He laughed. "Noted. And then, by corollary, I guess you wouldn't object."

"Um, yeah, sure. And who says, 'by corollary' in ordinary conversation? Are you on the debate team or something?"

"Or something," he said.

"Right. No talking about work. Fine."

"You seem disappointed in how this is going," he said, an amused smirk on his lips.

"No, not at all. I was hoping for a nap outside during my best friend's wedding reception."

"Good. Just want to make sure you're not disappointed."

"Absolutely not. And, I guess we're not making out, then. Just to be clear."

He turned toward me and those green eyes burned into mine. "I'm not ruling it out." He yanked hard on my lounge chair and pulled it right up against his. The movement made a scraping noise on the patio and added to the brute strength of the gesture. "But first I wanted to do this." He rolled away and onto his back and looked straight up at the sky. With the promise of a potential hookup still on the table, reluctantly looked up as well.

"Oh, wow. We had an unobstructed view of the sky and it was a perfect, clear night. The moon was full and hung directly above us like a big, smiling grandpa face. And around it, I actually saw stars.

"I didn't think it was possible to see a real night sky in LA," I said.

"Have you seen this kind of sky elsewhere?"

"Well sure, on camping trips in the mountains. But this is… it's pretty magnificent." I stared up until the brightness of the moon started to hurt my eyes and I had to close them.

When I turned my head to look at Finn, I saw his eyes studying me. I wondered how long he'd been doing that. He pulled me a little closer and I scooted toward the edge of my chaise. He did the same until we were pressed up against each other.

Neither one of us spoke. We just lay there, side by side, holding hands under the blazing white moon, for a long time.

That's why I wasn't expecting it when he brought my hand to his lips and kissed it. And when he turned on his side to face me, I wasn't expecting him to do anything more than talk more about the sky or propose another arcane activity that no one did at a wedding reception ever.

And I was good with that. I'd begun thinking of him in a completely different way than I had been a few hours earlier. I actually liked him. He was different. And interesting. And definitely not the kind of guy who was just looking for a hookup. But he was still so reticent, I wasn't sure what he was looking for exactly.

"You'd be crazy to think I haven't been wanting to do this for the past two hours," he said, pressing closer to me, which had the effect of scooting me over so both of us were facing each other on my lounge chair and the distance between us had disappeared. Then his lips swept across mine, just hinting at more but withholding it. He licked my bottom lips and sucked it gently before backing away. "I just didn't want you to think it was *all* I wanted."

"What else do you want?" I asked, surprised at how breathless I sounded after one kiss.

"Ah babe, the list is long." He kissed me again, deeper this time and I felt every part of body shudder at his touch. I tugged his dress shirt free from his pants and ran my hands over his abs, which felt like they were carved from marble.

His tongue tangled with mine and his hands were in my hair, brushing it away from my face. But there was nothing frantic or hurried about his pace. He wasn't trying to get to a finish line. He was the frustrating sort who wanted to admire the view.

That had never been my priority. I was all about the accomplishment, the checking of a box, even when it came to sex.

"Hey," he said, pulling away and focusing his eyes on mine. "Relax."

"I am relaxed."

He laughed and rolled his eyes. "You're not relaxed. The question I have," he said, running a finger over the contours of my cheek until the skin tingled with goosebumps. "Is what it will take to get you there." He followed the path of his finger with a row of kisses which ended at my neck. He followed that with his tongue.

"I... I could maybe get there," I mumbled, my brains scrambling and willing to agree with whatever he proposed. His breath was hot on my skin. Then his lips followed. He held my cheek in his palm and kissed my forehead, my nose, my chin. Finally, my lips.

And I was gone.

***

Then I was back.

"Shit." Finn pulled away from me and shoved a hand in his pocket. I assumed it was a panicked attempt to check for condoms.

"It's okay I have one in my—"

"Shit," he said again, only this time he'd pulled out the sexy nerd glasses and his phone. "I'm so sorry to have to do this, but I can't stay. I didn't realize how late it'd gotten." He seemed perturbed and more ruffled than I'd imagined possible from a man who'd seemed so calm and thoughtful all night.

"It's okay. Can I do something?"

"No, no. It's fine," he said, backing away from me. That made me want to chase him for some reason, but I didn't get the chance. He doubled back and pulled me to him. His lips crashed onto mine and he kissed me like it was his last kiss on earth. Forever.

Then he turned and jogged—almost ran, actually—down the hallway and out of sight.

I could still feel his lips on mine and a part of me felt so whiplashed by his abrupt departure I had to do a double take to make sure we weren't still kissing. My fingers went to my lips in a futile effort to connect. But he was gone.

I retraced our steps and wandered slowly along the path and back into the reception. Once in the room, I was immediately pulled onto the dance floor by Nikki who was glistening with the sheen of a beautiful bride but smiling the way she ha been all day. I wondered if her cheeks would be sore in the morning. She linked arms with me and we danced to all here eighties favorites until I was mopping plain old sweat from my face and begging to take a water break.

It didn't seem worth trying to find Table Ten when there was a perfectly good—and now empty—bar with cold glasses of water. I downed several and looked around at the other guests. Most of the people who were still on the dance floor or nursing drinks were Nikki and Chris's close friends. I felt a little guilty that I'd missed half the reception, but not that guilty. Nikki wouldn't care, and I'd been there for the first dance and the toasts.

I didn't want to hassle Nikki with questions about Finn on her wedding night, but I also really did. It was just so weird. The reception was starting to wind down but Nikki couldn't be pulled from the dance floor. Even Chris had sat out the last few songs.

I decided I could just as easily ask him my questions. He probably knew most of Nikki's friends by this point, at least friends who were close enough to merit an invitation to their wedding. So I pulled a chair over to his and sat down.

"Congratulations, Mr. Nikki," I said, giving him a kiss on the cheek.

"You got that right. I definitely got the better end of the deal here."

"Oh, I'm not so sure about that. I'm pretty sure Nikki would call herself the lucky one."

He smiled and I almost had to shield my eyes from his charisma. It was really no wonder he could take over a movie screen. "You enjoying your night?"

"I am. Actually, I enjoyed a certain friend of Nikki's who I wanted to ask you about."

"Oh yeah? Ask away."

"His name's Finn. Do you know him?"

Chris didn't answer immediately. I turned and saw his gaze fixed firmly on Nikki, who was now barefoot and dancing in a circle of friends. The smile on his face said more about their future together than any of their vows. And their vows had been beautiful.

When he finally tore his attention away from her his smile had dimmed a bit. "Wait, you hooked up with Finn?"

"I mean… a little. Why, is he married or something?"

"Did you two not talk at *all*?"

"We talked a little. But then he abruptly had to leave, which was kind of strange. And now you're freaking me out."

Chris shook his head. "Well, I'm not surprised he left abruptly. He has a ten o'clock curfew."

"What kind of man has a curfew?"

"The kind who's wearing an ankle monitor because he's under house arrest."

Gah…what happens next? PREORDER In Trouble with Him, a standalone romance in the Summer Heat series